ATOMIC ANGEL

An **ASTRAL HEAT** ROMANCE 3

LAURA NAVARRE

CHAPTER ONE
The Captive

"I know you're awake."

Hearing the crisp observation made in a voice that sounded like her lover's but emphatically wasn't, Kaia of Kryll released her held breath in a slow hiss and opened her eyes.

She couldn't be sure how long she'd been lying sacked out on the icy floor of the Hurricane, Dex Draven's turbocharged space shuttle weapon of mass destruction. Huddled on her side with wrists shackled behind her, ankles chained together, head swirling with dizziness, and mouth rusty with the chemical tang of a knockout drug, it felt like forever.

She was terrified it could've been clicks.

Not days, because at least she wasn't lying in a puddle.

Not days. Which means you're still strong, samurai. Still functional. Still capable of getting yourself out of the oven before someone cranks up the heat.

Without moving, her eyes searched the shadows. Far as she could tell, she was alone with her captor and streaking through space. Alone with the coldly forbidding Dex/not Dex imposter seated at the captain's console wearing a gleaming Mogadon uniform whose accolades he hadn't earned and packing an illegal nerve gun the real Dex wouldn't touch.

In place of Dex's electrifying psychic presence, her head hummed with the blank white buzz of static.

Which meant she was alone with their mortal enemy. The shapeshifter.

Alone with Proteus.

"I know you're awake," the Dexlike figure repeated, without even bothering to turn his tawny head. Beneath the stern black jacket of her lover's imperial uniform, Dex's controlled stillness inhabited the imposter's powerful frame. "Your heart rate has nearly doubled."

Kaia cleared the nasty taint of anesthetic from her throat and wished passionately for a slug of Kryllian firewater to blast away the fumes. "You telling me you can hear my heartbeat?"

Proteus placed a calm hand on Dex's biometric panel and toggled a command into the console. "My neurological senses are what, to a lesser species such as yours, would seem to be preternaturally acute. In short, I'm an apex predator. I'm not at all surprised you're terrified."

Angels and asteroids.

She'd been fighting like hell to control the surges of dread and panic that swelled and ebbed like sine waves in her drug-clouded head.

But she couldn't control her heart rate with a thought. She wasn't the galaxy's most powerful psychic—not by a long shot—just a barely competent telepath. In other words, she wasn't her psychic lifemate Ben Nero.

Great merciful gods, Ben. Do you even know I'm missing? Does Dex know this thing did a snatch-and-grab and kidnapped me from the Inevitable *right under the Mogadon Empire's imperial nose? Are the two of you all right? And what the flip has Proteus done with Zorin? If he hurt him—hurt any of you—just to get his shapeshifter hands on me…*

I swear to every god I know he'll die for it.

And being so terrified for the men she loved—so desperately clueless about all three of their fates—was more than enough to flip her off.

Way better to be furious than terrified.

"Think about it, smarty-pants." She blew a burgundy curl out of her eyes and forced a scowl instead of a whimper. "I've just been drugged and kidnapped. And I'm not exactly comfy chained up down here in deep space on an ice-cold floor in this tissue-thin cybersuit you hustled me into. So my vitals are a little hinky. You want a medal for noticing?"

"Oh, you can keep your medals. But I should think I've earned your respect as an adversary, haven't I?" Her captor sliced her a glacial glance, a flash of cobalt that read and cataloged the clamoring fear all the snark in the galaxy couldn't conceal. "I'm a meticulous student of human behavior, darling. Makes me more effective at the hunt."

That familiar endearment spiked her through like a hypodermic to the heart.

Comets, he sounds like Dex. Dex as he would be if he'd grown up like his psycho dad. But he isn't Dex. He's Proteus. God of the farking Swarm.

What in the nine unknown realms is he planning?

She fought to clear her head and master her fear before it mastered *her*. The shapeshifter looked like Dex and sounded like Dex. Enough like Dex to fool the biometric scanners that ran the Hurricane.

But he wasn't Dex.

He emphatically lacked the crackling vitality and interstellar army and carefully contained command presence of the First Indomitable—the galaxy's paramount military power. And unlike Dex with his battle sense, Dex who displayed remarkable telepathic sensitivity for a Mogadon, Proteus was headblind. Student of human behavior or master of the universe, he couldn't see inside her head.

Which meant he had a weakness.

A weakness even a hybrid half-telepath like Kaia could use.

Now she needed to master her fear and probe for more. Not to mention suss out where they were, where they were headed, and what in the seven devils he was planning.

"I can tell you're not him." Wincing, she wiggled her weight off her throbbing shoulder—the same shoulder Dex's would-be assassin had shot all to shit with that blaster two days ago—now a fiery vortex of discomfort. "If I hadn't been high as an orbiting satellite, I would never have left the *Inevitable* with you."

"I'm well aware of that. Which is precisely why I utilized the opiates in Dr. Cato's dispensary to drug your drink before we vacated the battleship." His heart-stoppingly familiar profile—all strong jaw, hard face, and sun-bronzed skin—was still averted.

But she knew he was acutely vigilant. Cautiously she curled and twisted and scooted her acrobat's body up to an awkward sit.

Before her befuddled eyes, an impressive array of combat screens and flashing lights swirled in a dizzy blur. Under her ice-cold derrière, the shuttle's microreactor hummed and thrummed. Against the aft wall, the indigo glow of the cyberport pulsed.

The cyberport.

And the one foggy impulse I managed to heed when Dex/not Dex hustled my drugged-out booty into this cybersuit in dead of night was to buckle on my utility belt.

Which she was still wearing. She even had the transcription chip, her mating gift from Zorin, tucked away inside. But—and this was a *big* but—she'd been tinkering with the cyber chip, experimenting with the coordinates Zorin's cyber samurai had programmed into it. She didn't think it would take her to Zorin's *Relentless* and his space pirates anymore.

After all her tinkering, it might not take her anywhere.

Because she hadn't had time to test it.

Even if she managed to get her arms and legs free and overpower the preternaturally observant shapeshifter long enough to use it.

One asteroid at a time, angel. Keep him talking. You're probing him, remember?

"Anyone who knows Dex could tell you're not him," she repeated. "Your ears are too big. Your face is… I don't know… off-kilter somehow. You definitely smell different. And you sound a little different too. It's not your timbre so much as your tone."

"I've acknowledged my replication of this specimen is imperfect." One corner of his mouth turned up in a flicker of sly satisfaction that was nothing like Dex. "Although you'll observe it proved more than adequate to bypass the biometric locks on the First Indomitable's quarters. Dex Draven has been quite fortunate to elude my… intimate scrutiny. The sustained experimentation I require for fully successful replication. All in all, a reprieve for which he should be exceedingly thankful."

Unlike Dex's brother. Poor Cato. The guy Zorin thinks you kidnapped and locked up and tortured—maybe for years—to make a model good enough to fool everyone. Even Cato's own brother.

Already chilled to the bone from however long she'd spent conked out on the floor, Kaia couldn't suppress a hard shiver.

"Has it all been you?" Fighting the deep-space chill, she hunched her shaking knees to her chest. "Those Kryll who tried to kill Zorin—who were poisoned in custody before Ben could interrogate them? All those assassination attempts? Not to mention the mole back on Mogadon who tipped off the Swarm and sent those spacebots after me?"

"Very clever of you, darling," Proteus murmured, typing a command into the console. "Not just a pretty face, are you?"

And having him look so much like Dex and sound so much like Dex, while feeling so telepathically, overwhelmingly *off, other, inimical* to everything Dex had ever stood for, was a nightmare she couldn't seem to wake up from.

Get a grip, angel. Ask him the million-credit question.

"I can't believe you went to that kind of trouble just to flip us all off." Yeah, she wanted to keep him talking, but her mystification was genuine. "What the punk are you trying to get out of all this? I'm a circus acrobat. A runaway kid with a bad attitude and a samurai sword."

"You're the prime maharani. Heir to the Kryll theocracy. The closest thing to a goddess to inhabit this benighted galaxy." Proteus frowned over the sensor bank. "And your three chosen consorts—the First Indomitable of the Mogadon Empire, the galaxy's dominant Valyrian telepath, and the formidable chieftain of the Syndax pirates—well, they *are* this galaxy's premier powers. United, they pose an unlikely but not entirely implausible threat to my designs. You're the centripetal force that brought them together. That binds them together. That keeps them together.

"Without you, darling, they'll splinter and fly apart."

"Don't call me that." She really didn't like the disadvantage of sitting at his feet. Using her core since she couldn't use her hands, she uncoiled to her knees. "And don't count on it, funny face. I might be the reason we all hooked up—me and Dex and Ben and Zorin. But there's plenty more than me holding the four of us together."

"Careful." The sharp-edged glitter of his Dexlike eyes sliced over her action-ready form. "I have a syringe already loaded with more of the same opiate that's already sent you once to dreamland. In fact, the dose in the syringe is quite a bit more potent. If I inject you, you're likely to wind up an opium addict. Like half the women in your father's harem."

And thank you very flipping much for unleashing that closet monster.

The horror of that old childhood nightmare snuck through her. Along with a swirling cloud of chemically induced dizziness that made her sway on her knees at the memory of all those vacant-eyed beauties in chains in her father's harem. But she knew better than to show fear to an apex predator.

Her father the so-called god had taught her that.

Which was why, instead of sitting at her enemy's feet like the good girl she wasn't, she unfolded to her full height—which admittedly wasn't much—and watched his pupils dilate.

Tracking her.

"Don't lose your cool. I'm just getting off this cold-ass floor," she muttered, standing ten cubits away so she wouldn't trigger him. "For flip's sake, my hands and feet are shackled. What exactly do you think I'm gonna do? Hop over there and head-butt you?"

"You're a Prime Class samurai, even without your cyber saber. I won't make the mistake of underestimating you." Cold as liquid nitrogen, those impersonal eyes slid over her. "Sit over there at the navigation console before you fall over. And don't even think about trying to operate the nav computer. This shuttle is programmed to respond to Dex Draven's biometrics alone."

Nimbly she shuffled over to the seat and dropped into it. Awkward as all get-out with her wrists chained behind her booty.

Still, the vantage gave her a peek at the nav computer, which was part of what she needed. The familiar coordinates leaped out at her like a laser and burned through her brain.

"We're going to *Kryll*?" Blazing with suspicion, she twisted to confront her captor. "What the punk for?"

He said the one thing she'd never expected. "Why, we're off to see your father. His High Holiness the Patriarch."

"My father?" She gaped. "He… isn't even on Kryll. He's at Quorum Central Starbase. That's where he and Dex agreed to meet to wrap up my mating contest. You're going the wrong way."

Lightning flickered in his eyes. "I'm afraid there's been a minor… incident on Quorum. The entire starbase is now a hot zone of contagion for spacepox."

Kaia's heart lodged against her sternum in a spasm of alarm. "At Quorum? But they were warned! I warned Zorin's pirates you were coming."

"My fighting force was stealthed, darling," he reminded her softly. "The biological agent I deployed from Dex Draven's stolen Zephyrs was genetically modified to elude the station's biosensors, and microencapsulated to slip through the starbase filters. Thereby enabling the pathogen to wipe out, well, everyone. Even those wary pirates hunkered under their biohazard bubble."

Horror spiraled through her, twisting her stomach and icing her palms. Suddenly she was fighting to breathe.

"*That's* what you did with the novicide? My gods—there's, what, twelve thousand people living on that starbase? Not to mention the seat of the galactic government, the home of the Mogadon Imperator, the council of the Quorum of Four—"

"Not anymore." Again that flicker of sly satisfaction she found so hideously unDexlike invaded her lover's familiar face. Except he wasn't her lover. He wasn't Dex. "But not to worry, love. The Patriarch survived. In fact, all available evidence suggests he's the only member of the Quorum to do so. I warned him just in time to make his escape."

She was still way too appalled to untangle how her tyrannical father's survival made her feel. Not to mention the apparent obliteration of the entire galactic government.

But more pressing needs than an eval of her emotional damage clamored to be spoken.

"You warned him against your own attack? Why?"

Before her horrified eyes, Dex's familiar features rippled and ran with blood. Muscle writhed, bone cracked, skin stretched, joints popped. Fingers clenched in agony, hands lengthened with the crackle of sinew and the crunch of cartilage. Finally, his burnished hair lightened to gilt.

Only his imperial uniform and his blue eyes remained unchanged.

Watching her without blinking the whole time.

"Because, my dear," Pontius Cato said gently, in the diffident voice of the Mogadon Empire's chief scientist, "my brother the First Indomitable has just proclaimed Pontius Cato one of the final candidates for your bed. Dex will fight to the death in the blood games tomorrow to protect my place in your mating contest."

He was talking about the Tombola. The galactic mating contest, enshrined and enforced by millennia of sacred Kryll tradition. The monstrous fate she'd fled her Kryll homeworld to escape. The prison sentence she'd finally—reluctantly—accepted.

Because that was the only way to spare her innocent kid sister the same fate.

She squared her shoulders and buttressed her resolve. "My father—the Patriarch—he'll never agree. To him, the Tombola's sacred. A holy ritual."

"Why, to the contrary. The Patriarch and I have already reached an acceptable arrangement. If I can endeavor to bring you before him on Kryll myself—and I do very much believe I shall—well, to his way of thinking, that's a portent. A sign of divine favor. He'll proclaim me the victor. Granting to me and me alone the right to become your immediate consort."

Her gut twisted with a squirm of revulsion. Her throat burned with the sour churn of bile.

The imminent prospect of mating anyone other than the three men she'd chosen—much less this cold-blooded reptile whose alien presence inhabited the cockpit, this predator whose cannibalistic race was ravaging the outer colonies like a hatch of maggots—sent panic arcing through her with an electric shock.

She swallowed down the acid taste of fear. "Dex named the real Cato as a Tombola finalist. Not you."

"I am the real Cato now. I am more Pontius Cato as this galaxy knows him to be than the original specimen. Certainly more than the real Cato as he exists today."

In the midst of her flailing panic, her brain seized on his use of the present tense for balance. "The real Cato—he's still alive?"

Her captor hesitated. "Technically, yes. I've kept him alive for you."

"For me?" She struggled to clear her head. "Why? I don't even know the guy."

"My methods may seem elaborate, but my motive is simple—and old as time. I can assume the form of Pontius Cato or any sentient being I've had sufficient opportunity to study." Deliberately he rose to loom over her, eyes burning like nuclear warheads in the young scientist's mild-mannered features. "But I can't procreate, Kaia. I can't make you conceive."

Thank all the Ninety-Nine Gods for that.

Even though she didn't like him looming over her with his radioactive presence, the breath she was holding rushed out in a snort.

"Neither can the real Cato, I promise you, even if he's virile as a Mogadon satyr. Get with the program, Proteus. I'm half Valyrian. For Valyrian telepaths, conception is an act of will. In order to conceive, I have to *want* the man I mate."

Three measured steps brought him to her side. A warm hard hand—Dex's hand, oh gods, Dex's touch firing his fake brother's body—gripped her chin to hold her. Those volcanic eyes seared through her.

"Quite simply, my dear, your very fertile body craves a mate. In the Swarm hive he now inhabits, Pontius Cato will be your only human option. He hasn't had a woman in years, since shortly after I took him. And he is Dex Draven's brother. Physically… sexually… you'll find the two are much alike."

Now he was really freaking her out.

Gritting her teeth, she twisted free of his violently disturbing touch.

"Not that this is a conversation I want to be having. But how would you have the first farking clue what either of them likes in the sack?"

He towered over her. Close enough to kill—if she had her samurai sword. Or close enough to grab the nerve gun at his belt—if she had her hands free.

"Because I've observed them. With scientific detachment, I assure you. Dex… performed… at a Mogadon saturnalia some time before he met you. Whereas Cato obligingly bedded the women I sent him early in his captivity. One of my standard bank of experiments when I study a new specimen." Her captor assayed a slow blink. "You'll fancy him well enough, my dear. Trust me."

"Trust you?" she scoffed, though she was flat-out horrified. "Not flipping likely! And it won't work because I'm not in love with him. I'm in love with Dex. Not Cato."

"As you like, of course." Indifferent to her horror, he swung back to his console. "All the same, your body does require a mate. And after years of rigorously enforced celibacy, believe me, so does Cato. It's my studied belief the two of you will contrive to find a way."

Rigorously enforced celibacy? Sounds positively sadistic.

And she didn't like thinking about the reasons the shapeshifter would have for keeping his prime Mogadon specimen in such a state.

Blindly she stared through the viewport. Directly before them against the starry void of space, the twin suns of the Kryllian system had swelled from diamond specks to platinum marbles. That much of what he'd told her was apparently true.

They were definitely headed for Kryll. The theocratic homeworld-slash-prison she hadn't gone anywhere near since she lit out of there years ago.

Now the nav computer claimed they'd be back in less than a day.

But according to the blinking console, their Hurricane shuttle was fully stealthed. Which meant even Dex's *Inevitable* with its powerful sensors, and Zorin's *Relentless* with its pirated scanner, wouldn't be able to track them.

"You don't even care what your little scheme would do to me—or Dex—do you?" she demanded. "Having me betray him with his own brother? Two of the only people in the galaxy he trusts? You don't care that we'd destroy him."

Cato crossed his legs and steepled his hands. "My dear, destroying Dex Draven is the entire objective. Far more effective than simply killing him, which was my original impulse. Destroying him this way in particular—driving the First Indomitable of the Mogadon Empire mad with jealousy and rage—will spur him to wreak immeasurable destruction and spread utter chaos across the galaxy. That chaos creates optimal feeding conditions for my precious children. Those same children you consider a galactic infestation."

"You mean the Swarm." She couldn't wrap her head around what he was saying. She couldn't. Because none of it made any sense.

But at least her questions were keeping him talking. Sooner or later, he'd say something she could use.

"If destroying Dex is the goal," she said carefully, "why not just kill me?"

"Well, for two reasons, really. First, I intend to study you. Perhaps even replicate you." With utter dispassion, his cold eyes ran over her huddled form. "You've proven to be a remarkably effective catalyst for your three would-be consorts—all quite powerful and entirely different sorts of men. Clearly all three find you compelling. I find myself rather powerfully curious to discover why. To take you apart in my laboratory, if you will, and put you back together. To learn what makes you tick."

Now that's just… nasty.

She literally didn't think she could get any colder. She pressed her knees to her chest and hunched over them with a shiver.

"That's why you want to be my consort? To *experiment* on me in your laboratory of horrors?" She pushed out a shuddery scoff. "You did say you were wedded to your work. I just didn't think you meant it literally."

"It's quite true I'm immune to sexual desire. When we spoke on the *Inevitable*, I wasn't lying about that." He still projected that clinical detachment that chilled her right down to her DNA. "Traditionally, my Swarm have always reproduced asexually. Rather like a virus. Which is precisely the life form we ourselves most resemble."

Guess I should count my blessings.

"So you don't fuck," she said flatly. "Then what turns your crank?"

"I operate by mathematical logic and infallible instinct." His pupils swelled to black. "What I do feel—what my Swarm feel—is *hunger*. A hunger more consuming than any carnal passion. But not to worry, Kaia of Kryll. I have recently… eaten."

In the twilight gloom of the cockpit, shadows writhed. For an eyeblink she glimpsed… something… a monstrous image in her telepathic mind. A flash of the shapeshifter's natural form. A mass of thrashing tentacles. The gape of a cruel beak dripping with human viscera. The high shrill chitter of a hunting cry that was anathema to human life.

The siren song of an apex predator.

Summoning his Swarm to feed.

A scream clawed its way up her throat. Before she could voice it, the image blinked out.

Meteors, she was streaming with sweat. Her cybersuit was sticking to her clammy skin. Kaia pressed her forehead to her knees.

Get your game on. Hold it together. Keep him talking.

Frantically she sorted through her jumbled thoughts. "You said there were two reasons you—haven't killed me. What's the second reason?"

Gently he told her, "I'm keeping you alive for your child."

My child.

Her child who didn't even exist except in prophecy. And for the daughter of a self-proclaimed god, Kaia'd never been particularly superstitious. Or even particularly maternal. A fugitive samurai had zero time and zero patience to muck around with kids.

Yet, somehow, she couldn't seem to breathe. A vise of dread closed around her lungs and squeezed.

Fighting for calm, she pushed out one word in a strained whisper. "Why?"

"Oh, come now. I too have heard the storied Valyrian prophecy. Your son will rule the galaxy."

That farking prophecy. I wish to gods the Senate of Psychics had kept its prophetic mouth shut.

She swung her booted feet to the floor with a thud. "What exactly are you saying? You plan to *replicate* him too?"

"Oh, I intend to do far more than replicate him." Like a lecturing professor, the shapeshifter leaned back in his chair. "My dear, yours is hardly the only sentient life form that yearns to procreate. I am the last of my kind. My beautiful Swarm are an ancient race. Once fecund, they are now quite sterile. And, like children, they are heedless, unthinking, ruled by hunger and instinct. I alone carry in my core the raw genetic material—the triple-stranded RNA—of the fully viable Swarm virus. With Cato's scientific expertise, I intend to modify your son's genetic makeup. To splice his genetic material with mine.

"In short, it may be Cato who lies with you. But I'll be your son's true sire."

Kaia didn't think she'd ever been so terrified. Terrified for the son she hadn't yet conceived and wasn't even sure she wanted.

Terrified for this whole punked-up galaxy.

"Feeling paternal?" she jeered. Because way better a jeer than a wail.

Even a jeer he ignored.

"Once I own your son, with his singular destiny and hybrid abilities—a child who will be part Valyrian, part Kryll, part Mogadon, part divine, and raised to be all Swarm—why then, as you can imagine, he won't be anything human."

"Humor me." Though her thoughts were anything but humorous. "What exactly do you imagine he'll be?"

"Quite simply, he'll be a god." Cato spread his slender hands. "Like me."

At least this was terrain well-traveled.

"I grew up with a guy who thinks he's a god. Godhood's not all it's cracked up to be." When he smiled and said nothing, she shifted tactics. "You've been planning this a long time, haven't you?"

That topic seemed to bore him. He turned back to his console. "I came to this galaxy decades ago. After my Swarm used up the last one. I've been, well, preparing to conduct this latest experiment ever since."

"Decades, huh?" That didn't make him a god. Just a long-lived species. "You got that kind of time to burn?"

"My dear, time is one resource I possess in staggering abundance. A few decades are an eyeblink of time to a being like me." He sliced her a canny look. "Of course, the original plan was to abduct the prior maharani—your eminently more malleable twin sister. I do regret her rather spectacular death."

Because of course he was responsible, the bastard. What with the demands of the current crisis, his culpability for the earlier tragedy had taken a tick to register.

Now, his offhand admission pulverized her heart like a headlong flight through an asteroid field.

"Right. My sister. You're head of the Swarm." Desperately she reminded her staggering, mortally wounded heart to beat. "Which means *you're* the one who murdered Kira."

"Murder? Not at all. I never meant her to die, you see. It's true my Swarm are often, shall we say, overzealous? Precision instruments, they are not. However, Kira of Kryll proved far more resistant to capture than her reputation for docile compliance could possibly suggest. In fact, I fear I misjudged her."

"Everyone misjudged her," Kaia said in a voice like tungsten. "Kira was way stronger than she ever let anyone know."

Deception. That was always her survival strategy. Just like defiance was mine.

"Clearly my mistake. And it *was* a mistake." He tutted a rueful apology. "Under the circumstances, your twin's unfortunate demise might best be considered, well, death by misadventure."

Which is the same line he'll use when I buy it trying to escape.

Not that it changed much when it came to her plan. To the vague extent she *had* a plan.

But to know what she needed to do, she didn't need a plan.

Because her father, the fanatical Patriarch of Kryll, was just whacked enough to see Proteus's mad vision as divinely ordained. To see the so-called god of the Swarm as the perfect antidote to the toxic poison of war. The perfect counterweight to the Mogadon and the Syndax, who already teetered at the brink of battle. Maybe even the perfect nemesis to the Valyrians, the dying race of telepaths, who'd hurl themselves to pieces against the Swarm to win her back.

Her abduction would ignite the very war she'd sworn to prevent. Millions—even billions—would be incinerated in the blaze.

And that was if they won.

No point at all appealing to her father for help. The Patriarch would consider her sacrifice to a Swarm consort the ultimate expression of neutrality. The sacred virtue he earnestly believed he'd been incarnated and destined to impose across the galaxy.

Which boiled the stew of her roiling panic right down to the bare bones. Before they landed on Kryll in a few clicks, she had to escape.

Had to.

Even if it killed her.

CHAPTER TWO
The Gamble

"Absolutely not," Dex Draven bit out.

He loomed over the cyberport in the *Interstellar Angel*, Kaia's souped-up little cruiser, still berthed in his battleship's hangar bay. Before him, Ben Nero lay on his back tinkering with something on the underside of the *Angel*'s CPU. The blue flash of a laser drill illuminated the scorch marks still browning the wall where Dex had fired his blaster days ago in his laughably futile bid to keep Kaia, equipped with Zorin's prototype cyber chip, from jumping through cyberspace to the *Relentless*.

Damage that Ben was now repairing, while the cruiser's antimatter drive hummed under his boots and the command computer whirred through its preflight checklist. Dex stood in the midst of this controlled chaos and fulminated.

An emotional expenditure that was having absolutely zero impact. Ben wasn't even looking at him.

And it made him frantic.

Between the howling fear for Kaia he barely held in check, his twisting sense of guilt for failing to protect her, the consuming imperative to *find her, save her, fight kill get her back,* and now Ben's blind determination to go jetting off on this suicide run to rescue her without him, Dex was about a whisker away from losing it.

And the haunting scent of Kaia's ozone and jasmine fragrance lingering like a ghost in the air was an agonizing reminder of the woman he'd lost.

"Ben." Fighting to modulate his volume, he gritted through clenched jaw, "I assure you I'm not in the habit of repeating myself. Are. You. Hearing me?"

Over the soft whine of the laser drill, he barely discerned a sigh.

"I hear you, Dex. I'm just not listening. This isn't up to you."

Dex barely mastered the overwhelming urge to grab his lover by his booted ankles and drag him out from under that infernal thing. "The devil it isn't. This is my bloody ship."

Ben switched off the drill and slithered fully into view, his sculpted face granite with resolve. "You may own this battleship and half this galaxy, but you don't own the *Angel* and you don't own me. She's my lifemate and it's my call. *I'm going.*"

Dex wanted to pull his own hair out by the roots. He settled for extending a hand and pulling Ben somewhat forcefully to his feet. When Ben would have blown past him on his next preflight errand, he kept his hand locked around the guy's forearm to hold him still. Beneath his grip, that arm was corded sinew. Taut and vibrating with purpose.

Every instinct Dex possessed told him this was one battle he was losing.

"Ben, I forbid it." He locked eyes with his boyhood best friend— the only man whose bed he'd ever shared—and saw his own desperate determination mirrored in those amethyst depths. *Damn it to hell, neither one of us is thinking clearly.* "If anyone's jetting off on some suicide run after the god of the Swarm, it's going to be me and my whole bloody army. For the love of Juno, the *Inevitable*'s running full-bore on their tail as we speak."

Ben tried to twist free, but Dex wasn't having it. The Valyrian flicked a single narrow glance at Dex's opposing hand.

Suddenly his fingers were tingling and Ben was free—all without moving a muscle—dropping the drill into Kaia's open toolbox and beelining for the pilot's console.

"This floating fortress of yours is too flipping slow, Dex," the telepath tossed over his shoulder, stripping off his leather gloves. "And flying blind on the bearing the Hurricane took clicks ago when they stealthed isn't going to get it done. Even if they were on a collision course for Kryll when they vanished, we can't assume that's where they're going. They could be headed anywhere in the Gamma Sector. The lifebond's the only way I know to track her."

Dex stared down at his tingling hand. Ben had just given him a warning. The smallest possible reminder of what the galaxy's most lethal telepath could do.

Too bad for him Dex didn't scare easily.

"The Hurricane's a fuel hog. She was built for attack, not marathon space flight. Which means she can fly fast but not far. When that shapeshifter comes up for air, this battleship is eminently capable of outgunning one nuclear-armed shuttle in head-to-head combat. And that's precisely what I intend to do." Dex curled his stinging fingers into a fist and strode for the exit ramp. "You're not going off alone and that's final. We're done here."

"Is that so?"

Ben's silken whisper brought him pivoting back. His lover's slim hands were dancing over the console, initiating the sequence that would spool up the hyperdrive. Purple light spilled between his fingers and the psi-powered cruiser purred under his touch like a kitten.

But his electric eyes were narrowed on Dex.

"Careful, space cadet," Ben murmured. "Just because I let you run the show in bed doesn't mean you're going to run the rest of my life. This showdown is god versus god and I'm the only guy here who qualifies. I'm going, Dex. I'm going and there isn't a force in this galaxy strong enough to stop me."

"Aren't you forgetting the Butcher of Beta Prime?" Dex demanded, sharp with frustration. "One man. One Mogadon. Not even a telepath. If I'd arrived any later, he'd have bashed your telepathic head in." Dex speared him with a warning finger. "Damnation. I'm trying to protect you. Because you. Are *not*. A god."

Magenta light spilled from Ben Nero's eyes and his raven mane floated around his shoulders in the psychic wind. He might not be a god in the technical sense, but with parapsychic powers like his, he could damn well pass for one.

"Think you can stop me?" Ben whispered.

Dex never could resist a challenge.

Which was a defining trait for a First Indomitable.

Not that Dex would ever, ever hurt him. But the thought of pinning him down and fucking him until Ben came to his senses—or at least until the engine spooled—held a definite appeal.

"Take it easy, kid." From somewhere behind him near the cruiser's entrance, Zorin's big hand landed on Dex's shoulder before he could indulge that rash, futile, testosterone-fueled impulse. "You too, gorgeous. Let's all take a deep breath."

Despite the fear for Kaia churning like ground glass in his belly, Dex's nerves—bowstring-taut and humming with tension—eased a notch under that steady touch. And apparently the older guy had a similar effect on Ben, whose hair stopped floating and whose hands stopped throwing purple sparks.

"Glad you're back," Ben muttered, turning back to his preflight checklist. "Didn't find any trace of her on that contraband scanner you've got set up on the *Relentless*, did you."

"Nope. Our girl and the big bad are still MIA." Zorin gave Dex's knotted shoulder a comforting squeeze. "But I reckon we expected that, didn't we?"

They had, but the knowledge did nothing to stem the tide of bitter disappointment that scoured Dex's struggling sense of hope like salt.

Hold on, darling. We're coming to get you.

"It was worth the attempt." Dex actively resisted the insidious temptation creeping through him to lean back into the Syndax pirate and let Zorin wrap both massive arms around his waist the way he knew his boyhood hero was longing to do.

Because they all needed a little comfort after the way they'd lost Kaia.

But Kaia needed them to *act*.

Right.

Bloody.

Now.

Zorin pushed out a breath and dropped his hand. "Talk to me. What's our game plan?"

Looking annoyed, Ben opened his mouth to speak. But Dex beat him to the punch.

"Ben's entire battle plan consists of taking on Proteus and the whole bloody Swarm in this two-man cruiser. A suicide run I've flatly forbidden. Perhaps when it's you saying it, he'll actually listen."

"And Dex's whole caveman complex has gotten way out of hand." Grimly Ben toggled a switch, and the engine throbbed with eagerness. In just a few ticks, he'd be ready to launch. "Kaia needs me. I'm her lifemate. And both of you need to stay the punk out of my way. Consider yourselves warned."

"Okay." Zorin slouched against the wall and crossed his arms over his armored chest. "Here's my two bits. I guess I got as much drive as either of you to get our girl back, on account of I'm crazy in love with her, I swore to protect her, and she disappeared on my watch. But we gotta be smart.

"Let's face it. We all want her back. But we can't all find her. Bridge log says the Hurricane stealthed soon as she took off. That scanner's the best gear I ever pinched. Costs more than a small planet. It'll pick up anything—even a stealth ship—if it's close enough. And I got zilch. Which means they're flying lickety-split and already outta range. We logged an initial bearing before they stealthed and that's it.

"We wanna find her? It's gonna take Ben and that telepathic lifebond he's got with Kaia to do it."

Dex knew in his bones the Syndax was right.

But he couldn't bring himself to admit it.

Faced with his stubborn silence, Ben threw up his hands. "Look, that Hurricane's the fastest ship you've got. Kaia's souped-up little cruiser here is the only thing that'll outfly her. The only reason that shapeshifter left the *Angel* behind and functional is because he didn't know what she can do—and still doesn't."

Ben's gaze went remote, his focus shifting inward. "Right about now, he's feeling pretty cocky thinking we can't catch him. Which gives us a minuscule advantage. But only if we don't waste it."

"I'll admit you've a point about the *Angel*," Dex admitted grudgingly. "But it should be me who flies her. I'm the best pilot in this sector. And both of you damn well know it."

"This cruiser's custom enhancements run on psi tech, space cadet. Another reason it has to be me. And don't forget the other pressing business Kaia's counting on you and Zorin to finish."

"You can't possibly be talking about the bloody Tombola." Dex snorted. "I don't give one flaming damn about the Patriarch and this barbaric mating contest—"

"Aw, c'mon, kid." Zorin straightened from his slouch and gave Dex a friendly push.

Because, even jolted like they were by this hammering crisis, they were both having trouble keeping their hands off each other. Neither one of them had forgotten what they'd finally been in the middle of doing when they discovered Kaia was missing.

"Our boy's the Valyrian Precursor, ain't he? Rumor says he's the strongest telepath they've had in centuries. He's just what Kaia needs right now," Zorin murmured. "You and me? We gotta win our bouts in the fighting pit in a few clicks and mosey on over to Quorum Starbase like we planned. We gotta finish the game. Or else we void the mating contest and the old man puts Kaia's kid sister in play. And you know Kaia won't want that."

What Dex knew was that he hadn't had a single sensible notion run through his head since the instant he realized Kaia was missing. He knew Ben wasn't thinking much better. He knew Ben was running on pure instinct—but Ben's whole precognitive, clairvoyant, telepathic race had been bred and conditioned from the womb for that.

And Dex retained just enough sanity to know Zorin's clear head and hard-nosed practicality were what they all needed right now.

"Admit it, kid." Zorin gripped his shoulders and gave him a bracing squeeze. "You know I'm right. Now you go on over there and kiss Ben good-bye before that engine spools. So he can get the heck outta here and bring our girl home."

Peeling off from pursuit of the only woman he'd ever loved for what amounted to a glorified publicity stunt on Quorum felt all wrong. Sending Ben flying off after the girl he might already have lost forever on what could very well be a suicide mission felt even worse.

But Zorin gave him a little push to get him started.

Ben met him halfway, same as always, enveloping him in a silken embrace that smelled of sandalwood and determination.

Dex dragged him close and kissed him with all the pent-up passion and clamoring panic he felt roaring in his head. A kiss Ben met with the same scorching heat, kicked up to combustion by the searing shared knowledge that Zorin was watching them both with hungry eyes.

"Bring her home safe." Dex cradled his best friend's sleek black head and stared deep into his glowing eyes. "Promise me, Ben. Because I swear to all the gods in the Mogadon pantheon I won't lose either one of you."

"I promise." Ben leaned in to nuzzle his cheek and whispered in his ear. "You promise me something too. About this thing between you and Zorin. You two need to work it out. Pretty sure that'll be easier if I'm not around."

"Why not?" Dex mumbled, wrapping one hand in Ben's soft hair to hold him close.

"Let's just say, when the two of you finally get horizontal, I doubt you'll be calling the shots." Ben spared him a long-lidded smile. "Oh, you'll be in good hands. And I'd pay real money to watch. But trust me when I say the first time's easier without an audience."

Well, after the way his boyhood hero had taken charge during their almost-encounter in his bed, Dex didn't need to be a rocket scientist to entertain a razor-sharp awareness of just who'd be giving the orders when he and Zorin finally gave in to all that smoking heat that had been building between them for a decade. Speaking as the bloke who was comfortably accustomed to commanding the pilot's seat himself during his erotic encounters, Dex still didn't know how he felt about that. But this moment was all about Ben.

Ben, whom he'd loved for a lifetime.

Ben, who was flying off and leaving him.

Ben, who might never return.

Dex burned with an overwhelming drive. The drive to mark him, take him, possess him, claim him. Physically and in every other way.

But they were flat out of time.

Ben said in a whisper, "Hold that thought for me, okay? Hold it till I bring back our girl. Then it's all four of us."

His gaze flickered over Dex's shoulder to Zorin, and his face softened in a way that twisted Dex's already aching heart to a pulp.

You too. Ben's mental murmur sounded in his head. *Come over here, big guy.*

Zorin pushed out a strangled sound that told Dex more clearly than speech how much he was yearning for the invite. A breath later his solid strength was enfolding them in the feral scent of steel and predator. Dex realized with a jolt that a healthy whiff of the exiled Mogadon's mating scent was rising from his own skin. That bloody pirate was *claiming* him.

Any Mogadon with a nose was going to know exactly what he'd nearly let Zorin do to him tonight.

"Sorry," Zorin muttered into his hair, pulling them both into his broad chest for a rough hug. "Don't have much choice, do I? I know it's a lot to adjust to, kid—"

"We like it." Ben swooped in to press a swift searing kiss—over in a heartbeat—to the pirate's startled mouth. His violet eyes dared Dex to disagree. "Don't we, Dex?"

Dex was eyeing the look of dazed pleasure spreading over Zorin's craggy features. Which was probably a dead ringer for the way he'd looked himself the first time Ben kissed him.

He'd thought maybe he'd feel jealous, seeing Ben all over another guy. But seeing him all over Zorin, seeing how happy Ben made his boyhood idol, electrified Dex with a flash of floating euphoria that made him feel—just for a tick—suspiciously similar to happy himself.

"It's… an adjustment," he said, meeting Zorin's patient gaze. "But I'm not objecting. The Mogadon army, as you well know, is another matter entirely."

Even though it's been years since the Mogadon Empire, at my father's command, crucified men for doing what the three of us are contemplating. But my father's been dead a long time. Somehow my army will have to accept this… new reality. The reality of me—their commander, Max Draven's son—taking not only Kaia, but these two men as consorts.

"You and me, we got time." Zorin's square jaw hardened and his blue eyes darkened to oxidized steel. "But Kaia doesn't. Let's get this show on the road, gorgeous. You go on out there and bring back our girl."

#

She had to keep reminding herself he wasn't really Dex.

Or else she'd never be able to kill him.

From her awkward position—fingers tingling, arm throbbing, shoulders cramped with confinement—Kaia stared grimly over the Hurricane's nav console at the rusty orb of Kryll, the desert planet now swollen in the viewport to the size of a gravity bomb. The last time she'd seen her homeworld, it was through the porthole of a smuggler's ship the day she ran away, her heart still reeling for Ben Nero, believed dead with the rest of his race in Max Draven's genetically targeted biowar.

The day her father first threatened her with the Tombola.

"I can sense your discomfort." From the pilot's console, Dex's familiar profile angled toward her. Because Proteus needed to be Dex to authorize the landing sequence on the Hurricane. "Your pulse and respiration are elevated. Do you require the toilet?"

"Too bad for me if I did, the way you have me hogtied," she pointed out, tone acid with resentment.

Don't think of him as Dex. Think of him as someone you'll have to kill. Because you know better than anyone that not even a god lives forever.

Anyway, angel, the galaxy isn't going to save itself. Right now that appears to be your job.

He sliced her a cool cobalt look—which made her *really* grateful that, unlike the real Dex, this scary 2.0 knockoff couldn't read her mind.

"I won't unshackle you, samurai. But I'm quite thoroughly acquainted with the noisome and unsanitary biological elimination requirements of the human body. I'm prepared to render the necessary assistance."

As.

If.

"Appealing an offer as that is," she said dryly, "I'm gonna take a pass."

"As you like," he murmured, indifferent.

His dispassionate courtesy was giving her chills. That dispassion was almost worse than uncontrolled cruelty. Because passionate people made rash mistakes, while relentlessly logical and patient ones did not. His dispassion gave her a window into what he'd be like standing over her in his laboratory.

With her strapped to a table screaming.

Somehow I've got to get out of here. Before my father gives me to him for keeps.

Settling back in her chair like she was rebooting her brain with a catnap, she watched through lowered lids while Proteus initiated the comms sequence that would snag them a landing berth on Kryll. Familiarizing herself with the functions of the console—especially the secondary functions she wouldn't need Dex's biometrics to access.

Those functions delineated the limited range of options she'd have to distract and contain him once she made her move. Because if Proteus had Dex's honed strength and lightning reflexes at his command, she couldn't be confident in her ability to get her hands on that nerve gun.

Not long enough to use it.

Without Dex's biometrics, the weapons console was entirely off-limits, as was the nav computer. But she was willing to bet she could trigger emergency systems like life support in a pinch.

"Kryll Capital Spaceport, this is Mogadon shuttle *Ascendant*." Dex's coldly authoritative voice gave her a jolt. "I require priority docking privileges and immediate transport for two to the Patriarch's palace."

A burst of static nearly drowned out the reply, spoken in a youthful voice edged in caution.

"Negative, *Ascendant*. We're on full planetary lockdown due to the, ah, incident on Quorum. All incoming traffic is diverted to Helix Starbase until the situation has stabilized."

Kaia's chest clenched in a vise of nerves. This was bad news. Because it validated what Proteus had said about the spacepox outbreak on Quorum—that hot zone of contagion her men were flying straight into. An invisible, almost invariably lethal menace about which she had precisely zero ability to warn them.

If the Hurricane was locked in limbo out on Helix, she'd be stranded in space with Proteus.

She'd rather be stranded in a smuggler's hole with a nest of stinging scorpions.

Still, any starbase was a dicey place, rife with gangsters and smugglers and desperados for hire. Part trading hub, part opium den, part maintenance depot. Starbase barons—of all genders—wrote their own rules and enforced them ruthlessly through a murky system of hired mercenaries and vigilante justice. Often those hired guns were Syndax.

Which meant the baron of Helix Starbase might be signing their paychecks, but those would be Zorin's men—

"This shuttle is captained by Commander Dex Draven, First Indomitable of the Mogadon Empire. Perhaps you're familiar." Stars and comets, the shapeshifter was getting better at this. He'd refined the real Dex's icy imperial authority to alarming perfection. "I have the Kryll maharani in my custody, eager to consummate her Tombola mating ritual. I'd advise you to consult your commanding officer. You'll find I have full transit privileges personally authorized by His High Holiness."

They waited through a pause that conveyed the junior officer's consternation.

"Stand by, *Ascendant*."

Way better for her if they were diverted to Helix. But whether they were cleared to land planet-side or sidelined to starbase, Kaia needed to act. Because it was nice to imagine Dex's *Inevitable* or Zorin's *Relentless* racing to her rescue…

But waiting for someone else to save her hide had never been her style.

Her first order of business was sleuthing out a way to shimmy free from these handcuffs.

"*Ascendant*, this is Spaceport. Proceed on landing approach Kappa to the executive docking terminal. We'll be waiting." The youthful voice went vibrant with suppressed emotion. "And tell Her Holiness—on behalf of the entire planetary congregation—*welcome home*."

Her Holiness.

Angels of Anaxos. That was the captive title and crushing fate she'd fled millions of Mogadon miles in a cargo bin to escape. Her heart kicked up its anxious tempo—a telling physiological response she knew her captor was reading like a flight manual. Her breath roughened and her palms turned to ice.

I have to get out of here. Have to.

As in yesterday.

Her gut churned with roiling panic. Grimly she battled it back. Self-mastery was the foundational first skill they taught at the Psi Academy. As a half-Kryll hybrid, she'd been hopeless at her psychic studies. Until she met Ben. Who'd tutored her through the rough spots.

Ben.

Gods, Ben! You have to be coming for me. Because the only guy I know who has a snowball's chance in a solar flare at tracking a stealthed ship through deep space is a Valyrian Precursor with a lifebond.

But I can't wait for you to get here.

Her heartbeat was slowing. Her breath leveling. And self-mastery wasn't the only skill she'd picked up at the Psi Academy. Even with Ben's help, she'd never been much good at the mental dexterity required for fine tasks like telepathic surgery or mechanical manipulation. Her full-blooded Valyrian teachers had totally written her off. Told her she just couldn't do it.

But she'd never been this motivated to blow past her own limits and prove them all wrong.

Carefully Kaia steadied her jumpy pulse and eased her cramped muscles. Then, with the delicate lightness of a feather settling to the ground, she attuned her telepathic awareness to the tiny mechanical complexity that made up her handcuffs.

And the lock.

CHAPTER THREE
The Seduction

Zorin planted a heavy palm against the rusting biometric panel outside his digs on the *Relentless*.

Relieved as always when the aging tech on this pirate ship of his kicked in and the door actually opened.

He trudged into the industrial icebox clutter of the captain's quarters he'd learned to call home, littered with battered comforts from a bygone age, cloaked in the fake blue twilight that blurred the wear and tear of exile and softened the harsh edges of war.

The familiar weight of his starmetal armor dragged him down like ten Gs of gravity.

He'd just killed a man in the blood games, and killed him with savage pleasure. Some Kryll bastard in the Tombola contest who'd sneered about clapping Kaia in chains. Then he'd stood guard like a damn watchdog while Dex cited some obscure provision he'd dredged up from the Apocrypha for taking his absent brother Cato's Tombola bout. And watched Dex bludgeon to death some snarling Mogadon jackal whose cruelty would've killed Kaia on their mating night. Watched Dex take care of business armed with nothing but his own capable fists and a First Indomitable's battle-honed brutality.

A feat that would boost Pontius Cato to the final ten.

Along with Zorin himself.

Finally, back on board the *Relentless* and way too amped up to sleep, Zorin had wasted half the night fiddling like a fool with his subspace scanner. Fueled by the clattering hum of nerves and worry rather than the unforgiving logic of his famously cool head.

Trying without success to get a fix on Kaia. Some whisper of coordinates he could beam to Ben, last seen streaking toward Kryll in

Kaia's souped-up cruiser, running on blind faith and whatever subliminal whisper of instinct the galaxy's most powerful telepath could discern in the still, silent void of space.

While Zorin and Dex in their battleships peeled off to protect Kaia's kid sis the way they knew she wanted. If they couldn't placate her Pops the Patriarch, he figured maybe they'd spring little Kylie out of his custody.

Even though turning away from their girl, knowing Kaia was in desperate danger, tasted bitter in his mouth as betrayal.

Now, before he hit the rack for a few clicks of badly needed shut-eye, he needed to get the *Inevitable* on the horn. Because he and Dex needed to cobble together some kinda game plan before they reached Quorum and the Patriarch.

The door rattled shut behind him. Rolling his tired head on his aching shoulders, unbuckling his utility belt with hands made clumsy by exhaustion, Zorin was halfway across the living room before his sluggish brain kicked in.

And told him he wasn't alone.

A fully armed and uniformed First Indomitable was sacked out on his couch.

Snoring.

All cleaned up from the fighting pit and sitting straight up—clearly waiting for Zorin when he'd conked out. Hands slack on knees, lips parted in sleep, burnished head tipped back at a wicked angle that was gonna give the kid one hell of a crick in his neck when he finally came to.

Zorin stood like he'd taken root and just stared at the guy. Reading the terrible toll of guilt and grief for losing their girl chiseled like print in Dex's furrowed brow and haggard features.

The same guilt he saw etched in his own ugly mug whenever he got a gander in the glass.

Still, the kid was way too much a soldier to disarm before he crashed on a Syndax ship. A ship he had to believe in his bones, after eight years of lightning raids and running skirmishes, to be enemy turf.

Yet he'd come here anyway.

He'd trusted Zorin to honor the uneasy, unwritten truce that hung by a nanofiber between the ruling Mogadon race and the upstart Syndax horde. Maybe he'd told himself a story before he hopped on the transport shuttle. The same tall tale about strategy and battle tactics that'd had Zorin reaching for the horn to call him.

When the plain truth was he was hurting and lonely.

They both were.

Their girl was gone—snatched on their watch—and their boy had jetted off into jeopardy to bring her back.

As he stared down at Dex—the prize pupil he'd trained to fight, the trusted comrade he'd refused to kill, the solitary kid he'd spent a lifetime telling himself repeatedly he loved like a son—Zorin felt his poor old ticker turn over with a convulsive heave he couldn't call anything but what it was.

Neptune's knickers. Why the hell fight it. He's not a student or a subordinate or a kid anymore. Even if he is your best friend's son and even if you whacked his dad out of mercy for the crazy bastard.

You're in love with him, knucklehead. You're so many fathoms deep in love with Dex Draven you've forgotten how it feels to breathe.

And why the hell that struck him as such a gods-damned revelation he'd never have a clue.

Moving like he was sleepwalking, he wrestled off his clunky space boots and peeled out of his armor. Later he needed a shower, but now he was dead on his feet. Barefoot in fighting leathers, he padded silently across the floor and eased down next to Dex.

He'd have liked to get the guy off the couch into an actual bed—even if all they did there was sleep—but he figured if he woke him up there was a level chance Dex wouldn't even agree to stay. Way too much unfinished business between them for Dex to rest easy in his arms the way he wanted.

The way he ached for, if he was being honest.

Zorin settled for unbuckling Dex's blaster so he wouldn't shoot himself in the hip while he slept, then wrapping a careful arm around the kid's shoulders to ease the awkward angle of his head.

His own familiar scent seeped through him, laced with the dusty sage of Mogadon soap and the dark bracing spice that meant Dex. He'd only had the guy under him for one unforgettable tick in Dex's bed—that dizzying, singular instant he'd spent breathless with anticipation, believing a lifetime of hidden dreams and fantasies was finally about to come true.

But Zorin had been so crazy turned on and scenting so hard it had only taken a tick to mark him.

Damn straight I marked him, he thought with a degree of protective ferocity that surprised him. *He's the alpha male of the galaxy's dominant race. There isn't a Mogadon alive who doesn't want him. But the only Mogadon… ex-Mogadon… whose bed he's gonna be sharing from now on is me.*

Even dead on his feet, he was already half-hard with anticipation. But nothing he couldn't handle. And he'd slept in his fighting leathers before. Wouldn't do him any harm. Besides, Zorin would rather sleep sporting a boner in full rig with Dex on his couch than sleep comfy, spent and solo in his own cushy bed.

Dex looped a sleeping arm around his waist and turned into his neck with a deep, trusting sigh.

And Zorin's battered heart just about stopped beating.

"Damn," Zorin whispered. "Just damn."

He'd fought like all seven devils for a lifetime not to fall in love with Dex Draven. But an old warhorse like him had way too much savvy not to own up and admit it when he'd flat-out lost the fight.

#

Something was tickling Dex's face.

Something soft and warm as a feather was brushing his cheek. In time with the rhythmic buzz of someone's snore.

Ben never snored.

And neither did Kaia.

Dex's eyes flashed open to find himself sprawled full length across a battered orgy couch, facedown over the warm powerful bulk of the Syndax leader's sleeping body. His arm draped across Zorin's muscled torso. His fist gripping Zorin's stretchy shirt. His head pillowed on Zorin's bulky shoulder.

And the slow warmth fanning his face was Zorin's sleeping breath.

Dex grunted in surprise. The guy lay so close, their foreheads were practically touching. But Dex felt way too comfortable—way too warm, way too relaxed, way too—well, peaceful—and somehow way too *safe* to budge. None of these sensations at all common, in his experience, to the short danger-packed life of a First Indomitable.

At least not until recently.

A handspan away, the pirate's silver eyes opened.

"Howdy, kid," Zorin rasped, husky with sleep.

He lay close enough for Dex to see the tawny glitter of stubble, salted with silver, along Zorin's rugged jaw. And it felt like the most natural thing in the world for Dex to lean in until their mouths met.

Every kiss they'd ever shared was about sexual domination. Which both of them were comfortably accustomed to wielding. Based on those scorching, no-holds-barred kisses, that same relentless, unstoppable sense of possession Zorin exhibited toward Kaia was also what he felt toward Dex. And Dex definitely wasn't used to being dominated or possessed in bed or anywhere else. The fact that submitting to Zorin had started to feature in his nocturnal fantasies— fantasies from which he woke aching and hard enough to spill in his own hand—was a secret truth he was still grappling with.

This kiss, in total contrast, was gentle and tender as a baby's breath. Even when Zorin's big hand wrapped around his head to hold him, the guy kissed Dex like he thought he'd break.

It was a kiss Dex had never in his life felt anything like. A kiss that rendered him speechless. Breathless. Downright defenseless. He sighed into the careful heat of Zorin's mouth, tasting the bitter sweetness of *chaco* the Syndax must have been quaffing to stay awake, and rested a hand against the rough stubble of Zorin's hard face.

"Howdy yourself," Dex whispered against his mouth. Because this was a kiss he was strangely reluctant to end.

"Wha' time is it?" Zorin mumbled, without moving a muscle to check.

Dex tilted his arm to read his wrist unit without lifting his hand from the pirate's face.

"Six clicks to Quorum." He tried to wake up. Tried to think about what needed to be done. Tried to think about anything but the way he was lying in Zorin's arms, the pirate's fingers stroking slow soothing circles against his back. "There could be news from those fighters we sent ahead to scout. Or from Ben…"

"My boys woulda pinged me either way. So would yours. Which means we got nothing. But we still got time." Zorin's battle-hardened hand smoothed over Dex's hair. Tenderness softened his sleepy face. "Kid, I'm more than happy to spend the rest of the night cuddled up with you right here, but this couch isn't doing my back any favors. Any chance we could maybe shift over to the bed? We don't have to do anything but sleep."

"What if I wanted to do more?" Dex heard himself whisper.

The pirate's eyes darkened to navy.

"Do you?" he said in a low visceral growl that shot straight to Dex's cock.

Suddenly Zorin looked as dangerous and predatory as the space pirate he was. A sexually aggressive whiff of wolf and metal rose from his skin. Dex's cock tingled and his balls tightened, making it harder than blazes to think.

Still, he tried to keep his head together and articulate what the other guy needed to know.

"You'll need to… take it easy," Dex said gruffly. "I mean it, Zorin. I'm still fairly new to all this. The only man I've ever been with is Ben." Roughly he cleared his throat, feeling heat creep up his neck. "You do, I trust, comprehend what I'm getting at?"

Zorin's lashes dropped over his knowing eyes. "Sure I do. With Ben, you call the shots. That's how both of you like it. It's gonna be different with me though, ain't it?" When Dex said nothing, Zorin pressed their foreheads together. "Ain't it?"

"Why else do you think I've been fighting this thing between us like the very devil?" Faced with Zorin's patient gaze, Dex closed his eyes and breathed, "But… yes… with you, it will indeed be quite different."

"Good lad." Zorin leaned in to kiss his forehead. An avuncular, oddly tender gesture that did strange things to Dex's heart. "I'm not in any big rush. That's the advantage of being with an old guy like me." The pirate's face creased in a wry smile. "Shoot, we can just do this if you want. Gods' honest, I don't think I'm ever gonna get tired of kissing you."

His hands cradled Dex's head—crazy gentle for a pirate—and steadied him for another of those leisurely, exploratory kisses that were making him lose his mind. One slow synapse at a time.

By all the gods of Olympus, he'd wanted too much for too long with this man to leave things between them at kissing.

"What if I wanted to do more?" Dex repeated, harsh with urgency. "A lot more. Could we still take it slow?"

Zorin took his time finishing the kiss, teeth scraping gently along

Dex's lower lip. "We can take this as slow as you want. Stop anytime you want. You can tell me to tap the brakes often as you want. Otherwise, all you need to do is kick back and enjoy the ride."

That was something else Dex had never known. Because you couldn't exactly kick back and enjoy the ride when you were always in the pilot's seat. Just the notion of doing that now, yielding the yoke and ceding control to Zorin's firm hand…

Sexual craving clawed through him, sharp and savage as a feral cat.

Clumsy with demand, Dex leaned in to kiss him again, and Zorin kissed him back slow and easy. This time, his hands slid down Dex's back to fit their hips together. Dex seized the moment to straddle Zorin's leather-clad thighs. He was already hard enough to lose it, scenting hard enough to make them both crazy. And it wasn't only Dex smelling like Zorin now. It was Zorin smelling like Dex.

A state of affairs that filled him with ferocious satisfaction.

Because gods knew he wasn't going to tolerate any other Mogadon in his guy's bed. Just them and Ben and Kaia.

He thrust without shame against the rigid bulge under Zorin's leathers, hearing his own breath harsh and urgent. In fact, he sounded as desperate and breathless with Zorin as Ben sounded with Dex. And when Zorin finally had his way with all three of them, he was really going to blow Ben's Valyrian mind.

A visual so potent it just about made Dex come in his trousers.

"Jupiter, kid, you're driving me nuts," Zorin said. "I swear I'll take care of you. You just need to be honest with me. Tell me what you do and don't want. And it'll help me out a lot if you can bring yourself to trust me."

The pirate's molten eyes burned into him. "Think you can do that for me?"

Dex had to clear his throat before he could answer. Even then, his voice sounded like a stranger's. "I can do that. I mean—I can—trust you."

Zorin's hands curled around his ass and held him steady against the slow rhythm of his thrusts. Dex clutched his shoulders with desperate fingers and thrust back without finesse.

"Oh—stars, kid—just like that," Zorin groaned. "You have absolutely no idea—how long I've wanted this."

"Me too," Dex panted, tongue meeting tongue in an electric openmouthed kiss. "You've been the star of my… locker room fantasies… for a really long time. Even though I fought like hell never to admit it. Even to myself. If I'd ever—let it slip—my bloody father would've had me crucified."

"Me, he woulda castrated with his bare hands," Zorin muttered grimly. "Fed my balls to his fighting dogs. Then crucified me. But that wasn't the reason I held back."

"You had to know though, didn't you?" Dex frowned against his mouth. "Yet you never—gods, you taste good—took advantage."

"That should tell you something about me then, shouldn't it?" Hands cradling his ass, Zorin leaned into him for another slow, deep, bittersweet kiss. "I'll always have your back. No matter what. So, for tonight, we got a deal?"

Dex's heart was pounding and his mouth was dry. But he couldn't have turned back now if it killed him. "Right." Gods, was he blushing? "We've got a deal. Tell me what you want me to do."

"Up." Zorin gave his ass a squeeze and released him. "Bedroom. And I'm tempted as heck to bargain for a back rub after."

"I believe I can accommodate that." Dex pushed up to sit, his pulse kicking up and his stomach doing backflips.

Zorin uncoiled to his feet, graceful as a panther in his fighting leathers despite his monumental size, and pulled Dex up after him. The pirate paused to peel his shirt over his head.

And Dex thought his heart would stop.

In their locker-room fly-bys growing up, he'd always done his level best not to notice what Zorin looked like naked. Which hadn't been all that often, because Zorin had always been a lot more modest around him than most Mogadon males bothered to be—obviously for reasons like ethics and decency that were finally starting to crystallize in Dex's head.

All of which meant that a shirtless Zorin, all bulging biceps and hulking shoulders and solid slabs of pectoral muscle scored with battle scars, was largely uncharted terrain. That Syndax tribal ink was definitely a recent add. Now the sight of all that smooth tattooed skin, as Zorin stood before him barefoot wearing nothing but a pair of leather pants stretched straining over the bulge of a massive boner, was definitely making Dex's mouth water.

Feeling like he was dreaming, his fingers drifted to the buttons of his uniform jacket.

"No, don't. I'll do all that," Zorin rasped. "I'm gonna take good care of you, kid. I promise. Just mosey on over to the bedroom for me."

It was his first command, but easy enough to follow. Especially when Zorin turned him gently toward the bedroom door and nudged him along, hands resting on his shoulders, strong thumbs kneading the tension from his neck.

By the subdued blue light oozing from the ceiling panels, they padded through the decayed splendor of the captain's quarters, all rusting arches and crumbling pillars and battered furnishings that still managed to project a sense of lived-in comfort. Through an open door, he glimpsed the echoing mosaics and steaming waters of a Mogadon *thermae*. He entertained a sudden flash of Zorin pinning Kaia to the slick tiles and pounding into her until her eyes went ultraviolet and both of them cried out in desperate pleasure.

His cock jerked and swelled. No doubt about it, watching Zorin ride Kaia was going to get him off like a rocket.

But that was for later. Now was for them. Now was for Dex and Zorin.

Now was the pirate's bedroom, a faded echo of imperial power, dominated by a bed the size of an armed Zephyr, mattress piled with an untidy tangle of thermal silver blankets to retain heat. Because this rust bucket Zorin had absconded with from the junkyard on Mogadon eight years ago when he fled imperial justice was more than a little drafty.

But the bed smelled like Kaia—like cyberspace and jasmine and a woman's passion. His own woman's unmistakably familiar fragrance.

That scent throttled his heart in a fist of longing.

"Ben's gonna get her home for us," Zorin whispered in his ear. "We gotta trust him to do that, kid. But if you don't—don't wanna do this right now—"

"No. I want this. I *definitely* want this."

There was so much he still didn't know about where the four of them were going. But this much he knew beyond a doubt.

Right now his boyhood hero, naked and scenting and hard for him in that big tumbled bed, was *all* he wanted.

"Okay then." Zorin's big hands left his shoulders to span his waist. "Remember—you need me to hit the brakes, you just let me know."

The pirate's calloused fingers, nimble for so large a man, worked open the gleaming buttons of his jacket and deftly slid him out of it. Then peeled him out of his shirt just as neatly. Dex stood like he was dreaming, the recipient of these capable attentions, flat-out incapable of recalling the last time he'd let anyone set the pace like this. The first time he'd had Kaia, she'd pulled at his clothes with a desperate, untutored eagerness that turned him on like blazes—but he'd been her first. He'd been utterly in command of her pleasure.

He'd been the one doing the seducing.

This time, he was the one being seduced.

Zorin's powerful arms wrapped around him from behind and eased him back against his broad naked chest. A devilish vulnerable placement—no place he'd ever tolerate a man he couldn't trust—especially one so much bigger than he was. And, technically, their armies were still at war. A hard shiver of arousal skidded through him. The pirate bent to nuzzle his neck, all sandpaper whiskers and soft lips and the tender scrape of teeth.

"Tell me what you're thinking," he said huskily against Dex's skin. "I'm no telepath like Ben and Kaia. You need to tell me if you're losing it."

"I'm thinking you're bloody good at this. I'm not the first man you've seduced, am I?" Dex turned his face into the hard plane of Zorin's chest and felt the heavy thud of a mighty heartbeat against his cheek. A flicker of surprise sparked the trace of a smile. "Your heart's pounding like a drum. Possibly I'm not the only one feeling a trifle skittish?"

"Are you kidding? I'm nervous as all get-out that I'm gonna screw this up," Zorin muttered, hard hands sliding over his ribs in a caress that made Dex shiver all over again. "Even if it's not my first go-round. It's my first go-round with you. I want you to want this like crazy. Same way I do."

Somehow knowing Zorin too was jumpy—that he cared enough about Dex's nerves to be nervous himself—was precisely the reassurance he needed. It eased the worst of his first-time jitters. When the pirate's fingers found the tight nubs of his nipples, twin jets of sensation streaked straight to his cock. His gasp of surprised pleasure was all the encouragement Zorin needed to linger, tweaking and rolling and finally pinching hard enough to elicit the moan Dex had been trying like hell to contain.

"Juno," he breathed, hands finding Zorin's leather-clad thighs and clutching hard. "I'm no woman, but damn if that doesn't bloody blow a man's mind."

"Good to know," Zorin chuckled, breath warm in Dex's ear. "Not every guy likes it. But you like it rough, don'tcha? Just like Kaia. I guess I know what both of you need, don't I?"

The thought of Zorin making love to him the way he did to Kaia shouldn't turn him on. Dex figured he should find it… somehow… unmanly. Still, the hungry sting of Zorin's mouth marking him, sucking a bruise into the side of his neck, sent a heavy surge of weakness down his legs. Particularly coupled with the play of hard, knowing fingers tweaking his nipples. Jupiter, he was already hard enough to explode inside the trousers Zorin still hadn't gotten around to working him out of.

Panting with need, he rocked back into the colossal bulge of Zorin's shaft, hands sliding over leather to find the hard muscled swell of his ass and pull him closer. Which was all the pirate needed to finally—gods, yes, *finally*—slide a hand south to find the rigid blade of Dex's cock wedged hard against his zipper.

A deep groan rumbled through Zorin's powerful chest. Skilled fingers wrapped around his length to work him through the fabric. Dex gasped and rocked into his touch.

"Ready for more now, ain'tcha, kid?" His voice was hoarse in Dex's ear. "You ready for more of me?"

Dex lost track of his own response. He thought he was panting words like *more* and *gods* and *please*.

And if it was unmanly to beg, he didn't give one combustible damn.

He pushed into Zorin's hand, ready to explode with frustration. The guy eased down his zipper and patiently worked open the slit in his combat briefs. Finally his cock sprang free, jutting into prominence, already slick with eagerness. Zorin's big hand wrapped around him and gave him a long slow stroke from base to tip that only made him wetter.

"There you are," Zorin whispered in his ear. "Is all this for me?"

"You know it is."

"Shoot, Dex." His breath roughened. "If you knew how many times I've dreamed about this… about *you*… hard and moaning under my hand…"

"Yeah. Me too."

Guttural with craving, he watched the guy's hand work up and down his length, slow and easy, building layer upon layer of surging need until he could barely even think, much less speak. If Zorin's arms weren't solidly around him, holding him up, he was fairly certain his knees would buckle.

This was when he would have shackled Ben's hands. Before he teased Dex to the breaking point. The fact that he couldn't do that to Zorin, that he had zero recourse except to grit his teeth and pray he didn't humiliate himself by spilling in the guy's hand like a bloody teenager on his first date, was slowly driving him berserk.

"For gods' sake, Zorin," he moaned, giving up every last pretense of self-control and bucking into his hand. "I can't—can't wait—oh gods—"

"Sure you can, kid." The pirate squeezed his base to slow him down. "You and me, we're just getting started. I'll tell you when to come. You'll wait till I say, won'tcha?"

"Yes." Dex panted. After all, this was a game he knew how to play. "But hurry the hell up."

"Impatient for me, ain'tcha?" Zorin chuckled and pushed him gently toward the bed. "That's what I like to hear. Now what about these boots, soldier? Should we call in a prefect to help?"

Dex muttered an expletive, but didn't protest when Zorin sat him on the bed and knelt between his feet to deal with the boots himself. Watching those hard, capable soldier's hands wrestle him out of his boots was another kind of turn-on, especially with his still-desperate cock jutting eagerly in plain sight the whole time. He had to grip the blankets in both fists to keep his hands off his own shaft.

When his blasted boots were finally dealt with, Zorin turned his attention to his trousers. Now his touch turned gentle, coaxing, careful as though Dex were some virginal girl he had to seduce to keep from fleeing.

And damn if that didn't do it for him.

His own breath came ragged and audible—too audible—in the

artificial twilight. Especially when Zorin eased him out of his combat briefs without ever touching the part of him that was burning for it.

Now he was naked and helpless as the boy he'd once been. The boy who'd lain aching in his lonely bed at night, on fire with shame and craving, and dreamed of this very moment with hopeless longing. His long-ago idol knelt between his knees, still wearing those damn erotic-as-a-heart-attack leather pants, hands resting on his thighs, face rugged and gorgeous and harsh with need under his tousled hair.

"Please," Dex got out somehow.

"Please what?" Humor sparked under the sizzling heat in Zorin's mercury eyes. "Am I going too fast? You said you wanted to take it slow."

"Slow, yes. This pace is positively glacial." Dex had never been any good at submission. He leaned in, cradled the guy's face in his hands, and kissed him the way he was dying to do. With all the openmouthed hunger of a man who was starving.

Zorin groaned into his mouth, their tongues sliding together in a swirl of wet heat, the bitter bite of *chaco* mingling with the smoky slug of whiskey Dex had pounded before he flew over to the Syndax ship.

Wanting exactly what its captain was now giving him. But not having the first clue how to ask for it.

Breathing hard, Zorin pushed him to his back and climbed on top. Big hands pinned his shoulders to the mattress.

"This isn't up to you—remember?" Powerful hips pushed his thighs apart like he was a woman and rocked into him. The shock of friction all down his shaft wrenched a groan from his throat. Dex had the foggy certainty he was leaving precum all over the man's expensive leather. "It's your first time and I'm a big guy. This is only gonna work when you're desperate for me as all get-out. When you're begging."

"I don't beg worth a damn," Dex growled.

Zorin gave him a wolfish grin. "First time for everything, kid."

Then the guy just went to work on him. Dragging his tongue over Dex's panting neck and sweat-slick chest and—oh gods—grazing sharp teeth against his nipples. His massive size and muscled bulk pushed Dex into the mattress. An experience utterly different from tussling with Ben's lithe wildcat ferocity or driving into Kaia's supple quicksilver heat. By the time Zorin worked his way down his abdomen, Dex had forgotten what he was supposed to be fighting. Between those searing kisses and the words of praise the guy was whispering against his skin, he'd practically forgotten his own name.

"Gods above, you're gorgeous like this," Zorin said thickly. "Eight years of exile and I never forgot you. Never stopped wanting you. Tell me what you're thinking."

"I'm thinking… this is what it's like," Dex gasped, "being ravished by a pirate."

"Too much?" Battle-hardened hands caught his thighs and spread him wide. "Or not enough?"

"Not nearly enough."

He realized he was gripping Zorin's head in both hands, gripping hard enough to pull his hair, back arched and hips riding from the mattress in desperate demand. He could barely bring himself to believe one of those utterly unattainable bucket list fantasies from his long lonely youth could possibly be about to come true. With Zorin running the show, he'd fully expected to be on his knees working the guy over himself.

He hadn't expected to be coaxed and seduced and, well, ravished. In fact, he was starting to realize he hadn't had the first damn clue.

About anything.

Hot breath caressed his aching length. Right before Zorin whispered, "Well, kid? What do you say?"

The word ripped from his straining throat.

"*Please*. Juno and Jupiter—please—stop bloody talking and suck my cock."

For an agonizing instant, Zorin hesitated. "Been a long time for me. I might not be much good at this."

"Somehow I doubt that's going to be a problem," Dex gasped out with a laugh.

"You asked for it. Remember not to come till I say." The other guy's voice was harsh with desire and menace. "Which won't be till I'm buried deep inside you."

Not long ago, a statement of intent that explicit would have had him bolting for the door.

Now it only made Dex shudder with need. "I promise."

"Good lad."

Liquid heat engulfed the head of his cock. Dex's eyes rolled back in his head as blinding pleasure surged down his length. Zorin's slick tongue slid down the underside of his shaft like they'd been made for each other, firing every nerve and hitting every switch on his console. That tight suction worked up and down his cock, taking more of him in with every stroke, until Dex thought he would lose his mind. He wanted to rut with frantic need into the hot tight heaven of the guy's mouth.

But Zorin's strong hands pinned his thighs to the mattress and kept him firmly in command.

Dex could only clutch the man's head as it rose and fell along his shaft, low wordless cries exploding from his lips with every downstroke. When his tip nudged the back of Zorin's throat, he nearly lost it.

By that point, he was so far out of his infernal mind with need and pleasure that seeing the guy raise his sandy head and slide a finger in his own mouth to wet it just made him hotter.

"How'm I doing?" the pirate mumbled around Dex's aching cock. Just the sight of his own swollen length, shiny with the other guy's saliva and jerking with need, ripped another moan from his throat.

"Jupiter's flaming bollocks," Dex panted. "This is supposed to be—you rusty—out of practice?"

"Mmm-hmm." Satisfaction smoldered in Zorin's silver eyes as his mouth slid back down Dex's shaft. The indescribable sensation of his throat tightening and swallowing around Dex's cock nearly pushed him over the edge.

Which made it surprisingly easy not to protest the careful finger that teased him open from behind, playing with his pucker until he softened and yielded to the first slow penetration he'd ever experienced. He absorbed the unavoidable sense of pressure, the intimate invasion he couldn't oppose, the hot burn of accommodation as that thick finger breached the tight ring of muscle to fill him. Stretching and readying him one knuckle at a time to accept another man's cock.

To submit to an act he'd always been told was the ultimate humiliation any man could endure.

And why in the seven hells that thought inflamed him and swelled his own cock nearly to the spilling point, he couldn't for the life of him explain. All he knew was he'd kill to keep Zorin's mind-blowing mouth moving up and down his shaft. He'd accept the slow thrust of the finger riding his rear passage.

He'd even submit to the second finger working its way inside to stretch him even wider.

And anyone watching him writhe with pleasure in the Syndax leader's bed, hearing the sharp urgent cries of encouragement and entreaty he couldn't contain, would have to be forgiven for concluding that he liked it.

That he loved it.

That he couldn't get enough of it.

Of being dominated and violated and made to submit to another man's passion.

By the time Zorin got him good and ready to take the third finger, he knew he'd reached his absolute limit. He'd never felt as full, as stretched, as close to losing his mind in his life. When the pirate released his desperately throbbing cock and came up for air, Dex's breath rushed out in a sound that was half sob of relief and half long shameful moan for more.

Now he had to wait what felt like bloody *eons* while the other guy shucked his leather pants. And that first mind-shattering sight of Zorin's thick shaft—swollen and rigid and eager for him, a shining tendril of precum already drooling from his tip—wrung out another desperate groan.

Because he couldn't imagine how on twelve earths he'd ever be able to… well… accommodate all that.

"Gods of Olympus," he said hoarsely.

"All rumors to the contrary, kid, I'm far from godlike." In Zorin's tone, wry humor fought with raw need. "If you want me to stop, I need you to tell me right now. Otherwise I'm pretty sure we're going all the way."

"What if I don't?" Dex whispered. "What if I tell you—I need more of it? All of it? All of *you*?"

Zorin's rugged features softened with tenderness. "Then I'm gonna need you to stand up for me. I reckon this'll be easier for you— psychologically, I guess—if you're not underneath."

Strong hands pulled Dex to his feet. His legs were shaking so hard he could barely stand. But the hard, hungry kiss Zorin pulled him into— a kiss slick and salty with his own copious precum—got him across the floor to where Zorin wanted him. Standing braced between two pillars, staring at the twin rings soldered into stone, desperately aware they'd been designed to hold a woman bound and spreadeagled for a man's pleasure. With Zorin close behind him, hands guiding his to the rings, cock dripping and swollen and flushed with violent need, he could only bow his head and wait panting for the other man's pleasure.

"Jumpin' Jupiter, you're gorgeous like this," Zorin rasped in his ear. "But I'm not gonna tie you up like some kinda war prisoner. Even though right now you'd let me do that to you, wouldn't you?"

"I do believe I might. If you asked nicely." Dex's throat was so dry he could barely manage a whisper. Especially with the wet sounds of Zorin lubing himself up behind him. "But—speaking solely out of curiosity—why aren't you?"

"Cuz I don't wanna scare you away." The pirate's big hands spread his legs and eased his head down. "Cuz I want you to want this with me again." Warm lips brushed his ear and made him shudder. "Cuz I'm so crazy in love with you I'd rather cut out my own heart with a dull blade than hurt you."

The slick invasion of his well-lubed fingers opened Dex wider and wrung from him a long moan, raw with craving.

After that, he could barely pull his reeling head together.

"You—you love me?"

"I'm outta my head in love with you. You gotta know that, don'tcha, Dex?" The slick head of his shaft lodged against Dex's already tender hole, and Dex clenched his teeth to keep from spilling. "It's okay. You don't have to say it back. But I do wanna hear you beg for my cock. It's one of my pet fantasies. Will you do that for me?"

Dex swallowed hard and closed his eyes. "You want me to beg? I'm bloody begging. I've wanted this with you as long as I can remember." He wet his dry lips. "I want your cock inside me. I want you to come so hard and deep inside me neither one of us will ever forget I'm yours."

"Oh baby. You're so perfect for me."

Zorin's reverent whisper kept him still for the slow, mind-splitting pressure of the massive cock sliding inside him, stretching his tight hole until Dex was gasping, fighting to submit, to accommodate that prodigious length that just kept pushing relentlessly inside.

The burning *pop* of the pirate's knob breached the tight ring of muscle, sparking a starburst of adrenaline—electric pain spiked with blinding pleasure. A startled curse exploded from Dex's throat.

"Deep breath for me here," Zorin whispered, gentle teeth grazing his lobe. Dex shivered and fought to comply. "Sweet mother, you feel like heaven. But we—we can stop—if you want."

Even with the all-systems alert zipping through every synapse, Dex knew stopping was the last thing he wanted. Hearing the other man's breath ragged in his ear, feeling those big hands steady against his hips—knowing however close to the jagged edge they were both riding, his boyhood hero would never let him fall—Dex pushed out a cautious lungful of oxygen and leaned into the pulsing ache of penetration.

Against his sweating back, a low moan rumbled through Zorin's massive chest. The pirate panted into his neck and eased deeper.

Just when he thought he couldn't possibly take any more of the stretching burn that filled him, when a whimper for mercy slipped out, Zorin wrapped a hand around Dex's cock and started stroking him.

"Neptune's knickers. You feel out of this world," his lover rasped. "So hot and tight and ready for me. You just tell me—tell me if I need to stop."

Because Dex knew that's what Zorin was now.

His lover.

And the fact that he *would* stop if Dex asked him, despite all his tough guy bluster, eased Dex's incipient panic. The steady friction of that knowing hand, jacking his aching cock in time with his own noisy breath, coaxed him to take even more.

Dex found himself rocking into the guy, taking more of him with every careful stroke, fighting to relax around the rod that stretched him to the breaking point.

And hearing his idol moaning words like *amazing* and *incredible* and *oh stars, kid* in his ear just made it hotter.

At long last, Zorin was fully seated inside him.

"How's this feel, baby? You haven't said a word. I need you to talk to me."

"It's, ah, tolerable," Dex whispered, barely breathing.

Zorin's soft chuckle rumbled through him. "I'd like it to be a little more than that. Try to relax a little for me."

The steady pressure of Zorin's hand, stroking his shaft slow and easy, in time with the steady rhythm of the pirate's well-oiled cock sliding in and out of his hole, made all his limbs go liquid. Dex gripped the rings and moved with him, acquiescing to this total violation, encouraging his lover to take his pleasure. The rhythmic slap of flesh on flesh and the quickening slide of the hand around his shaft chased the harsh tempo of their labored breath.

"That's it. Just like that. Talk to me," Zorin urged, thrusting faster and harder, tone rough with barely held restraint.

"Better," Dex breathed. "Oh Mars—oh *gods*—you're bloody spectacular—"

He forgot all the words he knew. Forgot everything except the mind-blowing friction around his shaft and the electrifying impact of the cock pegging his prostate. Forgot all his old hang-ups and the erotic sizzle of humiliation and everything that wasn't the pirate's powerful, sweat-slick body slamming into him, rocking him on his feet with every stroke, the hard hand slick with his own urgent need riding his desperate rod.

"Please—I can't—can't wait," he managed to get out. "You're going to make me come—so hard."

"I'm not gonna—last much longer—myself," Zorin panted in his ear, his swelling shaft stretching Dex's hole even tighter. "Oh baby… oh gods, baby… come for me now. Right *now*."

His climax pounded through him with the cataclysmic strength of an avalanche. Gouts of creamy release shot from his shaft in an explosive display of his own submission. Drenching the other guy's hand.

As if either of them needed any more proof of how thoroughly he was getting off on being ridden and filled and used for another man's pleasure.

His hole tightened and fluttered with spasms of release that wrung a hoarse shout from the man behind him. Zorin's pace grew jerky and, finally, frantic. He seated himself to the hilt, wringing another sharp cry of pleasure from Dex's lips. The rhythmic spurt of the other man's climax flooded into Dex again and again.

He never wanted any of it to end.

His knees were buckling. His sweaty palms slipping from the rings. The warm trickle of the other man's release spilling down his thighs. Zorin slid free with a long sigh, his heavy frame half collapsing against him, half holding him up. He wasn't entirely sure how they managed to stagger together to the bed and fall into it.

"Just gimme a sec. I'll getcha cleaned up," Zorin mumbled, flopping onto his back and pulling Dex clumsily down over him. "Oh stars, kid… were you ever… worth the wait."

"Good to hear." His own voice was husky with strain, making him wonder with a flash of heat just how loudly he'd been shouting. "I, uh, believe we'll have to wait… just a bit… before we endeavor to undertake that particular act again."

"Yeah, you'll be feeling me. For a good few days. Sorry about that."

The sound of masculine satisfaction mingled with honest chagrin in his voice made Dex grin even as he panted. For some damn reason, he didn't seem to mind the fact that Zorin clearly felt—and had just fully exercised—that possessive right of ownership.

He didn't even seem to mind, under this limited set of exquisitely intimate circumstances, being called *baby*.

The pirate's hand curled around his head to hold him close. "Lay it on me. Was I too hard on ya?"

"If you're asking whether I intend to invite an encore performance, the answer is decidedly *yes*. And I don't intend to wait very long." Dex wrapped an arm around the big man's waist and listened to the powerful heartbeat thud against his ear. "Would you ever consider, ah, allowing me to return the favor?"

"Hmmm." A rumble of interest rolled through Zorin's broad chest. "Tell you true, I haven't been on the other end all that often. But for you, kid—yeah. If that's what you want. For you, I'd do just about anything. You gotta know that by now, don'tcha?"

"I am acquiring that impression, yes." Sated and saturated with the warm weight of well-being, Dex turned his face into Zorin's neck. The soothing spice of his lover's mating scent enveloped him. Feeling the friction of the pirate's blaster scar chafing his cheek, Dex mumbled, "Sorry I shot you. Should've said it sooner."

"Aw, shoot." Zorin chuffed out a drowsy chuckle. "Worth being shot… just for this."

As he spiraled down toward sleep, Dex whispered on a sigh, "In the event you're somehow still wondering… I bloody well love you too."

CHAPTER FOUR
The Lure

The lock released with a tiny *snick* too soft for the human ear to detect above the microreactor's low rumble.

But Kaia's captor wasn't human.

Which was why she held her breath.

Now the cuffs that clasped her feet were like the ones that held her hands. Draped loosely around her limbs as she sat curled in the navigator's chair. Ready to spring open the moment she leaped into action.

Action that needed to happen pretty damn quick.

Under lowered lashes, she slanted the console a cautious glance. Through the shimmer of heat as the Hurricane nosed into the friction of the planetary exosphere, her desert homeworld filled the viewport like a calamity. Frying under the unrelenting blaze of the Kryllian system's twin suns, burning inexorably hotter with every millennium, easing closer to the conflagration that would eventually incinerate the doomed planet.

Framing that alarming panorama, the uniformed figure that looked like Dex—but wasn't—never turned from the weapons console where he labored, jacket and saber hung tidily from the wall clip beside him. In fact, the guy stayed focused on that weapons console with an intensity she found nerve-racking.

Considering the Hurricane's nuclear payload.

Thanks to the shapeshifter's preoccupation, she was cautiously optimistic her small telepathic triumph with the cuffs had escaped his scrutiny. A heady cocktail of elation, spiked with a jigger of apprehension, surged through her synapses like a contraband stimulant. It also goosed her vitals.

Which, at this juncture, came as a definite bonus.

Because it was absolutely true that picking a lock demanded the mental serenity of a mendicant monk. Luring Proteus in close and personal, so she could arm herself and launch the rest of her thrown-together, neck-or-nothing strategy, demanded the opposite.

Still no sign of Ben or anything remotely resembling a rescue. But if I don't act right flipping now, we're going to land on Kryll. Then I'll have to deal not only with Proteus, but with the punking Patriarch.

Kaia closed her eyes and swallowed, jonesing hard for anything liquid to lube her arid throat. Because once this crazy plan of hers kicked into gear, if it didn't go exactly the way she hoped, odds were she'd either have to kill the god of the Swarm—

Or be killed herself.

Either of which was preferable to spending her life as some genetic experiment in his laboratory of horrors.

Showtime, samurai.

Deliberately Kaia turned her thoughts to Ben Nero. Ben, her lifemate, who she had to hope was coming for her despite their erratic history. Ben as he was when she'd fallen for him that long-ago summer. Ben who was already gorgeous and graceful and deadly—even at that age. Effortlessly gifted, maddeningly arrogant, forbiddingly aloof, the secret terror of the teachers whose talents he'd already far surpassed.

Not to mention the secret crush of just about every student at the Psi Academy.

Ben could've had anyone he wanted that summer.

But he'd only ever wanted Kaia.

Later, he'd told her about the Mogadon crush with intimacy issues who'd just stomped on his heart at the youth ashram. When she first pitched up on Hegemon, Ben later confided, she was the only student at the school who clearly felt even more wretched than he did. The only person on the planet he could stand to be near.

Sullen, defiant, already burning with resentment over the ritual auction for her bed that loomed like an apocalypse over her future even then—Kaia was also the only person on the planet he wasn't supposed to want. The misfit, the rebel, the half-Kryll hybrid. The running joke. Because according to tribal superstition, she was supposed to be some kind of god back on Kryll. But she didn't even have enough psi talent to light a candle on Hegemon.

Until Ben started tutoring her.

In secret.

Because every student at the Academy was supposed to sink or swim on her own strength.

Before long, those late-night tutoring hookups morphed into something more. First an intimate friendship, itself a novelty to a desperately lonely girl who'd been isolated her whole life, worshipped and revered as a deity. Her twin, never sent for training since Kira herself showed none of Kaia's latent telepathic gifts, was the only intimate friend she'd ever had.

Soon another kind of intimacy developed between Kaia and Valyria's most freakishly gifted telepath.

"Love you, angel," that youthful Ben—still so young, but nearly a man—whispered in her ear as they lay entwined on the starlit beach under the six moons of Hegemon. "It's the lifebond. This is it! And I want you in my bed so bad I can't breathe. We both know you're already mine."

He could have seduced her a thousand times that summer. But he'd respected that solemn vow of chastity she'd sworn to her prophetic mother.

Not that his careful respect or her dutiful promise kept them at arm's length for long.

He'd known—intuited, discovered, explored, and finally enthusiastically affirmed—every way there was to flip her switch without crossing that uncrossable line. She'd been getting off half her life on the memory of Ben Nero's silken lips coaxing her mouth open and teaching her how to kiss, his diabolical hands easing under her shirt and teasing her nipples until she lost every molecule of restraint and begged for more, his tongue tasting her wet heat over and around and through the virginal panties she'd been burning to ditch.

The first time she ever climaxed, she'd come crying his name. Riding his hand and crying out her pleasure into his mouth the very first time he eased a finger into her tight, soaking channel.

And the first time she'd ever felt his mouth on her clit through the thin drenched silk of her panties, she'd come so hard she cried.

She was still shuddering with release in his arms the first time he whispered in her ear that he loved her.

Even a lifetime later, trapped on the Hurricane with her mortal enemy, that smoking hot memory still packed a powerful punch. Her pulse kicked up, her breath went rough, her nipples jutted hard against her cybersuit. Slick and aching with remembered need, she curled her knees to her chest and shifted in her seat.

And if Proteus was half the supreme predator he claimed to be, that fistful of bloody meat she'd just waved under his carnivorous nose ought to be plenty to—

"What in blazes do you fancy you're about?"

Icy with suspicion—Dex's tone rendered with terrifying perfection—the demand brought her eyes flying open to find her captor standing at the weapons console. Her captor, who got better at pretending to be Dex with every breath he spent in his body.

Now he'd pivoted away from his nukes to confront her.

His biologically agitated captive.

Under the circumstances, it wasn't at all difficult to produce a blush.

"I'm only doing what any fertile Valyrian girl would do who's standing in my cyber boots," she told him, husky with suppressed nerves. "Which is, to answer your question, wondering whether the only biological male in her vicinity is anatomically functional… in every respect."

Those keen eyes narrowed to neon slits.

"As we've already established, this construct of Dex Draven— unlike the original specimen, presumably—is incapable of siring viable offspring. However, if you're asking whether this construct is biologically capable of physical arousal, I assure you there is no deficiency."

Absolutely nothing in his voice encouraged her. But if she leaned into her instincts and pretended like hell he was Dex, she might just manage to encourage *him*.

"Care to undertake a little science experiment?" She moistened her bone-dry lips and let her gaze slide over the quiet, contained force buttoned into the imperial authority of Dex's Mogadon uniform. "I'm fertile, which means I'm horny, even if you're the only outlet in sight for all this sexual sizzle I'm packing. I know you can… smell it on me… if your senses are as keen as you claim."

"Rest assured that they are." His nostrils flared. "And that I do."

In any other circumstances, that revelation would be downright distressing. Right now, with any luck, her physical arousal would supply the bait she needed to reel him in.

"Well, the real Dex wouldn't be standing six cubits away. Knowing I'm hot to trot? He'd be hard as a titanium rod." Her gaze dropped to his trousers. "Are you?"

He wasn't Dex. He'd never be Dex. But he *was* walking around wearing Dex's relentlessly virile body.

And Dex's body was, like always, plenty happy to see her.

For the first time since this whole circus started, a note of strain threaded her captor's crisp tone. "As I've noted, this construct is anatomically functional in every respect."

Without raising her head, she lifted her gaze to meet his burning stare. "Have you ever made love as one of your *constructs*?"

"Why would I bother?" he countered softly. "I've already stated I can't procreate."

"But the point of life isn't merely to survive. The point is to enjoy it. Surely, with that scientific brain of yours, you must be a little… curious?"

"On an intellectual level—perhaps. Nevertheless, I haven't deemed pursuing that particular line of inquiry to be, shall we say, advantageous."

"I'll show you advantageous." She let her hair tumble forward over one shoulder and watched his eyes track the wine-red cascade. "Because right now—with you packing a boner in that body, and me going supernova in this one? You've got what I need, and I've got what you need."

She perched her chin on her knees and gave him a look so sultry she would've had the real Dex unzipped and sliding into her slick heat before he could say *sexy setup*.

"Come on, Proteus. One kiss. One itsy-bitsy physiological field trial. If I'm right, you'll know exactly where to take this. If I'm wrong and you're not feeling it? Well, there's your data. The scientific validation of your whole no-sex-needed hypothesis."

"I'm not a fool, Kaia." His voice deepened to a Dexlike growl that made her shiver. Even while he kept his distance. "You can't possibly expect me to believe you find this body, knowing what's inhabiting it and knowing my intentions, to be even remotely arousing."

For a heartbeat she was back on the beach with Ben Nero. Pushing him into the sand. Her untutored fingers, clumsy with craving, finding the rigid blade of his cock through his breeches. Hearing his low throaty moan echo in her ears. Stroking his taut length until she found the rhythm he couldn't resist. Feeling the thrill of his lean supple body thrusting desperately into her hand. Savoring the intense satisfaction of making him lose all that perfect telepathic control. Making him cry out and spill for her.

"What do your superhuman senses tell you?" she murmured, chest tight and core aching. "I need you inside me. When you feel what it's like, you won't want to stop. Why bother living if you don't feel alive?"

"*That* is an entirely philosophical argument." His face hardened with sudden purpose. "But damn if you haven't sparked my interest."

Before she was even remotely ready, he swooped in and claimed her mouth in a primal kiss.

The hard heat of Dex's mouth, the whiskey bite of Dex's breath, the sudden spice of Dex's scent flooded her senses with overload. Her body kindled with an inferno of pounding need. A surging need that shocked her soul—

Her curled legs lashed out and kicked him square in the chest. The guy flew back with a pained grunt. Kaia exploded from the chair, handcuffs falling away, and scrambled over his body. Driving him down across the console, booted feet punching into his gut, cybersuited body catapulting over him.

He was already reaching for her, Dex's superb conditioning and lightning reflexes springing to his defense. Which made the nerve gun holstered at his hip an asset way too risky to grab.

So much for Plan A.

Barely evading his wrathful grasp, she vaulted onto her hands and cartwheeled over the console, flipping every switch she could. Comms, navigation, weapons were dead without Dex's biometrics to trigger them. But life support and emergency functions, for safety reasons, could be triggered by anyone.

And when a ship's emergency systems were tripped, its protocol automatically deactivated the stealth feature to facilitate rescue operations.

Her tumbling run plunged the cockpit into darkness, barely lit by the reflected glow of the twin suns from the planet's dusty surface. The orange hazard lights flashed in alarm. The fire suppression system filled the cabin with its urgent hiss. The cool spray of chemical vapor poured through the jets. The air split with the undulating *ah-ooh-gah* of the danger claxon.

Wreathed in a swirling cloud of vapor, Kaia landed blind on the cabin floor—an impact that jarred the healing lacerations on her feet and ripped a cry from her lips. Somewhere behind her, Proteus was wrestling to his feet with a clipped curse. With the last few ticks of advantage her little surprise had bought her, she fumbled the cyber chip from her utility belt and pressed it into the jack at her temple.

Hello, Plan B.

The world went gray around her—a nightmare graphic of shifting shadows and jetting steam and flashing alarms. Heart thundering, adrenaline spurting, she shot to her feet.

"There you are," Dex whispered in her ear. A powerful arm wrapped around her throat. Trapping her in a stranglehold strong enough to snap her neck.

Well, she wasn't a Prime Class samurai for nothing. She tucked her chin to keep her airway open, slammed her heel into his booted instep, and drove a hard elbow into the solid plane of his abs.

The air whooshed out of him.

But his crushing grip around her throat only tightened. Her pulse hammered in her temples and blood pounded behind her eyes.

"Do you know, that kiss wasn't half bad?" he panted, breath hot against her cheek. "Is this how you and the real Dex make love? All this fury and violence? For an apex predator like myself, all this desperation has rather whetted my appetite."

The bulge of his cock ground into her back. A thrill of horror shot through her system. All the more horrifying because it was laced with her own arousal.

He was scenting like crazy—this thing wearing Dex's body.

Maybe the smart thing to do was go with it. But now he was violently alert to her game. And he wasn't Dex. He was a homicidal psychopath and a gods-damned cannibal. And she wasn't.

Farking.

Doing this.

The heel of his palm ground into the slick heat between her thighs.

"What do you think, darling?" His quicksilver tongue caressed her ear. "Is it still considered rape if I make you like it?"

The whining *choom-choom* of a psi-powered cannon sliced through the claxon's wail. The Hurricane lurched sideways and shuddered like a wounded animal under the slam of impact.

They both reeled and fought to stay upright.

"What the devil?" Dex grated. Only he wasn't Dex. "Who the bloody *hell* is shooting at us?"

Hello, angel, a familiar tenor whispered in her head. *Is this a good time for you?*

"Ben!" she gasped.

Though, really, she ought to have kept that flash of insight to herself. She hadn't been ready for the jolt of desperate relief that slammed through her like a bolt of lightning.

Beyond the viewport, the sleek silver arrow of her own cruiser flashed past. A volley of purple fire spat from her cannon to pound the listing shuttle and—if she was lucky—erode its energon shield.

She'd never seen a sight so glorious.

Way to make an entrance, stud pony. I figured you'd find me. Even if you did leave this nifty rescue operation a little late.

"Ben Nero, I presume," the shapeshifter snarled, lunging for the weapons console. Which meant Kaia herself was free—at least briefly—to suck in the oxygen her body was screaming for. "Your telepath in shining armor. Flying to the rescue in your wretched cruiser. Does he fancy he can put so much as an asteroid dent in this vessel or its formidable shield with that piddling cannon? I can destroy a small moon with this ship's nuclear arsenal."

She didn't trust the god of the Swarm for way too many reasons to count. But that much of what he said was one hundred percent true. The *Interstellar Angel* might be able to outrun a Hurricane-class shuttle like the *Ascendant.*

But she'd never outgun her.

Which leads to Plan C.

Through a spray of chemical vapor and the flash of amber lights, Proteus was using Dex's biometrics to arm his weapons. In the elevated display screen, a row of crimson symbols flamed to life.

<<Nuclear warheads armed and loaded. Three ticks to launch.>>

I'm coming around for another pass, Ben said in her head. *I knew you were close, but I needed you to unstealth, angel—and you didn't disappoint. You're already wearing Zorin's chip. Why don't you jack into that cyberport and come on home.*

That is the general plan, she fired back. *The thing is—I've been tinkering with Zorin's chip. Trying to even out the ride. And I didn't get a chance to finish. I can use it, but I'm not sure it'll actually work. Or where it'll take me.*

As that revelation sank in, the lifebond between them hummed with tension. But Ben was quick in a crisis—always had been—and his response was instantaneous.

I'm the galaxy's strongest telepath. And the strongest telekinetic. I can't penetrate that shuttle's energon shields. But the cyberport on the Angel's *back in business. If you jump, I can… catch you.*

I think.

You think! Kaia bit back a hysterical giggle. *Asteroids, Ben, that's one hell of a risk. I've got a better plan… I think.*

The *Angel's* sleek silhouette flashed past, spitting ellipses of heliotrope fire. This time, Proteus was tucked into the pilot's seat, poised and ready. One quick twist of the yoke in Dex's jet jockey hands, and the shuttle went spiraling out of the kill zone in a tight evasive inversion.

The ocher orb of Kryll slid out of sight, replaced by the turquoise disc of the nearest moon and the pulsing menace of the twin suns.

Temporarily dismissed as a lesser threat, Kaia tumbled across the floor, turning her uncontrolled fall into a tight triple somersault that brought her to the wall and a safety harness. Above her, Dex's saber swung wildly from the clip where the shapeshifter had left it. Gripping the harness to anchor herself as the shuttle completed its maneuver, she snatched the blade from its sheath with a leathery hiss. And hoped the blasting *ah-ooh-gah* of the battle claxon would ensure even a self-proclaimed deity wouldn't hear a thing.

The shuttle finished its spin and snapped to a level glide. She got her legs under her, slanted the saber in a defensive angle, and spun—

To find Proteus pivoted in the pilot's chair to confront her, nerve gun fully extended and leveled at her chest from ten cubits away.

A range far too close to miss.

"I'm afraid I haven't the time for any more sexual foreplay, darling. Be a good girl and put the saber down."

Above his head, the console flashed its crimson warning.

<<Nuclear missiles primed and targeted. Two ticks to launch.>>

Angels of Anaxos. He's going to nuke Ben. And those missiles will wipe out everything in range when they detonate.

Including half of Kryll at this altitude.

She made her voice hard and confident to hide her screaming terror.

"You're not gonna fire that thing at me. Not when you need me and my hybrid DNA to procreate."

"This weapon's programmed to immobilize, not to kill." One shoulder lifted in a diffident shrug. "Still, it *is* a nerve gun. They're outlawed across the galaxy for an excellent reason. How truly unfortunate that even a glancing hit causes permanent paralysis." Her lover paused, head tilted to consider. "Do you know, I believe that outcome might actually render our future relations to be substantially less… dramatic. At least from my perspective."

She could only watch with a sickening surge of dread as his finger tightened on the trigger.

#

Ben watched through Kaia's eyes as the thing she thought of as Dex/not Dex tightened its grip on the trigger. Over the shadow of Ben's psychic vision, the dark wedge of the Hurricane floated against the turquoise orb of the Kryllian moon.

If the real Dex were here, he'd fling the *Angel* into some hair-rising daredevil maneuver and blast the Hurricane to subatomic smithereens.

After he'd rescued Kaia.

But Ben had never been much of a pilot. Even in a psi-powered ship. And Kaia didn't have time for him to learn. With his lifemate's terror howling through every pore, Ben acted on pure instinct.

Psi power couldn't penetrate the *Ascendant*'s energon shields—a defensive feature designed by the Mogadon to thwart their ancient enemy.

But he didn't need to penetrate the shields to change the future.

Holding the *Angel* steady with one hand on the yoke, he flung a glowing purple hand across the viewport. A whiplash of raw power coiled through him and snapped out with pulverizing force.

The Hurricane tumbled sideways like a spurned toy thrown by an angry child.

With his doubled vision, he watched Kaia and that Dexlike thing go flying. But, like the Prime Class samurai she was, his lifemate kept her saber and her head. Surefooted as a cat, she scrambled up the tilting walls, two steps ahead of the nerve gun's crackling burst as Dex—Proteus—fired wildly after her nimble form.

Channeling her acrobat's moxie, Kaia swung from a safety harness through the shuttle's twisting tumble and whipped through the turn with slingshot speed. Her booted foot struck Dex—Proteus—a glancing blow to the head that knocked the thing sideways.

Through sheer luck, the shapeshifter fell across the pilot's seat. Still gripping that blasted nerve gun, he fumbled to strap himself in.

Ben righted the ship with a sharp slash of his hand. Still clutching the saber, Kaia landed lightly on her feet.

"Angels and asteroids, Ben," she muttered. "Warn a girl next time."

Cyberport, he fired at his lifemate. *Right flipping now, angel.*

"He's going to nuke you! In less than two ticks."

He'll have to catch me first. Will you please. Just. Jump.

Through her eyes, the weapons console flashed its grim warning.

<<Missile tubes opening. One tick to launch.>>

Wrestling one-handed with the yoke, burnished hair falling into blazing eyes, the shapeshifter twisted in his seat. Ben watched the nerve gun's lethal muzzle swing toward her—

He lashed out with everything in him.

Under his telekinetic assault, the shuttle skidded sideways through space. Biting out a Dexlike curse, the shapeshifter sprayed the cabin with staticky fire. Kaia was already spinning through the air, a creature of impossible grace, saber a flashing blur as it whipped around in a whirling slice.

A scream raw with agony slammed through every synapse Ben possessed. And damn near stopped his heart.

Because that agonized scream sounded like Dex.

Blood was spraying through the air. The nerve gun tumbling through the air. Gods of Solaris, that grisly object fountaining blood as it pinwheeled through the air looked like… had to be… a severed arm.

Dex.

No. Not Dex. He's not Dex!

Chaos reigned in the stricken shuttle. Fire suppression vapor fogged the hectic flash of hazard lights. The claxon whooped with maniacal insistence. The shuttle inverted, struggling to respond to its pilot's frenzied grip.

Kaia was running across the ceiling, burgundy hair streaming in her wake, her pulse a frantic drumbeat in his head.

<<*Missile tubes open. Half a tick to launch.*>>

"You're out of time, Ben!" Kaia screamed. *"Go, go, go!"*

When Kaia sounded like that, Ben didn't hesitate. He throttled the *Angel* for deep space and gunned the drive. The hammering fist of acceleration shoved him hard in his seat as the Hurricane shrank to a speck in his scope. While the stars blurred around him, his head was with Kaia, sprinting across the ceiling for the cyberport, blind terror fired with desperate resolve.

Behind her in the pilot's seat, something writhed that was no longer Dex.

Something much larger than Dex or even Zorin.

Something made of rage and tentacles and the hook of a monstrous beak.

"Full marks for effort, Kaia of Kryll," the thing rapped in Dex's voice. "But I haven't given you permission to disembark."

Kaia flung herself through the air and hit the cyberport in full flight, hands stretching to seize the connection cables. Just as her hands made contact, a dark tentacle, thick as her leg, lashed through the air to wrap around her ankle.

In Ben's head, she was screaming. Neither fully physical not fully digital, her body and her avatar suspended in space, stretched between the shuttle and the cyberverse. That hideous tentacle, strong as a titanium cable, crushing her fragile bones.

Before the shapeshifter let her escape, that thing would tear her in two.

As the *Angel* whistled through interstellar space, Ben rooted himself in his lifemate's head. A helpless observer to her agony, her… split-second decision to die—just as her sister had died… rather than submit to an unspeakable fate. Ben bonded with his lifemate's body, feeling her nerves fry, seeing smoke rise from her skin—

With every erg of psychic power ten thousand years of Valyrian genetics had bred in his bones, Ben Nero poured his strength into her. Psi fire tore through his lifemate's tortured body and ripped into the thing that held her.

Kaia was screaming. The thing hissing. Ben snarling with a superhuman effort so strong he nearly blacked out. Blindly he channeled purple fire across the swiftly widening void of space between them into the tentacle that gripped her.

Until that snaky limb blackened and burst into flame.

For a breath, Kaia was nowhere. Not in the shuttle. Not in his head. Just the flicker of a dream hurtling through cyberspace at the speed of thought.

Not knowing what he did or how he did it, Ben flung his consciousness into the void and dragged her toward him.

Somewhere far behind him, the Hurricane was firing her nukes. The *Angel's* souped-up drive was howling to outpace a flotilla of missiles with megaton death written all over them. Six cubits back, the *Angel's* cyberport was spraying a fountain of purple sparks.

And Kaia's voice—her beautiful, unforgettable, irreplaceable voice—was shrieking in his physical ears.

Ben slammed on the autopilot to keep the juice flowing and flung himself out of the pilot's chair. Sprawled across the cyber deck lay a whippet-lean figure, sheathed in a singed black cybersuit and a tangle of burgundy hair.

Steam rising from her skin.

While the fast little cruiser flew her heart out beneath him, racing to outrun those nukes, Ben half crawled, half slithered across the vibrating floor. Somehow he got his arms around her—his lifemate, his heart, his soul, his life—even though she flailed and screamed and fought him in a frenzy. Her thoughts a riot of delirium and anguish.

He dragged her out of the cyberport before the contraption went up in flames.

Smothered everything on board that was burning with a thought.

Averted his eyes from the blinding ultraviolet flash beyond the porthole as the nukes reached their maximum range behind him and detonated.

Prayed to gods he'd never really believed in that the *Angel's* cybered-up engine would outrace the blast wave and that her radiation shields would hold.

But if the desperately injured woman clasped in his frantic arms didn't survive, nothing else in the universe would ever matter again.

"Gods and demons," he breathed, his soul blasted bare, the stench of seared silk and burned hair acrid in his nose. *"Kaia."*

CHAPTER FIVE
The Ultimatum

Kaia was floating in an oily sea. Warm as melted honey and sleek as cybersilk against her naked skin.

And the utter absence of searing pain, after a hellish eternity trapped in nothing but, was so blissful she never wanted to wake.

But she wasn't alone.

Her heart kicked and her pulse spiked. Half-lucid memories streaked through her brain like meteors. Memories of that chittering thing that looked like Dex. She sucked in a sharp breath—heavy with the dusty sweetness of desert lavender.

That aromatic clue whispered where she was.

Contained within the smooth curving confines of a stasis chamber. To be precise, the snug ovoid capsule of the stasis chamber on the *Angel*. The gelid warmth of curative oil enveloped her body, while the glowing dome of an energon shield arched overhead.

Sealing her in a cocoon of healing.

And the reason she felt so snug was because the recuperation unit on her one-woman cruiser was barely big enough to hold a single patient. But there were two of them tucked in here.

Which meant Kaia was tucked tight, back to front, against the sleek muscled hardness of Ben Nero's naked body.

"Hello, angel," he murmured, raspy with sleep. When she spasmed in surprise, his deft hands circled her waist to steady her. "Hope you don't mind that I'm in here with you. We both needed a little chamber time after that epic escape."

"Proteus?" she managed.

"Stealthed and skedaddled, as our pirate would say." Humor lurked in his tone. Giddy warmth spread through her to hear Ben calling Zorin *our pirate*. "I don't know where he is. Without you on board, there's nothing on the Hurricane I can track. How do you feel?"

She kept her eyes forward and her hands to herself and her mind focused on the question. Instead of focused on her lifemate's way-too-gifted fingers spread across her ribcage.

All but brushing her naked breasts.

"Like I've got a bad sunburn. And a bit of a scratchy throat," she admitted. "Probably from all that screaming."

"Let's see what we can do about that, shall we?"

The delicate tickle of telepathic manipulation soothed the raw heat in her throat and eased the hot tightness in her skin. Which pretty much addressed any lingering questions she might still be harboring about how she'd gotten through getting flayed alive by electron backlash in the cyberverse with nothing worse than a bad sunburn.

Because her lifemate, who happened to be the galaxy's most freakishly gifted telepath, had wielded that awesome power of his with the meticulous precision of a master surgeon.

First to save her. Then to heal her.

How am I doing? he whispered in her head.

Best not to give him too much.

Oh, you know, can't complain. You're a handy guy to have around in a fight.

Good to know I have my occasional uses. Like any god.

Well, her phenomenally gifted lifemate had never bothered much with modesty. After that stunt he'd just pulled, dragging her physical body through the cyberverse by her digital ankles—a feat of telekinetic legerdemain she'd bet no one had ever taught him to do because no one even knew it could be done—he was entitled to a bit of bragging.

But she wasn't really thinking about any of that.

She was thinking about the five-alarm fire of being wedged in alarmingly close confines with a naked Ben Nero. Even if he'd left her wearing the skimpy fig leaf of her barely there panties—his subtle signal that he hadn't tested the boundaries of her whole no-penetration decree while she was out of it—she was exquisitely aware that Ben himself never wore anything under his Valyrian breeches.

And of course he wasn't wearing breeches in the stasis chamber.

Which meant six-plus cubits of naked Ben pressed intimately against her backside. Capable hands spanning her waist, muscled thighs bracketing her hips—and the electric sizzle of a rapidly hardening shaft nudging her ass.

"Feeling better?" he breathed, lips grazing her ear.

He means your sore throat, angel. Not the slow burn of wanting him to slide all that taut oily heat inside you one gasp of pleasure at a time.

She cleared her throat and rested her cheek against his muscled shoulder. "Guess this is my cue to thank you for saving my life. Not to mention breaking the speed record coming after me in the first place."

His silken voice roughened. "I'll always come for you, Kaia. You'd better get used to it. My days of running—from you and from Dex—are history."

"What about the breeding program?" Her tone was more barbed than she wanted. Because that old heartbreak might be buried deep in her bruised and battered heart, but it still rankled. "Even before the biowar, the Valyrians were a failing race. Isn't that what you always told me? Valyria means everything to you. Isn't that why you left me in the first place?"

"I left you from duty, angel, after the Senate banned our mating. Even though it just about killed me, and I still don't know if you'll ever forgive me. I left you when I was a flipping *kid*. Since then, I've done my duty for Valyria and then some." He pressed his lips to her ear and breathed the words like he didn't want the universe to hear. "I'm leaving the breeding program. Forty-three offspring—not counting the ones I'll give you if you let me—are enough to give Valyria."

She circled the breathtaking possibility of their mutual offspring with excruciating care. Because if Ben abandoned her again, she didn't think it was a blow she'd survive.

"So any children we might have—hypothetically speaking— would inherit forty-three Valyrian half-siblings?"

"Forty-three telepathic half-siblings," he said pointedly. "Which is no trivial asset. There's a lot about Valyrian genetics we still can't decipher. All the other sires, even the best, throw duds from time to time. But I never do. They'll breed an army of telepaths from the offspring I gave them."

"But they just made you Precursor, didn't they?" Skepticism curled her knees tight to her chest. Which made the stasis chamber even cozier. "You think they'll let their prize stallion just sashay away?"

"No one *lets me* do anything anymore. When I said I'm the strongest consort you can find, I farking well meant it," he said with savage intent. "I'll keep the title until one of my offspring proves to me and to the Senate they're strong enough to take it. And that'll be decades."

She hugged her knees tighter. "Decades to rebuild their strength with you as their not-so-secret weapon. You mean to tell me you'd walk away from that?"

"No, but I'll write my own rules." His tone darkened with determination. "With Dex as my consort, the Mogadon won't be launching any more biowars. We won't regain our ancient status as the galaxy's master race anytime soon. A status we haven't held since the Mogadon rose. But our people will never again be helpless."

"*Your* people. They were never mine." And now she did sound bitter. "I'm a half-Kryll hybrid. They're racial purists. That's why they blocked our mating in the first place, remember?"

His hands spread across her taut shoulders and kneaded out the tension. Because there was nothing his hands couldn't do to her. Any more than there had ever been anything he couldn't make her feel.

He leaned in to whisper in her tumbled hair.

"You're about to become the galaxy's dominant power, angel. Not only the Patriarch's daughter, but the only prime maharani in interstellar history to take a Mogadon First Indomitable or a Syndax Voortrekker for consorts—much less both together. If you think Valyria won't want to be part of that, you're just not thinking."

She yearned more than anything to believe him.

But she'd never been good enough for the Senate, for her father, for her teachers, for anyone. As a samurai, she'd learned to make her own worth. Yet part of her would always be that sullen rebel who'd smuggled herself out of Kryll in a cargo bin. The runaway acrobat who'd joined the circus to escape being auctioned off and led away in chains.

"What if they don't?" she whispered, throat tight and aching with a decade of tears she'd always refused to shed.

"I'll make the farking Senate accept our union. Believe me." Ben's entire body vibrated with ferocious purpose. "But even if they balk—which they damn well won't—you're stuck with me anyway. You and Dex and that dreamboat of a pirate. I meant what I said. I'm through running. I'm sorry I ran before. And I'll do whatever it takes to earn your trust."

The certainty of his promise rang through her soul. Along with the sincerity of his remorse.

Which made her feel even more like crying.

She swallowed hard against the need, but her voice still came out wobbly. "I'm not saying I don't owe you. You did just save me from becoming some genetic plaything for the god of the Swarm. Without you, I'd be barbecued samurai at the cyberverse bistro. But damn it, Ben! That's one hell of a broken promise you're asking me to forgive."

Undeflected, he wrapped his arms tight around her and pressed his face hard into her neck. "I know I've got years of broken promises and broken trust to make up for. But I *will*. I swear to all Ninety-Nine of your Kryllian Gods I will. Because I can't do this anymore, Kaia. I *can't*. Can't watch helpless from a distance the way I have for years while you hurl yourself into one hair-raising adventure after another and cheat death by an electron. You're my lifemate. I'm yours. And you know that bond's for life."

Feeling the dark intent that fueled him like a fever, she shivered with her own rising heat. His arms around her clenched fiercely. Which only ground the searing blade of his shaft more fiercely into her ass. She knew he was about a breath away from proving his love for her the way they both burned for.

The way that had always been impossible for her to resist.

She tried like heck to clear her head. Ask the questions she needed to ask. So she'd know what came next.

But all she seemed able to do right now was snuggle into his arms like the passive fairy-tale princess she'd always sworn never to become.

"Whatever comes next," she whispered, "thanks for coming for me. I mean it."

"You're my lifemate," he insisted, as though she were in danger of denying it. "So, yeah, I farking came for you. That's what a lifebond means. Despite the fact that Dex with his overdeveloped caveman complex really wanted to come for you himself. Zorin barely talked him out of it. And that was only so they could finish your gods-damned Tombola and save your sister the way we all knew you wanted."

The thought of her men together, caring for her together, solving their problems together, made her smile in the stasis chamber's neon twilight. Even while the physical contact between the two of them—and the looming promise of so much more—banked the slow burn beneath her panties in a way that made her squirm.

His soft whisper in her head felt as intimate as the slide of a finger into all that hot craving.

Nine years of needing you is a lifetime, angel. How much longer are you going to make me wait?

Until I know I can trust you. Trust you not to walk.

The thought was pure reflex. But this time—for the first time—that self-protective instinct felt wrong.

"So…" she said cautiously, still circling that whole trust issue, "you and Dex?"

His ferocious tension ratcheted down a notch.

"Dex and I are good." A slow sigh seeped through him. "Dex and I are perfect. Actually, right now? Dex and I are more than perfect. I've loved him for so long… wanted him for so long… every time we're together, I can barely believe I'm actually allowed to touch him. Or be touched by him. That I'm allowed to let him see how much I like it. Much less believe he actually wants me for a consort."

The wondering disbelief that softened his voice brought back her sappy smile.

"Or that *you* do." His teeth sank gently into the curve of her shoulder to make her gasp. "Want me as your consort. Even though that's what Dex tells me."

That was Ben asking.

Asking if she could forgive him.

Again Kaia edged back from the brink. "How'd you leave things with Zorin?"

Frustration rippled through his exhale. But he let her evasion stand.

"When I buzzed the *Inevitable* and Marcus patched me through, Zorin answered Dex's comm unit. Said Dex was sleeping and he didn't want to wake him. Sounded pretty flipping protective of him, in fact. All stern and Mogadon, you know how they get." Amused affection colored his chuckle. "Sounds like they both survived the blood games."

A grinding tension she'd been carrying for days eased its grip on her beleaguered body. A shaking breath seeped out. "Thank the gods. All Ninety-Nine of them."

"They're still too far away for me to read, but you want my guess? From now on, Zorin protecting Dex is going to be a regular thing."

A bubbling rush of excitement jetted through her blood. The desperate relief of knowing they'd both survived the latest bloodbath. Fueled by the elation of learning that both these fierce, strong, ferociously stubborn Mogadon males she'd fallen in love with had finally found a way past their troubled history to love each other.

Not to mention a fresh hit of the purely visceral thrill of imagining them both in her bed.

But—

"That's what I needed to tell you!" she exclaimed. Comets, she had to be brain-dead. "They can't go to Quorum. Ben, they can't! There's a spacepox outbreak—Proteus used his novicide—"

She slapped a hand over the control panel to bring down the capsule's energon shield. And was gathering her legs underneath her to scramble out when Ben wrapped his arms around her to hold her tight.

"I know, angel. Zorin told me. Those scout ships he sent ahead came back with the intel and warned him not to dock. Besides which, you were raving when I dragged you out of the cyberverse. I know your father's back on Kryll. I told Zorin the score and they're coming straight here." He pushed out a breath. "At least, the *Relentless* is coming. I assume the *Inevitable* and those last wannabes, as Zorin calls them, will have to follow. So we can all finish the game."

"Great gods!" she breathed, that urgent burst of strength spilling out. Because it would take a while after her latest near-death experience before she got her moxie back.

She slithered back into the capsule with a sigh.

But her haphazard docking maneuver brought her around to face her lifemate at last. Confronting her with a searing glimpse of the naked Ben she kept trying like blazes to forget she was sharing a capsule with.

With the *Angel*'s internal atmospherics dimmed for rejuvenation, the crepuscular dusk of a Kryllian double sunset seeped from the ceiling. Which still gave her plenty of light to see him.

And Ben was a beautiful demon, same as always, oil gleaming on the smooth sculpted planes of chest and arms and shoulders. Water beading the tight ruddy nipples she knew just how he'd moan if she tongued. Raven mane floating on a shimmering liquid sea like ink poured from a pitcher. Framing the chiseled cheekbones and silken lashes and pouting mouth of a fallen angel.

She dragged her eyes away before she saw anything more inflammatory. Although it was way too late to keep Ben from seeing parts of *her* she usually kept hidden.

And he was way too well motivated himself not to look.

Heat tingled in her breasts, bobbing on the liquid surface, and tightened her nipples into taut buds begging visibly to be touched. Feeling an incriminating heat climb into her face, she wrapped her arms across her breasts and cleared her throat.

"I, ah, assume we're orbiting Kryll?"

His chin dipped in a slow nod. Under lowered lids, he watched her.

She kept her arms where they were. "When do our boys show up?"

"Few clicks from now. By then, Dex will have broadcast the names of the final ten over interstellar news." His smoking gaze never left her face. Even as he edged closer, breath by breath, a graceful menace she'd eluded far too long. "Which means we have plenty of time."

"Time for what?" she asked like a Prime Class idiot, although she damn well knew.

"Time for *this*."

Kissing Ben Nero was like kissing a tiger. A feral predator who'd kill to stake his claim. Never more feral than now, all tongue and hands and hunger, hellbent to possess what he'd been too long denied. The dark sweetness of cloves stole through her, spiked with the head-spinning spice of Solarian wine.

"And kissing you's like kissing a hurricane," he whispered against her tingling lips. "An unstoppable force of nature. Say you'll be my consort."

Just like that, she was kneecapped by crippling insecurity. The insecurity that flowed from a lifetime of rejection.

A lifetime of never, ever being good enough.

"Ben? You know you can be with Dex without being with me… don't you?"

"Why do people keep telling me that?" He pushed out a chuckle. "Use your head, samurai. I'd die for you. Just like I'd die for Dex."

With hypnotic slowness, he eased her into his lean strength until her nipples nudged his chest. And just that grazing contact made heat pool and pulse between her thighs. His voice deepened to a primal growl.

"Say it, Kaia. I need to hear you say it."

She watched her thighs drift open underwater to wrap around his waist. Because that was easier than staring into the smoldering inferno of craving in his eyes. "Promise me I won't regret it."

"I promise." His fingers hooked under her panties. "You know the reason you haven't conceived? It's because your body's been waiting for *me*. Your lifemate. *I'm* what's been missing. Say it."

Her lips parted, but she couldn't find the words.

Even when he drew her knees together just enough to ease her panties down.

The soul-deep knowledge that he was telling the truth—that if he did what they were both aching for, if he slid all that turgid length deep inside her and rode her until she sobbed with pleasure and they both climaxed, he'd plant his seed in her eager womb and she'd bear his child—all that made her want him so much she could barely breathe.

And of course he knew. Because you didn't take the galaxy's strongest telepath as a lover and expect to keep your secrets.

She let him do it. Let him coax her out of her panties. Knowing full well she was acquiescing to a whole lot more.

This is it. Ben and me. And if we do this, we're going to conceive. If only I can trust him not to bolt.

Her tongue traced her breathless lips. "Shouldn't we… wait? For Dex and Zorin?"

His determined face rippled with humor and impatience. "Angel, it's our first time. This is one time I don't need Dex looming over me growling commands." His voice thickened. "Not that it wouldn't have its appeal. But they'll have their chance with you… with us… tonight. Right here, right now, it's the two of us."

Feeling him want her the way he did—feeling the powerful vortex of need swirling through his head, sucking at his senses, making him lose his famous Precursorial poise one heartbeat at a time—glimpsing that window into her lifemate's yearning ignited a dizzying sense of her own power.

Mischief sparked through her. She tilted her head and pressed a finger to her chin. "Maybe we should wait."

Ultraviolet fire flashed in his eyes. His words smoked with intent. "No more teasing. I need to hear you say it."

And how he still managed to smell like musk and sandalwood in a lavender bath she had no idea. But that was Ben for you.

"You want me to commit?" Her hands were shaking. She spread them across the taut plane of his chest, felt his heart slam against her palms, and issued her challenge in a whisper.

"Convince me."

Kaia knew she was playing with nuclear fire and Ben's bomb was rigged to blow.

She just didn't care.

After a lifetime of loving Ben Nero, a lifetime of aching for his hard heat inside her, a lifetime of believing him dead and mourning him while he watched her from a distance and flipping said nothing, he was damn well going to work for the privilege.

And because he was a telepath, of course he picked up the promise.

With a growl, he dragged her into his arms. Her legs wrapping around his waist, their tongues meeting in an openmouthed kiss that tasted of cloves and desperation, his hands cupping her derrière to drag her right up against the danger zone.

His cock wedged against her slit like it was designed and certified to be there.

All of it spiced with the zing of the forbidden. Because all of it went light years beyond what her constraints and barriers would have permitted way back when.

And she might have said *convince me* to provoke him.

But she didn't think she'd need much convincing at all to climax.

In fact, as his mouth devoured hers and his hands spread her bottom and his fingers—oh gods—his diabolical fingers slipped between her slick folds to make her gasp and writhe against him, all he'd need to do would be to angle his hips to slide deep inside her—

"Slow down, samurai," he breathed into her mouth, rocking his length against her wet channel. "Last time, at the Blind Tiger, you ran the show. And you just about drove me to a damn heart attack. This time, we're going to do things my way."

"Your way's about to inundate my cockpit," she panted. "And I'm not speaking metaphorically."

He surged to his feet with her wrapped around him, oily water streaming down their bodies, lean muscle flexing under her desperate clutch. She knew he couldn't see a blasted thing kissing her like that, but somehow he muscled them out of the capsule and across the *Angel*'s cockpit.

When he settled her dripping body in the pilot's chair, she blurted a murmur of surprise.

"You want me to fly while you…?"

"Oh, I definitely want you to fly, angel." Voice gruff with passion, his predatory eyes prowled over her. "But I'll do the driving. While I *convince* you."

His agile hands eased her thighs apart and draped them over the arms of the pilot's chair before she could say *indecent exhibition.* Realization of just how much she was exhibiting shot through her and heat rushed into her face. Even if nothing was visible through her viewport but two suns, three moons, a scatter of stars, and the russet orb of the Kryllian homeworld they were orbiting.

She was still totally, shockingly visible to *him.*

Desperate to maintain some shred of control in this situation that had spiraled way too swiftly from her grasp, she drew her knees together.

His hiss of warning froze her in her tracks. Even as his hands closed around her knees and eased them still wider across the arms of the pilot's console. She squirmed in abashed protest, the well-worn polymer soft against her naked backside.

"For gods' sake, Ben…"

"You owe this to me, Kaia. You've been teasing me as long as I've known you. Admit it."

Well, that much was definitely true. Only she'd been teasing them both.

"Fine," she whispered. "Take a good look. I dare you not to lose it."

Dare or no dare, it was all she could do to stay where she was— breathless under that commanding stare with her legs spread wide and her vajayjay on display.

While he looked his fill and took his time doing it.

As he towered over her, brooding and beautiful, she traced her tongue over breathless lips and did a little looking of her own. Since the opportunity was just too good to waste.

Ben was shameless about his own exposure and always had been.

Now he stood gorgeous as a god, splendidly naked and utterly unabashed, feet spread wide, hands braced on hips, a glistening veneer of oil clinging to his sculpted chest and dripping down the hard plane of his abs and, all the Ninety-Nine Gods save her, coating well over a handspan of fiercely erect cock, long and curving and pretty much mind-blowing.

Especially at eye level.

All she'd need to do was lean forward and glide her tongue around that ruby head and he'd be in her mouth—

"That's not the game we're playing right now," he said huskily, plucking the thought right from the steaming synapses of her overheated brainbox. "You just challenged me, angel. I'm going to pleasure you until you lose your clever, reckless, fearless, feckless, impulsive, outrageous, too-stubborn-for-your-own-good, notorious rebel samurai mind. Until you're *convinced* to be my consort."

He paused, head tilted to consider her shamelessly spreadeagled form. "And aren't you a sight."

Those smoking eyes dropped from her flushed face to her bare breasts, nipples tight and begging for his touch. That potent stare slid down her tummy to check out her fully exposed pussy, already slick from the bath and growing more so by the moment. She snuck a peek at her swollen clit, that flushed and dewy nub jutting on wanton display, so obviously eager for his attention, and burned with another scalding flood of fever.

His chest rumbled in a low groan.

"Do you know how many times I've imagined you like this, Kaia? All wet and eager and aching? Begging me to take you?"

If we're going to be all honest? she shot back at him like a solar cannon. *You might've had a cameo appearance in the occasional fantasy on my satellite channel too, stud pony. Let's hope you measure up.*

She dragged her gaze from his mouthwatering length to the dark determination blazing in his face. Framed by a curtain of ebony hair, psi fire burned in his eyes.

For some damn reason, he always brought out the devil in her. She hitched her brows and held his stare. "I'm not begging yet, boy toy."

Amethyst lightning flashed in his eyes. "You will be."

And just like that, he was on her. Unleashed from all that godlike restraint and savage with need. A predator crouching between her legs, pinning her in place, hands sliding up her thighs to trap her.

"I want you to show me," he breathed. "Show me how you want me to touch you. Show me how you pleasure yourself when you fantasize about riding me in your bed."

Angels and asteroids, that ego of his.

Catching the thought she lobbed at him, he grinned at her but retracted nothing.

"Wouldn't you rather have me show you how Dex touches me?" She just couldn't seem to stop taunting him. "Or maybe Zorin? You haven't been in his bed yet, have you? Want me to tell you what he's like?"

"I'll find out for myself soon enough." His guttural tone scraped against her senses to make her shiver. Even as he nuzzled her inner thigh with heated lips and looked up at her with those infernal eyes. "Right now, they're light years away. Show me you."

Foreplay for the two of them had always been about temptation. Testing how hard they could torment each other without crossing that uncrossable line. Now, fueled by the fire of her fertility, they'd removed all the guardrails.

Which meant she could tease him… tease both of them… right to the edge of reason.

Her hands drifted to cup her breasts, already swollen and tingling with anticipation. Her nipples so tight and sensitive the first tweak made her whimper and sink her teeth into her lower lip. Knowing he was watching, knowing he was learning, knowing he was *feeling* what she liked, she rolled and pinched her nipples. When she paused to lick her fingers, his throaty moan almost made her come in her chair.

"Gods and demons," he breathed, dragging his hot tongue between her breasts. "You truly are a goddess. Your eyes are glowing. Just like those Valyrian torques I gave you. Kaia… you want my mouth on you, don't you?"

Shameless with need, she cupped her breasts and lifted her nipples to his mouth. He suckled hard, the way he knew she liked. She gasped in pleasure, the first deep throb of arousal lifting her hips from the chair. His ruthless hands held her spread as he tongued her nipples. Every flick of his tongue sent shocks of pleasure shooting down her thighs and stoked the slow hot ache of need in her clit.

Gods, he made her so wet for him. Moisture pooled at the mouth of her channel. Where her spreadeagled placement meant he'd be sure to notice.

Especially when her own cream trickled down her thigh.

Helpless with craving, her hips bucked. And still he held her wide and suckled her nipples until she started moaning.

Round One goes to the Precursor.

"All right, you've—made your point," she gasped. "I do believe I'm—ready for you."

"Not nearly as ready as you're going to be." He lifted his head to assess his work—taupe nipples jutting with impatience and shiny with his saliva, hips rising and falling as she writhed in the chair. "Show me how you get yourself off."

She really needed to resist that little diktat, because it was never good to give Ben too much of what he wanted. But the incomparable thrill of being here with him—her lifemate—feeling his own barely chained passion for her lunging at the leash—knowing he felt the keen edge of her pleasure slicing through his senses just like she felt his—tempted her further than they'd ever gone.

Right over the flipping cliff.

She held his gaze and breathed, "Are you ready for this, stud pony?"

She saw him swallow hard before he nodded. Not nearly as in control as he claimed when it came to this long-awaited consummation.

I'm going to break you, Ben Nero.

Her hand was already sliding down her tummy, head tilting back in her chair, eyes closed and lips parted. Her finger dipping into all that honeyed heat to swirl it around the vortex of craving at her clit. Two fingers spreading her folds to expose her even more, working that taut bud with shameless eagerness. A symphony of rhythmic moans she couldn't suppress slipping from her parted lips.

"Look at your pretty pussy, so wet and eager and needing me so bad," he groaned. "You're going to make me come just watching you and hearing your sweet sexy sounds."

His need pounded through her, a blaze of red heat against her closed eyelids, pulsing between them through the lifebond. His own hand wrapped around his taut length in a few slow strokes that made precum seep from his slit.

This was way too good to miss, so she lifted her head to watch. Watching him watch her rock her aching clit into her own eager hand.

Flaming fireballs, she could climax just from the sight of Ben Nero kneeling between her spread thighs with his cock in his hand, his hair in his eyes, and his driving need blazoned in every labored breath.

Her finger teased her wet hole, then eased inside.

"Yeah, that's right, angel," he rasped, one hand spreading precum down his shaft. "Work it in there good and deep. Show me how bad you need me."

The sucking sounds of her own foreplay quickened as she bucked into her hand, working her way deeper the way he told her, sweating with her own need. Her breasts bouncing with every thrust, moans sharpening to short urgent cries. Every ion of her mounting arousal exposed to his burning stare.

"Like this," she gasped. "This is how I get myself off. Imagining you inside me. Does this… satisfy your request?"

"I'm not even close to satisfied." His voice went dark and dangerous. "Why don't you let me try."

Which wasn't actually a question.

With a last long stroke, he released his shaft and pounced on her. He eased her hand free and encased the digit she'd been pumping inside herself with the silken heat of his mouth. His tongue swirled around her and lapped at her essence. A deep purr rumbled through him.

Dimly she wondered if that was what his mouth felt like wrapped around Dex's cock. If so, that wicked mouth of his must drive Dex insane.

"Have I mentioned how much I love your filthy fantasies?" he muttered, eyes smoking with heat as he eyed her through a sleek curtain of sable hair. "And yeah, Dex likes it a lot when I blow him. Pretty soon you'll see for yourself. You need me so bad, don't you?"

"Yes," she moaned.

No point lying to a telepath, was there?

He worked his own finger into her tight heat with more of that audible wetness that would have incinerated her with embarrassment if she'd been in her right mind.

But she wasn't.

At this point, she wasn't even sure she had a mind.

"Oh gods, Ben, just like that!" she gasped, feeling her channel tighten and release around his finger. Her voice spiraled high in urgent demand. *"Ben."*

One corner of his mouth curled up in a sly grin. "Have I *convinced* you yet?"

She bit her lip and shook her head.

Her hand fell away and his tongue—his talented, diabolical, insatiable tongue—slid up her slit. When he found her clit, she voiced an aching cry and wound her fingers in his hair to drag him close.

And wondered if it was possible to die of pleasure.

She'd never see the pilot's chair on the *Angel* the same way again. Not after she'd sprawled in it writhing, clutching Ben's head and fucking his hand and moaning under the relentless flicker of his tongue over her sweet spot. Stars above, the man knew just how to bring her to the paralyzing edge of pleasure and hold her there, suspended and sobbing with need.

She thought she was moaning words like *please* and *gods* and *oh, Ben, I'm losing it*. But maybe she was just thinking those things. And Ben was… doing something… something with his mind that made her insides glow and tingle like he'd flooded her with sparkling warmth.

This time when she climaxed, the entire sector was going to explode—

"Hold that thought for me." His arms were around her, lifting her from the chair, her limbs clutching him as she wiggled desperately to seat herself on his shaft.

"Blast it, Ben Nero, stop teasing! I need you—right *now*."

"Hold on… just a little longer…" Voice threaded with strain, he staggered across the cockpit with her frantic body wrapped in his arms. "We're not doing this… for the first time… in that flipping chair."

"Not the stasis capsule," she panted. "We'll make a monumental mess. This cruiser really wasn't designed for—"

"You took your samurai boyfriend here, didn't you?" he growled, savage with determination. "And that rotten little thief. Drove me demented to know you were with them. Even if you weren't really with them. I swear I wanted to murder both of them. Giving them what you should've been giving *me*."

Meteors, Ben. Just how close were you watching me all these years?

Obviously not close enough to keep you out of ten thousand types of trouble. An oversight I fully intend to remedy.

Her bunk was rising up to meet them, one of Ben's dappled furs thrown over her silver sheets. She caught a random image of him sprawled across it—sleepless and grim with resolve—as the *Angel* streaked toward the Gamma Sector, following her psychic trail like he'd been pulled on a string.

Her bunk had never been built for two.

But damn if they didn't find a way to make it work.

He tumbled her onto the plush fur and she pulled him down on top, legs wrapping around his hips to pull him close. His shaft nudged up against her channel, slick and pulsing with hunger. His face above her was fierce with focus, every sinew tight with restraint.

"Now," she moaned, hips rising to meet him. "We've waited long enough. Do it now. Please, please do it now. I need to feel your cock inside me."

"You asked for it," he whispered. *"Finally."*

After half a lifetime of craving and close to a decade of denial, the electric friction of his cock sheathing deep inside her felt like coming home.

Around them the planets stopped spinning. Their two minds pulsed and joined like astral bodies in conjunction. For a span of heartbeats, she wrapped herself tight around him and lay still, his breath harsh in the deep space silence, her cheek pressed to his. For no good reason, her eyes were swimming with tears.

"Oh gods, Ben," she whispered, broken with longing.

"I know, angel," he breathed in her ear, voice shaking. "I know."

He lifted his head to find her. Burning pure platinum with raw need, his eyes locked on hers like he'd never look anywhere else. Brow furrowed, lips parted, the chiseled lines of his face edged in starfire and shadow, harsh with intensity and intent.

Breath suspended, he started moving inside her.

Every stroke of his cock, already hard and full enough to spill, along her slippery sheath triggered slow shocks of sexual pleasure that made her gasp. He wasn't as thick as Zorin, but he was longer than Dex, and her body accommodated him like she'd been made to do nothing else, gripping his shaft in rippling spasms. She vibrated with the impact of every stroke. Pulse after pulse of pleasure rolled through him… through her… through the lifebond between them.

Even the antimatter drive of her psi-powered cruiser hummed and throbbed in time with their tempo.

"Gods of Solaris, the way you feel," he whispered, leaning in to find her mouth in a deep kiss salted with her own arousal. "Let me do this right for you."

She gasped out a laugh. "Right now? I don't think there *is* a wrong way."

His thrusts quickened, finding the driving rhythm designed to push both of them over the edge. Their bodies slid and twined and clung, sleek with sweat and oil. He moaned into her mouth, smooth tenor gone ragged with strain. His exotic fragrance, incense laced with Dex's mating scent, made her universe expand.

"Gods, Kaia. I swear I'll love you forever. Swear I'll never leave you. Have I—oh gods—have I convinced you?"

Her heels pressed into the flexing muscles of his ass to pull him in deeper. Her nails, sharp with urgency, dug into his shoulders to make him hiss. She met his incandescent gaze and the deepest secret of her heart spilled out.

"You convinced me—the day we met. Since then, I've hated you—but I've never—stopped loving you."

"Tell me you'll be my consort," he ground out. "Tell me or I won't let you come."

"That's playing dirty." She pressed her lips to his ear and breathed, "But it's an effective tactic. I'll totally be your consort."

The explosive crest of his climax caught them both by surprise. A cry, harsh with triumph, ripped out of him. Rigid and buried to the hilt inside her, he flooded her with jet after jet of potent release.

His climax filled her with liquid light. Her entire body ignited and pulsed around him like a heartbeat. Her hips undulated into him fast and eager, milking every last drop from his spurting cock. The force of her own orgasm slammed through her like a neutron torpedo, flinging her head back and wrenching from her throat a scream of release. Shooting stars streaked past her closed lids.

When her vision cleared, he was still sprawled across her, their gasping bodies still joined, sweat mingling on their skin. His hand spread across her tummy. Under his gentle mental probe, her whole body tingled with warmth and light.

"All right?" he murmured without lifting his ear from her chest. Like he was listening to the still-humming symphony he'd played on her body.

"Good gods." With a drowsy smile, she wrapped a hand in his sweat-damp hair and smoothed it back from his face. "That's one way of putting it. Are you?"

"Great flaming comets, Kaia. Do you know how long I've dreamed of being here with you like this? I don't think I've ever been this happy. As in… *ever*." He nuzzled her breast, long lashes falling over his soft gaze.

But that light probing touch along her insides never faltered.

She shuddered under a powerful surge of love. All the more satisfying for knowing they shared it through the lifebond.

She barely mustered enough post-coital energy to form the words. "What are you sensing?"

"Mmmmm." He lifted his head to find her lips in a leisurely kiss that still smelled and tasted of her own arousal. "Well, you've definitely ovulated. What we just did? That should certainly do the trick."

He sounded thoroughly satisfied, but the stakes were so high she needed to hear him say it.

"So… you think we might have conceived?" She held her breath and waited through his thoughtful silence. Hoping it would mean the Patriarch accepted their mating. Hoping it would mean they'd saved her sister.

And hoping the outcome wouldn't be too much of a disappointment for Dex. Or Zorin. Because they *all* wanted to sire her prophecy son. And she wanted that for all of them.

All three of her men.

Even though she knew what she wanted was impossible.

A slow sigh spread through him. "I'll check in a few clicks… do a full psi scan of your uterus. Tonight should be… all four of us. So we all have a shot. You won't mind that a bit, will you?"

"All four of us?" Her pulse of excitement met a ripple of surprise. "To be honest, I'm kind of amazed you'd want that. I thought you were pretty determined to be the father yourself?"

"Only fair if we all have a go." His murmur spilled out on a long exhale as he sprawled across her sated body and they both coasted toward dreamland. "Because Dex and Zorin are pretty determined too, angel. And you're not the only one who's fallen crazy in love. With both of them."

CHAPTER SIX
The Refugee

"I just gotta ask. How's it feel, boss?"

Marcus's casual question barely dampened the sizzle of anticipation or blunted the buzz of agitation that fueled Dex's rapid progress through the bracing hurly-burly of the *Inevitable*'s landing bay. Anticipation for what he'd find waiting for him on the *Interstellar Angel*, now settling into a shipboard landing berth under the gentle guidance of his tractor beam.

Agitation because, since Ben's initial transmission while Dex was sleeping sent both his battleship and Zorin's sprinting off to the Kryllian system for this rendezvous, Kaia's little cruiser hadn't been responding to hails.

"Hope you don't mind my asking," Marcus added.

Dex dragged his impatient eyes away from the *Angel*—seemingly none the worse for its incorrigible owner's latest adventure—to search his *optio*'s battle-hardened face.

"What precisely *are* you asking, Marcus?"

Best to grasp this looming dilemma squarely by the horns. Because it was obviously common knowledge among his army that he'd just spent his night on the *Relentless*. He'd rather hoped his romantic proclivities might be overlooked in the weighty press of the latest interplanetary developments.

Namely the imperial honor guard, twelve Mogadon bureaucrats clad in togas and mantles and full imperatorial rig, who'd boarded the *Inevitable* last night. All twelve of them now streaming in his determined wake.

Apparently, no such luck.

Damn it to hell. Over the years, he and his Number Two had

certainly had their differences. During the early years, the man hadn't always shown him much respect. To a rough-and-tumble army grunt like Marcus, Dex was a patrician to the manor born, a spoiled kid whose formidable advantages had been handed to him at birth with a flourish. Over the years, they'd learned to rub along together. Dex had come to fancy they'd developed a mutual respect.

And with it, a certain familiarity.

However, the extent of that familiarity between a subordinate and his commanding officer decidedly had its limits.

Surely his reliable right-hand man wasn't asking about his liaison with Zorin?

Embarrassed warmth climbed the back of Dex's neck. Last night his boyhood hero had bloody well shifted planets in his bed. Dex still hardened every time he thought about Zorin's hungry mouth on his body. Zorin's possessive hand on his shaft. Not to mention the unforgettable sensation of Zorin's monumental cock in his ass.

None of which were experiences he particularly cared to elaborate for an inquisitive subordinate.

"What exactly is it you're asking?" Dex repeated stiffly.

Marcus waved away a prefect with a tablet full of problems and met Dex's wary gaze with good-humored patience. "Not what you're thinking. I'm asking how it feels to rule the whole galaxy instead of only half of it, Imperator."

"Ah." Dex pushed out a breath. *"That."*

He supposed he ought to feel more grief over the newsflash he'd awoken to that morning. Grief at the news that his Imperator had just died in a virulent spacepox outbreak on Quorum. Even though he and Claudius had never been friends, they'd been allies.

At least, they'd been allies of convenience.

Instead, Dex found himself experiencing a certain sense of poetic justice. That novicide he himself had always felt so conflicted about inheriting and so desperately reluctant to use—a reluctance the ruthless Imperator had mocked—was apparently now responsible for the man's own demise. Spacepox had been one of Max Draven's favorite bioweapons.

Never again. I'm incinerating my father's arsenal of biological nightmares—down to the last microbe—the moment I'm back to Mogadon.

As they marched past a gleaming row of armed Zephyrs, his maintenance crew snapped off a salute to their brand-new Imperator. Dex nodded in grave acknowledgment.

Trying to keep his mind on his rapidly multiplying responsibilities rather than his steamy liaison with his Syndax pirate or his imminent reunion with his Valyrian lovers, Dex shot a keen glance across the landing bay. Just to assess the impact his glorified progress with this infernal cortège of encumbrances was having on shipboard discipline.

Blast it, no crewman in the landing bay was even pretending to perform his duties.

They were all standing rigidly at attention, wherever they were, watching the twelve togas flutter after their commander like bloody ghosts in a theatrical drama. Somehow, while he was down for the count in Zorin's bed, the whole damn dozen in their speedy sun clipper had managed to intercept the *Inevitable* and announce their confounding tidings.

Which meant they too were probably well aware he'd spent the night with Zorin. Despite the fact their two civilizations were still technically at war.

Damnation.

Well, if they expected *him* to wear a bloody toga—ever—he'd soon disabuse the lot of that notion.

Title or no title.

"I don't know that I *am* ruler of the galaxy, Marcus. The Patriarch of Kryll is the Quorum's sole surviving member—the only head of state to escape the spacepox attack. Even the Syndax succumbed in their biohazard bubble. Which makes the Patriarch the Quorum's ranking member. The Mogadon Imperator is merely one of four."

"The strongest one," Marcus pointed out, eyes canny. "The top dog."

"Too soon to say, really, how that dynamic will play out." Dex shrugged. "Zorin has yet to name the new Syndax rep. And who knows what the Senate of Psychics will opt to do about the vacant Valyrian seat?"

"Far's I know, that Patriarch might be rich as Midas in Mogadon myth, but Kryll doesn't even have a standing army. And as of today, you're the new Imperator." Marcus hitched his shaggy brows. "We're still the dominant superpower, ain't we? Sounds like ruler of the galaxy to me."

A reminder of his altered status Dex certainly didn't require. Since the twelve togas now dogging his every step were unlikely to allow him to forget it.

Ever.

"At the moment," Dex noted, crisply returning a flight crew's flurry of salutes, "humanitarian operations for the handful of survivors at Quorum and decontamination protocols for the starbase are the immediate priorities—along with finally concluding this interminable Tombola. As the Imperator-elect, I won't even have my coronation until we return to Mogadon."

Not to mention the fact the jury was still out on how willing the Mogadon rank and file—and the military Council of Indomitables—might be to tolerate the litany of traditions Dex was merrily in the midst of shattering.

Because he'd no intention whatsoever of tamely submitting to the crushing weight of Mogadon tradition and yielding up his military authority to a new First Indomitable merely to maintain the historical separation between civil and defensive functions.

That was a title he'd actually earned, damn it.

If the Empire wanted him wearing the imperial toga—figuratively speaking—they'd bloody damn well tolerate him continuing to lead the army as First Indomitable.

Him *and* his three consorts.

Assuming his three consorts wanted any part of the ceremonial hoopla of mating the Mogadon Imperator. Which might be rather a large leap.

And assuming the Patriarch bought into the Tombola outcome the four of them were scheming to orchestrate.

"You'll be the strongest Imperator we've had in centuries," Marcus said easily. "Plenty of folks—including me—figger we need fresh blood in the ruling house in the worst way. His Imperiousness started out with seven sons, didn't he? Not a one of them outlived him."

"No small thanks to me," Dex muttered. "Since I'm the one who killed his last living heir in formal combat."

A combat that, as it turned out, had been far too recent an event to allow the last Imperator to sire another son. The lack of which was directly responsible, according to the Mogadon Codex, for the fact that the ceremonial title now devolved to Dex.

The title he'd never in a million light years wanted.

"Young viper challenged *you*, sir, didn't he? His old man never held it against you."

That much was true. If the Imperator's last surviving son had managed to kill Dex, given the way the snake had already poisoned his own royal brothers, the Imperator himself would have been next to fall.

And the Imperator had known it.

Leaving Dex no choice but to crush the young viper's head beneath his boot.

"Like I said, we're the dominant power." Marcus hitched his burly shoulders in a shrug. "If you wanna run the whole show, boss, I'd like to know who's gonna stop you."

"I expect my three consorts will keep my tyrannical ambitions in check." Dex grinned, then realized with a jolt what he'd just admitted. Appalled by his own lack of discretion, he sliced his subordinate a sharp glance. "That intelligence is embargoed, by the way, until the Tombola outcome is finalized and formally announced. I, er, expect I've rather shocked you."

To his utter astonishment, his crusty, staunchly conventional, sexually conservative *optio* actually chuckled.

"I guess that woulda shocked me back in the day. And it woulda flipped me off. Just one more rule a guy like you can break, and a guy like me can't." Marcus hoisted his bushy brows. "Well, we've worked together a long time, ain't we? You've done one helluva job for us and the Empire. Me and the other boys who serve under you? We're mostly just glad to see you happy, boss. Reckon it's been long enough coming."

Dex's brain was still reeling with that unexpectedly ready acceptance of his wildly unconventional marital prospects when he reached the *Angel*.

At the foot of the lowered gangway, he slanted another grim look at the twelve togas, then shifted his attention to Marcus and the quartet of armed felons who'd replaced his praetorian guard.

"Keep everyone out until I emerge," he said briefly. "All of them, Marcus."

Because ruling the galaxy can blooming wait until I see with my own eyes if Kaia's on that ship.

He still hadn't forgiven Zorin for intercepting his calls while Dex was sleeping. And not only because that minor indiscretion had made glaringly apparent to his scandalized subordinates precisely whose bed their commander was sharing. The fact that he'd returned reeking of Zorin's mating scent merely confirmed their worst suspicions.

The more worrisome truth was that no one on the *Angel* had responded to a single hail since.

Leaving his men to secure his flank, he strode up the gangway—all the while trying to appear like he wasn't utterly frantic for his two lovers. Because this business of being out of his head in love with all three of them was every bit as complicated as he'd anticipated.

At present, it was all he could manage not to go sprinting up the ramp like a lovesick adolescent. Bad enough his entire crew had been bemused observers for days while their First Indomitable fell desperately in love, first with his Tombola ward and then with his boyhood best friend.

Now that he'd be walking around wearing not only the First Indomitable's epaulets but also the Imperator's toga… figuratively speaking… he supposed he'd need to be far more circumspect about all three of his tempestuous love affairs.

Not that his altered status changed his intentions one single nanoparticle. He was still taking all three of them as consorts.

He ducked into the narrow cylinder of Kaia's cockpit. The subdued mauve dusk of a Kryllian sunset seeped from the ceiling panels. The pilot's chair before the console's blinking lights stood empty. The glowing ovoid of the stasis chamber stood open.

Likewise empty.

Steps quick, heart thudding, he strode deeper into the cockpit.

If that infernal farking shapeshifter—

Past the looming structure of the stasis chamber and the obstructing bulk of the cyberport, the pilot's narrow bunk came into view.

Dex stopped in his tracks.

In a rumpled nest of slate fur and silver sheets, the one-woman bunk overflowed with a tangle of sleek naked limbs and the banner of Kaia's riotous wine-red curls, mingled with Ben's lush raven mane. Whole and unharmed, his woman slept on her back, tawny limbs flung everywhere in wild abandon. Ben was sprawled facedown over her, face buried in her neck, arm and leg flung possessively over her body.

As though, even adrift and dreaming, he couldn't bear to let her go.

Dex stood staring down at his lovers' entwined bodies and felt his heart—the steely, formidable, formerly impermeable heart of the galaxy's greatest general—contract in a spasm of wrenching relief.

None of which prevented him from noticing, and fully appreciating, that the arrangement yielded an outstanding view of Kaia's lush breasts. Not to mention Ben's sculpted ass.

Kaia's lashes lifted. A radiant glow suffused her sleepy face.

"Dex!" she breathed.

Thank every god and demigod on Olympus that shapeshifter didn't harm a hair on your beautiful, maddening, wildly willful head. I'm going to love you until the day I die. I trust that won't pose a problem for you, maharani.

Hearing the thought that blazed through his brain, a contented smile drifted across her drowsy lips.

Which was fortunate, because what came out of his mouth was a typically terse demand. "Why the devil didn't you answer my hails?"

"Cuz we didn't want to be interrupted, space cadet," Ben mumbled, one sluggish hand reaching to twine with Dex's fingers. "'S why I posted the 'Do not disturb' sign."

And despite the open door behind him and the imperial escort beyond and the wrathful Patriarch fuming planet-side, despite the god of the Swarm still at large somewhere in the galaxy and undoubtedly plotting his next attack, despite the handful of homicidal suitors still on the Tombola roster confined under guard to quarters in the belly of his battleship, and the rusting hulk stuffed full of Syndax tucked into planetary orbit like a stalking wolf at his flank—despite the whole damn universe, Dex let his two lovers pull him into that overcrowded bunk that was definitely not designed for three.

Kaia's ripe lips parted willingly beneath his, giving him all the access he needed to plunder her sweet mouth with his hungry tongue. Her supple curves yielded beneath him, full breasts pressing into his chest, slim thighs opening under the urgent drive of his hips. His cock shoved against his zipper like a starving beast.

Saturn, he was starving for her. Starving to reassert his claim and assure the whole galaxy she was his.

"Are you all right, darling?" he got out between desperate kisses. "I've been losing my mind. Tell me that creature didn't hurt you."

"Don't worry, Dex. I'm fine." Her silken tongue wrapped around his and her eager hands slid down his back. "Although we do need to talk about what I learned…"

She sounded breathless, probably because her fertile body was already responding to his driving need. Her thighs wrapped around him and, gods on the mountain, *all* he wanted to do was drag down his zipper and bury himself deep in her eager heat.

"Talk later," Dex muttered, finding the ripe swell of her breast. Oh gods, she filled his palm so perfectly, nipple rising taut and eager for his touch.

"Slow down a tick," Ben breathed in his ear, arms twining around his neck. "The door's wide open."

"Do you bloody think I give a damn?"

So much for his imperatorial discretion.

Besides, the angle was working in his favor. Thanks to the stasis capsule's looming bulk, no one lurking outside could see one damn thing.

Dex turned his head to find the quicksilver magic of Ben Nero's kiss, one hand clenching in his hair to hold him. Against his tongue, the dark spice of cloves mingled with the tang of Kaia's arousal.

The electrifying press of Ben's rigid cock, jutting into his hip, seared him with a fresh coil of lust.

"Sorry we didn't answer," Ben gasped between kisses. "Don't be mad for keeps."

"Don't you *ever* do anything like this again." Dex aimed this grim directive at both of them. "I mean it. Drove me demented when the two of you went dark."

"Why so grumpy?" Kaia whispered in his ear.

His lovers shifted to accommodate him between them. Legs entwined, hair everywhere, Kaia's soft lips against his neck, Ben's hand settling against his cheek. The sexy perfume of jasmine and the cyberspace zing of ozone mingling with his own predatory scent.

Even with the three of them wedged together tighter than Solarian sardines in a vacuum pack, Dex didn't think he'd ever been happier.

But they needed to be told, didn't they?

"Grumpy, am I?" He lifted his head to eye the open door and thought about that blasted entourage. "Speaking as the luckless sod who's about to be crowned the next Mogadon Imperator, I do believe I'm entitled."

#

Zorin piloted his own fighter from the *Relentless* to the *Inevitable*. Manning his own helm was a pretty rare perk for him these days. But Dex had just given him at-will landing bennies on his flagship. And Zorin darn well intended to make the most of them.

He docked neatly in Bay Six and scrambled out in a rush, leaving Tick Tock and Junior to make their own way behind. He figured Kaia could use a little heads-up before he sprang this one on her.

And, on a practical level, he figured it'd be good to make sure everyone had clothes on.

Kaia's cruiser wasn't hard to ID, and he beelined for it. But his first sight of that gaggle of toga-clad geese outside it, all honking with indignation at the sudden appearance of the notorious Syndax wolf in their millpond, definitely slowed his stride. Aghast, the whole kit and kaboodle took in the sight of his big body, all starmetal bulk and blaster.

Fully at ease and fancy-free on the Mogadon flagship.

One portly, balding bureaucrat hitched up his big-boy toga and waddled right up to get in his grille. "What in blazes are you *doing* here, Theodophilus? The Empire has declared galactic war on Syndax scum and traitors."

And hearing that mouthful of moniker he'd kicked to the curb years ago did nothing to improve his temper.

"Howdy right back, Antonius." Zorin sighed. "How's the missus?"

Neptune's knickers, wasn't this a humdinger? Especially since he had a sneaking suspicion he knew exactly why this gaggle of imperial geese had landed on Dex's doorstep.

Thoroughly dissatisfied with him—just like the old days—the paper-pusher goggled at Marcus. "I demand to know the meaning of this indignity, *Optio*."

Marcus folded his arms across his chest. "Afraid you're gonna have to ask the top dog, Your Magnanimousness."

Zorin had to hand it to him. Dex's Number Two had guts. Because flipping the bird to a Mogadon magistrate was rarely a smooth move for any guy's career.

Toga flapping, another bureaucrat waddled into the fracas.

Quacking words like *outrage* and *insubordination* and even that old reliable *treachery*.

Zorin had pretty much figured their new Syndax-Mogadon alliance wasn't gonna go over too good with the home crowd. Well, let Dex's man deal with it. That's what he was paid for. Right now, Zorin had way bigger fish to fillet.

Leveling a wry look at the besieged *optio*, he planted one big space boot on the ramp.

Marcus shifted his weight unhappily.

Looking so harried Zorin felt sorry for the guy.

"Better hold up, Zorin," Marcus advised. "The, ah, Imperator wants everyone kept out."

"Imperator, huh?" Zorin said glumly, silently resigning himself to the whopping shitstorm this latest whiz-bang was about to bring down on all their heads. "Well, toga or no toga, reckon he'll see me, don'tcha, Marcus?"

Without waiting for permission, he maneuvered past Dex's faithful watchdog and tromped up the ramp. Giving them all a good whiff of Dex's mating scent all over him—and hoping like hell the kid wouldn't hate him for doing it.

Trick worked like a charm. With a good noseful of their alpha's scent in their sniffers, the whole flock stopped pecking at him. He grinned at the appalled silence.

At least no one else tried to stop him.

Halfway up, he remembered Tick Tock and tossed over his shoulder, "You're gonna wanna let the next guy in too, Marcus."

Kaia's crib was way too small for a guy his size, but he managed to maneuver. Ducking his head so he wouldn't brain himself on the ceiling, angling his shoulders to squeeze between the stasis capsule and the cyberport, he breathed through the vise of anticipation and anxiety that tightened his chest under his armor.

Jumpin' Jupiter, the sight of all three of his future consorts crammed into Kaia's narrow bunk… naked limbs wrapped around Dex's dark uniform, burgundy curls and midnight hair mingled and gleaming in the artificial twilight, Ben sultry and tempting as a fallen angel, Dex's burnished hair falling in his face, atomic eyes smoking with sexual heat…

And best of all Kaia.

His girl.

Whole and healthy. Her eyes glowing lilac and her delicate face illuminated with joy just to see him.

He was so goddamn thrilled with the whole scenario, his beat-up old ticker just about exploded with contentment.

"Zorin," Kaia breathed, all throaty and sexed up as seven hells. "Is there a reason you're standing all the way over there, big guy?"

"I'm one lucky son of a gun," he said gruffly. "But I gotta get something off my chest. The four of us really go through with this thing? We're gonna need a bigger bed."

Feeling his shaft harden behind his armor at the prospect, he issued himself a stern directive.

Stay right where you're at, flyboy. Keep your dick in your dungarees. You got Tick Tock coming up right behind with Junior. You need more folks at this shindig wearing clothes, not less.

"Tick Tock's coming here *now?*"

Plucking the thought right from his noggin the handy way she did sometimes, Kaia giggled and wiggled her way out of the crowded bunk.

Giving him an eyeful of sleek naked samurai as she sprinted across the cockpit and threw herself into his arms for a hello kiss. And, Tick Tock or no Tick Tock, he wrapped his arms tight around her and dragged her soft clinging body up hard against his armored chest.

"Thank Juno you're all right," he muttered. "Just about killed me not knowing, sweetheart. Especially since I'm the one who let you wander off with Proteus in the first place. I'm too old for all this excitement."

"Missed you," she breathed. "You're not old. And it wasn't your fault, Zorin."

With a groan, he bent to claim the sweet warmth of her mouth. Her lush body wrapped around him. The mingled fragrance of jasmine and incense and pheromones—laced with his own familiar scent— shifted his orbit. Just like always. Under the buffering shell of his starmetal, his cock stiffened and rose in urgent need.

Gods, he needed to be inside her. He wanted to throw her down across that tumbled love nest that reeked of her arousal and Ben Nero's passion, spread her thighs wide, pull her legs over his shoulders, push his tongue inside her wet heat until she knotted his hair in her fists and thrust her hips against his mouth and moaned for him to let her come.

And he wanted Dex to pin her down and Ben to tongue her nipples and both of them to get her good and ready for him to ride her.

All of it—her yielding kisses, his primal need—heightened by the razor-sharp awareness of Dex rolling on his side to watch, a naked Ben twined around him. Both of them openly admiring the view of Kaia's pear-shaped buttocks cupped in Zorin's big paws.

Stars, this thing with the four of us is gonna take some getting used to.

"You're mating two telepaths," she gasped against his mouth. "This is how it's going to be. Do you mind?"

"Mind? I'm still trying to figure out what I did to be this lucky." By a monumental act of will, he managed to lower her feet to the floor.

Rather than backing her into the nearest bulkhead and burying his cock inside her.

"Listen," he told all three of them, scrubbing a hand against the back of his neck and thinking of cold showers. "You're all gonna wanna get some clothes on. I got news."

Kaia made a playful face at him—a look of pouting disappointment that made him burn to keep right on rolling with that whole four-way fantasy.

But she bent to scoop up the black scrap of her panties like the good girl she wasn't.

"Do tell," Ben murmured, stretching like a languid cat. Dex gave the Valyrian a quick hard kiss and rolled out of bed.

Watching those two kiss always made him hotter than an O-class star.

Zorin tried like heck to get his head back in the game.

"We got a landing window confirmed at Kryll Capital Starbase. My boys just beamed the coordinates to your bridge."

He lobbed this piece of intel at Dex. Because watching Kaia wiggle into those tiny panties, full breasts swaying as she shimmied, was way too distracting. And he kept his eyes politely averted from the still-lounging and naked Ben—who, after all, he still barely knew. He didn't wanna presume and just ogle the guy.

Even if it did seem like Gorgeous over there was all but daring him to look.

"Very well." Dex paused to mutter through his wrist unit to Titus on the bridge, one hand smoothing his tousled hair. "Have we been able to reach the Patriarch?"

"Yeah. We got an appointment bright and early at oh-six-hundred tomorrow. And, uh, we're gonna need to palaver about that…"

Now Kaia was sliding into her cybersuit, stretching the sleek black fabric over her taut golden thighs in a way that would drive any red-blooded male to drink. Still wearing that smug smile as she listened in on his head, though her lavender eyes were sharp with focus.

"Our negotiating strategy is entirely in order." Dex, too, was watching Kaia's sexy show as he tugged his uniform straight and adjusted the merchandise down below. "My, er, accession considerably strengthens our hand—but also limits our freedom. I presume that's something else the four of us should discuss. I'm well aware none of you signed on to mate the Mogadon Imperator."

"Don't be brain-dead." Ben yawned. "We're mating *you*. I can't wait to wear a toga."

"I still can't believe it," Kaia murmured, tucking her succulent breasts into her cybersuit. Zorin watched with regret as they vanished from sight. "But Ben's right. It doesn't change a thing—for any of us. What do they call an Imperator's consort anyway?"

"Imperatrix," Dex said, distracted, tossing an indolent Ben his breeches. "To be precise, that's the title for a female consort. No other Imperator in history has ever taken a male consort—at least not openly. To say nothing of *two*."

"First time for everything, kid." Zorin was feeling a little distracted himself as Ben finally rolled out of bed.

Still taking his sweet old time, the imp prowled past, brazenly naked and sublimely unconcerned, all silken skin stretched over supple sinew, hair a sleek curtain spilling down his back. Framing just about the most bitable ass Zorin had ever laid eyes on.

The Mogadon *thermae*.

That's where he wanted Ben Nero.

On his knees and slick with lather in a steaming shower while Zorin grabbed fistfuls of that glossy hair and coaxed that sulky mouth to wrap around his cock and suck him off until he saw stars.

But he didn't want to come. Not like that. Not their first time. Not until he was buried balls-deep in that perfect—

Cripes, at least keep your eyes off his ass, old man. Give the guy some privacy.

"You needn't be shy on our boy's account," Dex said in his ear, tone warm with amusement. "He'll be terribly disappointed if you don't at least look. Consider it a preview of coming attractions."

Our boy.

And the easy way he said it told Zorin at least one of his secret fears was unwarranted. Possessive and territorial as any Mogadon alpha in history, Dex miraculously didn't seem bothered by sharing Ben with Zorin.

At least not yet.

"Lucky us," Zorin rasped.

And boy, did he mean it.

He'd never been the needy type, but then he'd never hooked up before with a Mogadon Imperator. Which had to be why he found himself turning to Dex and pulling the guy into his arms.

Just to see if he still could.

And bless his heart, this particular Mogadon Imperator actually let him do it, hands settling possessively at Zorin's waist, their mouths colliding in a scorcher of a kiss. A hint of ruddy color rising in Dex's face that just about charmed the socks off him.

Even though Zorin tried like hell to keep it all in, those three needy words slipped out anyway. Against Dex's warm lips, he whispered, "Still love me?"

"Mmmm." Dex leaned his forehead against Zorin's. "Afraid you're stuck with me."

Which pretty much made Zorin's whole goddamn day.

"Me too." Kaia slipped an arm around each of them.

They turned in tandem to pull her close. And Zorin had never in his whole life felt happier than he did with an arm wrapped firmly around both his lovers.

Beneath his hand, Kaia's lean frame vibrated with a subtle current of tension.

"Wasn't there something you wanted to tell us? About my father?" Her anxious face peered up at him.

"Oh, Jupiter. Yeah." Zorin lifted his head to include Ben, who'd *finally* managed to slide into his breeches, thank you gods. "There's been kinda… uh… a development."

"What sort of development, damn it?" Dex stepped back to eye him, wariness invading his hard face.

"Yo." Before Zorin could pull his head together to explain, a youthful hail from the doorway behind him whisked the whole shebang right out of his hands. "Pretty sure he means me."

And, for the second time that morning, Zorin had the pleasure of watching an infusion of incredulous joy wash through his Kryllian lover and turn Kaia incandescent with delight.

"Kylie?"

He'd gotten a good gander at the junior maharani earlier, when the gal first pitched up on the *Relentless*. Just about gave him a damn heart attack. Far as he could figure, she'd smuggled herself aboard on the bunkering ship from the surface that had just hooked up with them in orbit.

He knew from Kaia that Junior was only twelve, but thanks to the Patriarch's hormone shots, Kid Sis over there looked and sounded at least sixteen. Slim and sharp as a bolt of lightning in the scruffy cargo leathers of a stevedore, copper hair swinging in a fiery braid down her back, freckled face narrow and intent under the brim of her battered hat.

But for a breath, with Kaia flying at her like a hurricane and hugging her hard enough to knock her hat off, the scarily self-possessed young urchin looked her actual age. Both sisters were crying.

And Kaia's happiness was so intense Zorin felt damn close to crying himself.

The normally composed Precursor, still shirtless and barefoot, boots dangling forgotten from one hand, stood staring at this teary reunion in astonishment. Beyond, Tick Tock and Marcus stood wedged shoulder to shoulder in the doorway. Both scoping out the sitch with their jaws hanging.

But, with typical quickness, Zorin could already see the electric awareness of this development's dangerous implications flashing across Dex's alarmed face.

He was still pretty new to this whole telepathy thing and so was Dex. But this was one time Dex's sharp thought knifed right through Zorin's noggin.

Gods of Olympus, the Patriarch must be hunting her. If he suspects for one bloody moment we're harboring her here—

"Dude, don't sweat it. He doesn't have a clue." Junior surfaced from her sister's clinging arms and pivoted to answer the question he'd never even spoken. "Believe me, you don't have to worry about my dad hunting me down."

"Telepath too, huh?" Zorin eyed her with some sympathy. "And a damn fine one, ain'tcha, honey?"

Unimpressed, Dex sliced the impudent newcomer a narrow look.

"Speaking as the Tombola master who's spent the past six days consumed with nothing else," he said dryly, "I'd be quite keen to hear precisely why you believe we needn't 'sweat it' about the Patriarch."

The gal cocked her skinny hip with plenty of sass. Just like her big sis, gods help them all. "You don't have to worry about him hunting me, Mogadon, cuz he thinks I'm *dead*. And I intend to make pretty effing sure it stays that way."

CHAPTER SEVEN
The Ambush

"Junior's down for the count," Zorin reported a few clicks later, schlepping into his digs on the *Relentless*. "Pretty wore out from all the excitement. Kaia's just kinda… tucking her in, I guess. She'll be along in a tick."

He hoped.

Because he'd been fully expecting to find Dex and Nero both kicked back in his quarters for the night, ready for all four of them to rumble the way they'd planned. Sharing a bottle of contraband thirty-curie reactor-fermented whiskey from the latest shipment he'd smuggled off Mogadon.

Instead, he'd just walked in to find gorgeous Ben Nero prowling his digs solo, restless and deadly as a caged panther. His lean limber frame barefoot and dangerous in sexy black breeches that fit him like a latex glove and a silky white shirt unlaced halfway down his chest.

The kind of shirt you wanted to peel off with your teeth.

And the plum in all that pudding, pouring loose and luscious down his back, the skein of glossy hair Zorin was dying to touch. Hair he was aching to feel spill down around him and tickle his face when he finally pulled the guy down on top of him for a long leisurely kiss that would leave them both moaning.

He took one look at Ben Nero, heard the slow scrape of a match, and felt the sparking sizzle of a flame ignite.

Jumpin' Jupiter. I think I'm in trouble.

"Dex was delayed on the *Inevitable*," Ben said casually.

Reading his mind again, of course, the way they both did. Both these erotic, exotic aliens Zorin was somehow miraculously about to mate.

Zorin cleared his throat. "Trouble?"

"Depends on how you define it." The hint of a smile softened Ben's brooding mouth. "Don't mind me. I'm sulking. It's Imperator stuff. He's been doing it all day—issuing executive orders and dictating press releases and planning his coronation. But he tore himself away long enough to promise me he's coming."

Which brought Zorin right back to the two of them.

Alone.

Together.

Casually he punched the button that left his door unlocked. Even though he'd already given passcodes to all three of his future consorts. For a bit he putzed around with the wall-mounted comm unit, scrolling through messages he could've ignored.

Which, for a delaying tactic, had to be pretty obvi. He figured his houseguest didn't need to be a telepath to sense he was jittery.

Lounging against the rusting titanium wall in a wash of subdued light—the cool blue glow that meant bedtime—Ben studied him, head tilted, face soft with that slight enigmatic smile.

"And what have you been doing all day, Zorin the pirate?"

"Pirate stuff." One corner of Zorin's mouth lifted in a grin. "Inventorying a cargo full of contraband from that Kryllian bunkering ship Junior hitched a ride on. Paying a boatload of bribes to cover her trail from Pops. And avoiding Kryllian excise taxes I really oughta be paying."

"Just another average day?" Ben's purple eyes drifted over his leather-clad body. A slow smolder flared in those stormy depths. "What, no abducting and ravishing helpless captives? Compelling them to indulge your every kink and pleasure in your bed? Or maybe in your shower?"

A vivid fantasy flared in his head. A fantasy of backing Ben Nero into the handy hip-high corner seat in his monster Mogadon shower, lubing them both up till they were slick and desperate, then easing the guy's legs over his shoulders and working his way one breath at a time into all that tight heat.

Because Ben Nero was way too gorgeous for Zorin not to watch his face when he climaxed.

Glad you like what you see, big guy. Because the feeling's more than mutual.

Under that intimate whisper that stroked him like a finger, a pulse of heat flared in his groin. His cock tingled and tightened and sat up to say howdy.

"Ravishing helpless captives, huh?" With a wry chuckle, Zorin logged off the comm unit. "Pirates always get a bad rap."

"Leather looks good on you, Syndax," Ben murmured, soft and husky.

Aw, shoot. Where the hell's Dex?

Sedulously avoiding the tanker-sized orgy couch where he and Dex had fooled around last night, Zorin moseyed over to the aging but fully stocked bar with its scuffed leather stools and contraband bottles.

One of the perks of being the galaxy's most notorious smuggler.

"Can I, uh, pour you a whiskey?"

"If you're having one." Reflected in the cracked mirror before the bar, his dangerous houseguest lifted one shoulder in a graceful shrug. "Normally I'm a Solarian red kind of guy."

Sure he was. This wasn't some Syndax pirate slouching around his digs. Not some casual conquest. Ben Nero was the superbly engineered apex of ten thousand years of Valyrian genetics. In the dwindling Beta Sector that Valyria had dominated for millennia, he was a lord of the ruling caste. An aristocrat.

Practically a god.

More to the point, he was Dex's lover and Kaia's lifemate.

Which meant Zorin intended to get their permission—and preferably their participation or at least their presence—for his first go-round with their Valyrian lover.

Who needed to be wooed, damn it. Zorin couldn't just fall on this guy he still barely knew like a starving wolf and ravage him.

No matter how much he burned to do it.

No matter how much the guy himself seemed to be all but inviting it.

"I'll have to remember that," Zorin said gruffly, splashing smuggled whiskey into a couple of glasses.

Meaning the wine… and other things.

Bare feet silent against the brightly woven Kryllian carpet he'd just installed for Kaia—one more luxury he hadn't paid excise taxes on—Ben slipped up behind him. A whisper of warm breath brushed the back of his neck. A thrill of erotic pleasure shot down his spine.

Straight to his shaft.

Rock-hard and swollen with need, it shoved against his fighting leathers.

"I'm not here to drink, Zorin," Ben whispered against his nape. "Tonight I intend to indulge an entirely different set of vices. What was it you were imagining on the *Angel* this morning? Me naked on my knees in a Mogadon *thermae*?" His velvet tenor deepened. "Remind me what it was I was doing to you."

Last night, alone in this very room with Dex, Zorin had been the seducer. Tonight, he was keenly aware, he stood in active danger of being seduced himself. Seduced by a guy who was half his age—which he had to admit was flattering as hell.

Seduced by a guy who was a goddamn master.

So much the master Ben didn't even need to touch him to seduce him. All he needed to do to make Zorin want him was stand behind him. Just close enough to give off a whiff of that sexy incense that rose from his silky skin.

Laced with the bracing bite of Dex's mating scent.

A lethal conjunction of both of them—the guy he'd finally claimed after half a lifetime wanting him, and the one he was aching to touch—that made the predator inside him sit straight up and howl.

Zorin tossed back a burning slug of whiskey just to clear his damn head. Its smoky caramel bite seared his sinuses. Glass dangling, he ambled over to the panoramic viewport, filled with the banded saffron and sienna orb of the desert world they circled.

Eight clicks till the Patriarch's party.

And if Dex doesn't stop fooling around with those togas and get his imperial ass over here PDQ, I'm gonna fly over there and fetch him. Cuz Gorgeous here's horny as all seven hells and hotter than a sulfur fire.

And this isn't happening without all four of us.

Tonight—this first time—we gotta do this thing right. And not only because that could damn well be what it takes to make Kaia conceive. We got a whole future, all four of us, that depends on it.

"Why don't we slow down a tick." Zorin kept his tone easy. "Don'tcha think we oughta wait for Kaia and Dex?"

Especially Dex.

Dex who was possessive enough to kill when it came to any other guy sticking his dick in Ben Nero.

Zorin would rather self-disintegrate than do anything to hurt Dex. Ever.

"Why should we wait? This is what Kaia wants. Comets, it's all she's talked about or thought about for days. She's my lifemate. You can trust me to know." Back at the bar, a mutinous note crept into Ben's tone. "And Dex doesn't own me, Zorin."

"That's not what I hear."

Yeah, that little rumor was all over the fleet. Because the *Relentless*, the *Inevitable*, the togas' sun clipper, and the Kryllian bunkering ship all orbiting the planet together did constitute a makeshift fleet. Rumor was Dex Draven was so crazy jealous of any guy who looked crosswise at Ben Nero he'd just *killed* one of his own farking men for putting the moves on him, for Neptune's sake—

"Don't believe everything you hear. Dex's man wasn't *putting the moves* on me. An idiom that implies consent." Reflected in the viewport over the Kryllian homeworld, Ben's eyes flashed a blinding silver. "And Dex wasn't the one who killed him."

With the delicacy of a master surgeon, the Valyrian inserted another lurid image into his brainbox. The image of one of Dex's jack-booted butchers, knickers around his knees, bleeding out through every orifice on Ben's bathroom floor.

"Mars," Zorin rasped. He tipped back a hefty gulp of liquid fire just to settle his roiling gut. "Remind me never to piss *you* off, gorgeous."

Leaving his own whiskey untouched, Ben prowled toward him. Taking his sweet old time.

But definitely still stalking him.

An elemental instinct made Zorin put down his glass and turn so the guy who'd just pulverized a man's insides to a pulp with a thought wouldn't be at his back.

He was taller than Ben, but not by much. The fact that Ben even came close to his height was actually kinda rare.

Zorin didn't often feel at a physical disadvantage. He'd never met a man he couldn't defeat in combat. Although Dex, back in their sparring days, had gotten strong enough and sharp enough and quick enough to give him a good scramble for his money.

The fact that here Zorin was falling for a guy who could literally squash him like a space bug with a thought?

Turned out it was one hell of a turn-on.

Who'd have thunk?

Two cubits away, Ben stopped. Almost close enough to touch.

"I shared that memory with you for a reason," Ben said softly. "And it wasn't to threaten you."

"It wasn't, huh?"

"I wanted to reassure you."

"*Reassure* me?" He snorted.

"Reassure you that you can't hurt me," Ben said patiently. "For a galactically notorious Syndax, you have a remarkably tender conscience. The pirate with a heart of gold."

"Yeah, I know. Don't tell anyone." Zorin chuckled. "For a Syndax it's kinda, you know, a defect."

"Your secret's safe with me." A wry smile flickered across Ben's mobile mouth.

The guy tilted his head down and looked up at him through his lashes. Looked up at him like he ruled the whole goddamn galaxy.

Even though that gig now officially belonged to Dex.

No wonder the kid can't get enough of this guy. When Ben Nero looks at a man like that, you feel like you can slay dragons.

"Don't get me wrong, big guy," Ben breathed. "I'm thoroughly charmed that you're actually worried about taking advantage of me. Worried about hurting me by being as rough as you want to be. Worried about offending me by coming on too strong. You're afraid I'll be… turned off somehow, aren't you? Turned off by how much you want me. By all the ways you want me." A breath. "Don't be."

Two slow steps eased the guy right past his defensive perimeter. Tempting and seductive as all seven devils. With his eyes that promised pleasure and his mouth made for sin. His deft hands slid up Zorin's chest. Every hair on his whole body prickled and rose in arousal.

Zorin said the name like a safeword. "Dex."

Ben's gaze flashed violet lightning with frustration. He knotted Zorin's shirt in his fists.

And just that whisper of sexual violence between them was enough to make Zorin shudder. His shaft jerked and lunged against his zipper like a fighting dog on a leash who smelled blood.

"You're obsessed with Dex. I'm obsessed with Dex. We're all

obsessed with Dex. Because we're all in love with him! But you need to hear me. *Dex. Doesn't. Own me.*" Ben's voice thickened. "You said a couple days ago, back at the Tombola when we danced, you said I could have your full attention anytime I want. You remember, don't you?"

His mouth too dry to speak, Zorin jerked his chin in a nod.

"Well…" Ben's eyes ignited with need. "I want."

He leaned in, plenty slow enough for Zorin to evade if he wanted. But he didn't. All the gods help him, he didn't.

What he wanted—*all* he wanted—right that moment was to discover how that sulky, succulent mouth of his would taste when Zorin finally kissed him.

Ben's lips eased over his, soft and smooth as silk. The dark sweetness of cloves slid through him. And all the ethics in the universe couldn't stop Zorin from leaning into him, demanding access, demanding more, coaxing his lips to part and meeting the slick heat of Ben's tongue with his own.

A husky moan slipped out between them.

His hands were hard on Ben's slim hips—too hard and he knew it—dragging him closer. Needing him off-balance and clinging to Zorin to stay on his feet. Ben's hands cupping his face to hold him. So compliant, so sweet, so yielding to the sudden hot need surging through him. Gods, he could do anything, the guy would let him do *anything*—

"Wait a sec." Zorin fought like the dickens to clear his head. "Wait. Why are you doing this?"

"I told you," Ben muttered between desperate, searing kisses. Kisses deep enough and dark enough to drown a man in an ocean of desire. "Because I want you. And yeah, I'll let you do anything. Anything you want. The rougher you are, the harder you'll make me come."

A hungry groan ripped out of him.

Their cocks collided, Zorin's hard bulge pressed against leather, Ben's rigid shaft straining his laces. He had just enough presence of mind left around the pounding need between his legs to know he couldn't wrestle off the man's breeches and ride him while they were plastered up against the lit expanse of his external viewport, with transports trundling back and forth between their ships and shuttles zipping up and down from the planet.

But not enough presence of mind to stop.

His hands had a mind of their own, wrapping around that tight, bitable ass he'd been fantasizing about all day to pull him in tighter. Just the thought of spreading him wide to expose that pretty pink hole. Spreading him wide for Dex.

Yeah, Dex. The guy they needed to wait for, remember?

"For punk's sake, Zorin." Ben broke off the kiss so suddenly Zorin wanted to roar in protest. "Look—I'm the Precursor, okay? Dex might run the show in bed, but he doesn't run me. It's the four of us. You're mating all of us. You've been with Kaia and you've been with Dex. But you're afraid to be with me unless Dex *gives his permission*. And, yeah, it's flipping me off."

"Sorry," Zorin said hoarsely. "Them's the rules."

In a quicksilver reversal, Ben loosened his demanding clench on Zorin's shirt. His hands threaded through Zorin's hair in a caress so sensual it made the roots of his hair tingle. Ben leaned in to slide his tongue—his slick, hot, diabolically skillful tongue—along the rim of Zorin's ear.

And all Zorin could think about was how much he wanted that skillful tongue wrapped around his cock.

"Don't you get it?" Ben's breath filled his ear and made him shiver. "When it comes to you, Dex wants what I want. Says he plans to spoil me. And I've been feeling everything Kaia feels for you, everything Dex feels for you, everything you feel for them for days."

His hot mouth nuzzled his way down Zorin's neck, teeth scraping skin, tongue licking sweat, lips seeking out all the sensitive spots that made him shiver. Zorin was losing this fight one breath at a time and he knew it. This yielding, clinging, pleading demon—this demon who thought he was falling for him—there wasn't a wall in existence that could keep this man out of his heart.

"I love the way you taste," Ben sighed against his skin. "Like making love to a wolf."

Zorin finally did what he'd been aching to do forever and slid a hand through the sleek soft fall of all that jet-black hair. While his other hand stayed right where it was, wrapped around the guy's ass, keeping Ben's slender hips and sinewy thighs and all that searing cock anchored right against him.

His fist clenched in Ben's hair, hard enough to make him whimper in mingled pain and pleasure, and eased his head up.

"Ah, pet, you're so young," Zorin sighed, his heart aching. He searched Ben's sculpted face. Ben's glowing eyes naked with needing him. Ben's perfect mouth swollen with kissing him. "You and Kaia both—but when has our girl ever done anything she's supposed to. She's young yet, crazy young, but she knows what she wants. Heck, I think she was born knowing."

"So was I." A stubborn spark flared in Ben's eyes. "You and Dex—"

"The kid and me, we fell for each other years ago. It just took us this long to admit it." Zorin swiped a thumb along the tender curve of Ben's lower lip and watched his silky lashes flutter closed. "You, though… why does someone like you want an old guy like me? When there's no one in the whole universe you couldn't have if you wanted?"

"What if the one I want is you?" Ben whispered. "All three of you."

Zorin shook his head and forced out the secret fear he was still fighting. "I told you before—if you and Dex—I won't insist—"

"No." Ben's eyes flashed open, incandescent with intent. "You're, what, afraid I'll *reject* you? Get a clue, big guy. When it comes to you? With your big hands and your silver eyes and your scourge-of-the-galaxy reputation? With the way you protect all of us, care for all of us, keep all of us safe and steady and sane despite ourselves?"

"Oh, I get that I'm the father figure in this whole setup," Zorin said dryly. "Shoot, gorgeous, you want me to take care of you, you don't need to sleep with me for that. I'm gonna do it anyway. But a guy like you—"

"Let me tell you about *me*." A flicker of humor softened Ben's mutinous mouth. "In case you haven't noticed, when it comes to you, I'm what you might call a sure thing. Even if I wasn't already out of my head in love with you."

That did it right there. He could just manage to withstand Ben Nero saying he loved him once, while the guy was trying to seduce him.

If he said it again and meant it, Zorin was a goner.

"I do mean it," Ben whispered. "I want you. I need you. For days I've been craving you. And I'm going to lose my flipping mind if you don't do something major about that. Right the hell now."

Hold on to your heartstrings, you big dummy. You can't just lunge at the guy and devour him. He's Dex's. And Kaia's. But he still isn't yours.

With his sweating back pressed to the viewport and Ben's lean length plastered all along his front, Zorin knew he needed to grab the yoke and seize control of this runaway shuttle they were riding before they shot straight to oblivion. He even straightened up to get his ass off the polyglass and got his hands on Ben's waist to move him.

But all he seemed able to manage was a sharp pivot, two decisive steps that backed Ben into the corner, and a palm planted against the wall to keep him from escaping.

Trapping his delectable houseguest between the viewport and his braced arm.

Eyes never leaving his, Ben looped his hands in Zorin's studded belt and dragged their hips together. The electric collision of their steel-hard cocks fractured his wavering resolve and damn near shattered him.

I mean it, big guy. I'm so deep in love with you I'm going to lose it if you don't love me back. You want to hear me beg for you? You want me on my knees?

A groan rumbled through Zorin's chest. "Have a little mercy. You're killing me here. Look, you're right about Kaia. You and me… this is what she wants. She's said so often enough, hasn't she. But we're still waiting for her and Dex."

He said it as firmly as he could manage. But any firmness of tone he'd mustered was pretty much obliterated by the hand he hooked under Ben's thigh to ease the guy's leg around his hips and hold him there. Not to mention the way his body started moving all on its own, rocking his cock into Ben's hard searing heat.

And, stars, the way he responded, undulating against Zorin, supple as a snake. Just the way Zorin knew he'd yield and accommodate and encourage him once Zorin finally got him naked and thrust home deep inside him.

Hot and hungry, Ben slid his hands around Zorin's ass and urged him on. The guy knew just how to cling to a man, didn't he? Like he was frantic for his touch and helpless in his thrall—all at the same time.

"Please, Zorin, please," he panted into his neck, that sinful mouth sucking hard enough to mark him. "I'm so close to coming for you. Please let me come for you."

"Aww, hells, gorgeous," Zorin groaned. "How am I supposed to say no to that?"

"Telepath, remember?" Ben gasped out a laugh. "I know what it takes to make you come. *Please* let me come for you."

Zorin's pace quickened, hard and desperate, palm shifting to pin Ben's shoulder to the wall, hips hammering into him, cock pistoning against his with driving need. Already slick and wet with precum inside his leather. His panting breaths roughened to rhythmic grunts of effort.

Because if there was any guy in the galaxy who could make him come in his pants like a newbie watching his first porno vid, it was this one.

"Gods, Zorin, just like that," Ben moaned, head tipped back against the wall, lips parted and gasping for air, eyes lidded and glowing with arousal. "Yeah—oh yeah—harder—I'm so ready for you. Please don't stop—"

We gotta stop.

Problem is, I've got no goddamn intention of stopping.

"You know just what to say," Zorin growled, leaning in for a punishing kiss, "to get a guy off. Don't you, Ben Nero? Even after I said no."

"You need to hear me on this," Ben got out, meeting his every thrust with a supple flex of his hips that was driving Zorin insane. "Dex doesn't own me."

"And you need to hear *me*." Stars, the man felt good against his cock. Way too good to stop rutting into him, heart hammering in his chest, breath ragged in his lungs. Gods, he wanted inside the guy. Wanted like blazes to shoot his load deep inside him. Even though it didn't exactly reinforce his message. "It's not about ownership. It's about communication. This thing with the four of us? We're gonna need—oh gods, Ben—one heck of a lot of it—to make this mating work."

"I'll stop whenever you stop, big guy. If you *can* stop." A wicked mischief flared in Ben's smoking gaze. "Or else… whenever space cadet and angel over there… tell us to stop."

"I pray you won't stop on our account." Dex's familiar baritone, deep and husky with passion, just about shot Zorin's startled, desperately aroused body through the Kryllian exosphere. "In fact, I do believe we'd very much like to join you."

#

If Zorin's living room was a Mogadon reactor, the core was about to go critical.

Kaia stood riveted just inside the door like her boots were bolted to the floor. With Dex at her back, hands hard and possessive at her waist, breath harsh with craving in her ear. Watching one of her five favorite fantasies play out in real life.

The one where Ben focused all that formidable sex appeal and seductive skill he'd honed over a decade as a Valyrian stud pony on making Zorin lose his steady-eddie composure and unchaining the ruthless, tenderly violent savage that lurked just beneath her pirate's easygoing exterior.

And Ben had definitely done it.

All tattoos and leather stretched over a mouthwatering expanse of muscle, Zorin pivoted from where he'd trapped Ben in the corner to confront them, massive chest heaving with effort, rugged face ruthless with arousal, lidded eyes burning with intent.

"About time you two turned up." He dragged a rough hand through his hair. "We were, uh, waiting for you. At least, *one* of us was waiting."

He slanted Ben a look that smoked with wrathful purpose—-the silent promise that he fully intended to give Ben Nero everything he'd just been begging for.

And then some.

Kaia's lifemate took his time smoothing back his raven hair and disentangling himself gracefully from Zorin's looming body. Looking sullen and debauched as a rock star, all gorgeously disheveled and barefoot, erection shoving against skin-tight black breeches. Not at all daunted by the pirate's hard hand still gripping his shoulder.

Pinning him to the wall like a sand wolf claiming captured prey.

Claiming him every way he could.

An aura of sexual aggression, charged with relentless intent, crackled in the air between her two lovers.

Asteroids, it's hot in here.

"We're fully aware *you* were waiting." Humor and arousal mingled with irritation in Dex's voice. His arms tightened around Kaia, easing her cybersuited derrière against his fully erect cock. "An awareness attributable to the fact that you were… I believe you'd call it… projecting? I've, ah, been listening in since halfway over on the shuttle."

"Aw, shoot." Clearly chagrined, Zorin scrubbed a hand over the back of his neck. "Sorry, kid. All this mind-reading mumbo-jumbo's still pretty new to me."

"He didn't mind," Kaia murmured. "And give yourself some credit. When it comes to telepathy, big guy, you're a damn quick study. Ben wasn't making it easy for you either, was he?"

Fighting to contain a smile while her Syndax was still so obviously worried over both of them and their supposedly injured feelings—a preoccupation she adored in him—she let her attention wander over his dangerously aroused body.

All Ben had really done was gotten him good and ready. Ready for all three of them.

She loved Ben for that.

You're welcome. Ben's wry whisper sounded in her head. *Since you're feeling all grateful, angel, why don't you shimmy over here and show me just how grateful you're prepared to be?*

Hells, the climate in here was so combustible the viewport was getting steamy.

Kaia swallowed hard past her dry and breathless throat.

Well, this is what you've been waiting for, isn't it? All three of your men loaded and locked and lusting. Lusting for each other and lusting for you.

Heart thundering, she eased down the zipper of her sapphire-blue cybersuit. The soft buzz echoed like a shout in the suddenly supercharged silence. She unzipped just enough to reveal a hint of cleavage. Barely enough to entice.

Just a preview of things to come. But plenty enough to rivet all three of her men. Dex rumbled in her ear—a deep-throated hum somewhere between a purr and a growl that only she could hear.

She'd never heard him make that sound before. But damn if it didn't kindle the slow heat building down below to a sudden slick need. A need for him so intense it made her weak.

She wanted him. She hadn't had him since before Proteus snatched her.

And if not for the constraining presence of her kid sister sleeping in the room where he'd just found her, she would've already had him.

"Anyway." She smiled at Zorin, knowing he'd hear her throaty rasp of longing. "You're a natural talent. Psychically speaking."

"Glad I'm making a good impression, sweetheart," Zorin said wryly, residual annoyance still sparking in his aqua eyes. Annoyance with his own susceptibility to Ben's little games.

Tread softly here, samurai. All four of us are rigged to blow.

"Actually," she breathed, "we're both impressed. Both with your… natural talent… and your self-control under fire. Aren't we, Dex?"

"Mmmm," Dex agreed, easing her still closer, voice husky with arousal. "Precisely the same way we know Ben feels I've been ignoring him for the exigencies of my work—and that he's consequently been in a towering temper all day. Haven't we known, darling?"

"He is my lifemate," Kaia agreed, leaning into Dex and rubbing into all that heat he was packing. Because her own self-discipline wasn't worth a damn wherever Dex Draven was concerned. "So, yeah, I pretty much had a front row seat for that whole seduce-a-pirate scenario you've both been rocking. Which *was* fairly distracting while I was coaxing Kylie to sleep."

She paused. "Which I did finally manage to do. She was pretty wired, but she crashed hard and she's finally out. With a parting directive to her big sis not to hover." She flashed a grin. "We won't see her till morning."

Behind her, she knew, Dex was borderline annoyed with Ben for acting out this way. He'd muttered as much under his breath while he was hustling her from Kylie's well-secured quarters down the hall straight here.

But she also sensed Dex's deep satisfaction that Ben felt as kid-with-a-crush possessive over Dex's time and attention as he obviously did.

For Kaia's part, she couldn't be happier. She finally had her three men right where she wanted them—alone in a room with an orgy couch. With all of them hard and both her Mogadon scenting. Just the pheromones they were pumping out were enough to jack her hormones through the roof.

Even without Dex's hot mouth nuzzling her neck and his rigid shaft nudging her ass.

Hair tousled in sandy spikes over his brow, Zorin watched them both with sexual promise burning like lava in his eyes. Obviously trying like hell to pull his head together.

And failing.

Which suited her fine. She wanted him. Wanted all of them. She'd wanted them forever.

Tonight, she was finally going to have them.

All three of them.

"Thanks for the sit rep on Junior." Her Syndax shot her a rueful look and cleared his throat. "What I'm trying to say is, uh, this isn't what it looks like. We were gonna stop."

Ben snorted and rolled his eyes.

No, we weren't. For punk's sake, Zorin. And if you're waiting for Dex's permission to know what it feels like to have my mouth wrapped around your disco stick, big guy, he just flipping gave it. Are you ready for me now?

When Ben tried casually to straighten from the wall, Zorin tightened his grip on his shoulder to hold him there. And slanted him a look so menacing it sent a shaft of raw craving straight to Kaia's already tingling clit.

"You'll stay right there till I'm done with you, gorgeous. If you know what's good for you."

Behind her, she sensed Dex absorbing the fact that, while Ben wouldn't tolerate being manhandled by Dex anywhere outside the confines of their bed, he seemed plenty willing to tolerate being manhandled by Zorin.

At least in private.

She felt the power dynamic among the four of them—the four of them finally together—shifting and settling into place.

Um, how about a little help here, angel?

With one last wiggle of her hips against his joystick just to keep him thinking about her, Kaia slipped out of Dex's arms. She sauntered across the floor, one hand trailing across Zorin's broad back in greeting as she wandered past.

Her pirate finally released Ben to slide his hand through the loose side ponytail spilling over her shoulder—a slow caress that heated her whole body.

"Howdy, sweetheart," he rasped.

She met his hot gaze with a sidelong smile. "Miss me?"

"You have no idea."

His heartfelt tone made her grin. Reaching Ben's side, she looped her arms around his neck to purr in his ear.

"Ben Nero, you are *such* a bad boy. You've got Zorin ready to come in his pants."

"Yeah, well, that makes two of us." Ben pulled her in for a kiss that crackled with sexual frustration. Tongue claiming her mouth, hungry and slick and forceful. Hands gripping her ass, spreading her cheeks and probing her hole with a casual privilege that made her gasp.

Seating her cybersuited pussy right against the rigid blade of his furiously aroused cock.

Need slammed through her and pulsed in her clit. Feeling the sweet ache spread through her, she writhed against him and moaned into his mouth.

Knowing Dex and Zorin were watching boosted all that raw craving from near-earth orbit straight into the stratosphere. Very soon, if she played her cards right, she'd have all three of them inside her.

"Bloody hell," Dex said hoarsely. Sounding quite a bit closer than where she'd left him. "The two of you together… you're too damn beautiful. Just the way I always knew you would be. Do you know I've been fantasizing about the two of you naked in each other's arms since the day you turned up on Mogadon?" Amusement softened his predatory edge. "Even though you were barely speaking to each other at the time."

Ben ended the kiss with a nip that left her lower lip stinging and glowered over her shoulder at Dex.

"Look, I know you're still annoyed. But you ignored me all farking day, space cadet. I'm not used to being ignored. Especially right after I've just changed my whole life to be with you—all three of you. So excuse the hell out of me for minding."

Kaia stifled a giggle at his surly tone. "You're used to being the center of attention, aren't you, stud pony? But he's ruler of the galaxy now."

"And, for your information, I wasn't ignoring you," Dex said gruffly. "You're on my mind all day every day. All three of you. I was toiling like a damn galley slave to clear the decks so I can sleep in your arms tonight without this comm unit going off every twelve ticks with some sort of administrative crisis. Are we entirely clear on my priorities?"

Ben grumbled under his breath.

But she knew he felt placated.

She slid her tongue down the sinewy line of her lifemate's throat, his heartbeat hammering against her lips. The taste of salt and longing zinged against her tongue. The head-spinning hit of incense and wolf, mingled with the lush sweetness of her own fragrance, stoked the furnace of her own arousal.

"We'll just have to get used to it," she breathed. "Dex being the center of everyone's universe. Won't we?"

Under her sustained attentions, she felt the sharp edges of Ben's frustration soften. One hand curled around her ass to hold her in place against the electrifying jut of his cock. The other wandered its leisurely way up her torso to wrap around her breast.

Against the tissue-thin cybersilk, her nipple tightened and peaked against his teasing thumb. A gasp slipped past her parted lips.

"I'm telling all three of you," Ben murmured, eyes heavy and glowing with passion, "someone had better be fucking me in about a nanosecond. Right now I'm not too choosy about which one of you gets me off. Looks like you're first in line, angel."

His clever fingers found the zipper dangling between her noticeably jutting nipples and eased it down. One micron at a time. Her limbs turned liquid with yielding to that slow, seductive slide.

"Strip out of this for me and show me your sweet pussy. I want to see how wet you are." Ben's breath in her ear went ragged. "Show me how much you need my tongue to make you come. Tonight I'm going to make you beg. Beg for my cock inside you."

A soft whimper slipped past her breathless lips. A whimper that mingled protest and surrender.

Because once she stripped out of her cybersuit and spread her thighs the way he wanted, she knew from the abundance of slick slippery heat down below exactly what he'd find.

The gusset of her panties already soaked with her own cream.

Of course he'd comment. About how she smelled and tasted. With her face on fire and her clit jutting stiff and eager for his touch the whole time—

"Hold on a sec, sweetheart." Behind her, Zorin's big body shifted. "Before we start all that, I gotta say something to Dex. Really didn't wanna do this without you, kid. You believe me, don'tcha?"

Still wrapped in Ben's demanding arms—seeing as he didn't seem anywhere close to ready to let her go—Kaia turned her head to watch. Because the searing sight of the Mogadon Imperator tucked up against the scourge of the galaxy, Zorin's muscled arm wrapped possessively around Dex, fingers buried in his tawny hair, while Dex nuzzled his neck and worked on the buckle of Zorin's studded belt, was way too good to miss.

Zorin's hand closed over Dex's before the buckle sprang open. "Look, I know you and gorgeous have a history. Know I'm the new guy—"

"Blast! Will you bloody stop apologizing?" Dex shot their pirate a rueful look. "I adore the fact that you want my permission, love. But Ben's right about that much. It isn't necessary."

Zorin's rugged face went soft with tenderness. "Come on, kid. We gotta be honest with each other."

"Oh, don't mistake me. I'll tear apart with my bare hands any bloke who—what was it?—sticks his dick in Ben. *Except you.*" Dex's voice deepened to a warning growl. "Similarly, I trust you won't be wanting to indulge in that sort of intimacy with anyone who isn't currently standing in this room."

Ben's hand stilled on her zipper. Stopping its calamitous course just before her breasts would have spilled out. Because this conversation was one she knew they really needed to have.

All four of them.

Warm and breathless with sexual charge, she slithered around in his arms to face the two of them. Ben's arms wrapped snugly around her waist, his chin resting on her crown.

All that heat between her legs would have to wait a little longer for his tongue.

"Stars," Zorin sighed, leaning his ass on the viewport ledge, space boots spread wide for balance. His big hands eased Dex down on one leather-clad thigh. Sitting half in Zorin's lap.

And just the sight of her two spectacularly virile Mogadon males—Dex formal and formidable in dark uniform gleaming with platinum, Zorin disreputable in Syndax tattoos and leather and exuding casual dominance—seeing the two of them together like that flipped every switch she had.

Maybe we should postpone this little convo for later.
Much later.

Clearly picking up the thought, Zorin shot her a look of wry appreciation. His eyes lingered on the golden swell of her breasts, perilously close to spilling out of her cybersuit.

"Shoot, sweetheart. You gotta realize the four of us still haven't palavered about how this mating's actually gonna work, don'tcha? Cuz there hasn't been enough time between interstellar crises around here to scratch our asses, much less negotiate a four-way mating."

She sighed against Ben's lithe frame. Feeling him shift by instinct to accommodate her body. Just the way he used to do in the old days at the Psi Academy when they'd lie dreaming and entwined, body and soul, under the six moons at sunset.

"We're all crazy in love with each other. We're all consorts and allies. You're all going to be the fathers of my children. And our chemistry is so off-the-charts it's practically pyrophoric." Sudden impatience spiked her pulse. "Not to mention the fact we've got less than eight clicks to conceive before we go planet-side to face my father. How much more do we need to negotiate?"

"For one thing," Zorin said patiently, "we gotta talk about what Dex just said. Cuz if he hadn't said it, I woulda. From now on, the four of us—all four of us—we're exclusive. Look, I can put up with a lot from you three. But not infidelity. Even if it's only fooling around. Afraid I don't share too well. In fact, when it comes to consorts, I'm downright possessive. It's a Syndax thing."

"It's also a Mogadon thing," Dex noted, his tone adamant.

"So." Face hard with determination, Zorin dipped his chin in a nod. "It's the four of us. *Just* the four of us. No one else in our bed. No one else in our union. No one else in our hearts. And that's a hard line for me."

Having found complete agreement between them on that score, both men turned in unison to look suspiciously at Ben.

"Don't look so skeptical! That's what we want too." Her lifemate spoke for both of them with the easy privilege he'd picked up from the lifebond they'd finally both embraced. "But the galaxy's a big place. What happens when we're not all together? Say you're off ruling Mogadon, Dex, with Kaia as your Imperatrix. Do I get to be with Zorin? The way I wanted to be tonight?"

"Only if you tell me all about it," Dex said huskily. "I want no secrets of any kind between any of us, all right?"

Kaia chuffed out a snort. "I have news for you, space cadet. You're mating two telepaths. Not to mention you and the big guy are turning into not-so-shabby telepaths yourselves. It wouldn't surprise me one bit if we've got some sort of four-way lifebond starting to crystallize—even though that's not supposed to be possible. Lifemates don't *have* secrets from each other. Not for long. Because we can't."

"Speaking of which…" Ben stirred behind her, a ribbon of resolve running through his supple frame. "You know that whole thing about us having no secrets? Lifebond or no lifebond, with two of us on the Quorum, not having secrets is going to be a whole lot easier."

For one of the perishingly few times in her life, Kaia experienced the novel sensation of seeing Dex Draven look downright gobsmacked.

"*Two* of us on the Quorum? What the devil are you saying?"

Ben's body rippled in a languid shrug. "I've just pulled out of the breeding program, haven't I? The Senate of Psychics had to do something with me. Today I volunteered… rather forcefully… to take Valyria's vacant Quorum seat."

That little news flash froze Kaia in her number nine boots.

"Neptune's knickers," Zorin breathed. "Don't tell me they went for it?"

"Are you kidding?" Ben aimed his reply at Dex. "Knowing you're on the Quorum and I'm mating you? They're hoping like hell I'll have a curbing influence on your militaristic Mogadon tendencies. It'll be announced at midnight on the interstellar broadcast."

Shaking free of her stunned stasis, Kaia twisted to look up at Ben. Just in time to see her lifemate give the thunderstruck Dex a playful pout.

"I figure it'll be harder for you to ignore me all day, Imperator, when I'm sitting right next to you."

Bristling with annoyance, Dex shot to his feet. "Damnation, Ben! A seat on the Quorum is no mere trifle—"

"You think I don't know that? Or do you honestly think I'm such a fool this truly is some childish ploy for your attention?" Ben's voice hardened. "Think it through, space cadet. With you and me both voting on the Quorum, and Zorin's new guy to back us, we can crush any stunt the Patriarch tries to pull."

For possibly the first time in his life, the First Indomitable of the Mogadon Empire seemed speechless. His confounded gaze settled on Kaia and narrowed. Clearly waiting for her response.

Well, he was going to have to wait a little longer.

She was still floundering through the sea of shock that engulfed her at the thought of Ben Nero—her flamboyant, temperamental, brazen, brooding, relentlessly sexual lifemate—sitting tamely in a Quorum seat.

"Huh." Brow creased, Zorin slanted Dex a thoughtful look. "Then you really will rule the galaxy. Won'tcha, kid?"

"Not just Dex," Ben growled, arms tightening around her. "It's *all* of us. All of us together who'll rule."

Kaia still couldn't seem to wrap her head around it.

Body wired tight with anticipation, Ben leaned in to mutter in her hair. "Snap out of it, angel. You wanted your consort to bring peace to the galaxy, didn't you? Wanted all four races united to fight the Swarm? This is how we get that done. No one's declaring war on anyone but Proteus with the four of us running the show."

Kaia tilted her head and studied the russet-banded orb of her homeworld. An unavoidable reminder of the imminent homecoming she was light years away from welcoming. Just gliding into frame in the viewport sailed the formidable floating fortress of the *Inevitable*, flanks bristling with solar cannons and nuclear-armed missiles.

An invading army.

A visual metaphor for Dex. The galaxy's dominant power. A power way too dominant, surely, for even the Patriarch to challenge.

Especially with the Valyrian Precursor and the Syndax horde to back him.

"I hope that's true," she murmured, letting them all listen in on her head. "Although, admittedly, I can't see how having two consorts leading the charge for law and order in the galaxy is going to work out at all for Zorin's whole smuggling and piracy operation. Not unless *you're* going to go all respectable on me too, big guy?"

"You let me worry about that." Zorin folded his arms across his broad chest. "I know what the Syndax need and I'm gonna make sure they get it. Same as always. I wanna know what you're thinking about all this hoopla. Cuz I'm not good enough yet at the mumbo-jumbo to read your mind."

What I'm thinking is having two consorts on the Quorum means we'll be talking a lot of politics at the breakfast table.

What I'm thinking is we'll be seeing a lot more of my father. And we still haven't figured out how to keep Kylie hidden.

Which is a pretty major risk.

What I'm thinking is I don't know whether having two consorts on the Quorum solves our big problem or makes it worse.

But I'm thinking it's worth a shot.

"Love you, angel," Ben whispered in her ear, the brush of his lips sending shivers cascading down her spine. "Now we'll always be together. And I promise not to bore you at the breakfast table."

"Speak up, sweetheart." Fixed on her face, Zorin's eyes creased in a smile. "I can see the gears turning. We all wanna hear what's happening in that clever samurai head of yours."

She wound her ponytail through thoughtful fingers, then shook her hair loose and swirling down her back with a flash of defiance. Having all three of them as consorts was more than she'd ever dared dream as a Tombola outcome. And if her unconventional choice came at a cost?

She'd live with that cost. Whatever it was.

Nothing worth having in life came for nothing.

"Honestly? Having two of my three consorts seated on the Quorum? Sounds like one spanking lot of trouble for a girl who was just a fugitive samurai a week ago." A spurt of mischief shot through her. Fueled by a heady hit of adrenaline. "If you really want me to agree to this dull and decorous life, you're gonna have to persuade me. And don't think I'm going to make that anything close to easy."

Hearing the gauntlet she'd just thrown down, Ben hissed in a breath harsh with primal need.

"I daresay that sounds like a proper challenge." Dex uncoiled to his feet, eyes blazing cobalt with intent as they slid over her half-exposed breasts. "And whoever said anything about decorum?"

Zorin rumbled in agreement, lids dropping over his predatory gaze.

A powerful pulse of arousal tightened her nipples and clenched her channel in a spasm of craving.

"She's asking for it, isn't she? Time for us to give our girl exactly what she needs." Dex's hand dropped to find Zorin's and pulled him to his feet. "Let's sire that prophecy son of ours."

CHAPTER EIGHT
The Consummation

Dex knew quite a lot about forbidden, fiercely stifled fantasies. In fact, he'd been intimately acquainted with them all his life.

Most of all he knew that, in all his years, he'd never been so savagely, damn near uncontrollably aroused as he was right now.

If he and Kaia had arrived any later, he harbored precisely zero doubt Ben would've had Zorin peeled out of his fighting leathers and buried fathoms deep inside him.

Obliterating every ion of conscientious objection from their mannerly Syndax lover.

Even now, after the pirate had done his damnedest to hold tight to his hormones and rein them all in from a headlong gallop to a measured walk, Dex was keenly aware of the colossal bulge shoved against Zorin's straining leathers, the naked need chiseled in his rugged face, the slipping restraint in his labored breath.

Through the conduit of Zorin's hand wrapped around his, Dex vibrated with the raw current of his lover's intent. All that wrathful sexual purpose locked on Ben Nero—who'd managed to entice him parsecs past the pirate's own famously unbreachable restraint—like a heat-seeking missile.

Dex's wary gaze followed Zorin's burning stare to Ben. The man whose every whispered breath invited sexual violence from his lovers. The man who coaxed savagery as effortlessly as kisses from Dex. The man who blithely beguiled brutes and killers like the Butcher of Beta Prime to his bed.

Ben had to know Zorin was rigged to blow like a megaton warhead. Yet there Ben lounged, lean and languid against the viewport, with Kaia nestled in his arms, her back pressed to his front.

Casually unconcerned about the ticking time bomb he'd just triggered.

Because Ben right now was all about Kaia.

The lifemate he'd lost through his own bitter choices. The lover who'd finally welcomed him back to her bed. Face buried in her burgundy hair, lips pressed to her golden skin, hands claiming her taut curves, Ben leaned close to breathe in her ear.

"How about it, angel?" His clever hands slid up her torso to cup her breasts. "Tonight's the night. The night we conceive. Are you ready for us?"

"Born ready," she said on a sharp inhale. "Isn't that what Zorin was just telling you? Gods, Ben—I've never *been* more ready."

Kaia's supple samurai body arched into his touch, head falling back against his shoulder, breasts all but spilling from her half-unzipped cybersuit and begging for his touch.

Dex couldn't drag his eyes off her.

By the reflected light of her homeworld pouring through the viewport, she was the distilled essence of pure seduction. She'd been that way since this morning when Ben brought her back: smooth skin glowing with vitality like just-poured honey, lustrous hair glistening with accents of deep ruby and hammered gold, lips fuller and curves riper than they'd ever been.

She was a goddess of fertility and seduction. Dex was still tungsten-hard and aching from the feel of her lush, clutchable ass pressed against his cock.

And all too clearly, he wasn't alone.

Ben's deft fingers found her nipples jutting against the cybersilk and pinched them. A soft cry of pleasure spilled from her lips and she writhed against him.

A low growl of craving rumbled through Zorin's big chest and sent all the blood racing to Dex's groin. The pirate's hand clenched around his and dragged him hard against his muscled side. In the pheromone-drenched air of Zorin's shadowy quarters, all rusting titanium strewn with smuggled luxuries, the desert world burning in the viewport like a dragon's lidless eye, the flash of physical contact slammed through his overstimulated body like an electric shock.

Dex wrapped an arm around his lover's waist and leaned into Zorin, eyes never leaving the incendiary tableau Ben was orchestrating with their all-too-willing girl.

"Lose the clothes," Ben said hoarsely. "All of them, angel. You're going to get all of us off long and hard tonight."

Kaia's breath hitched audibly in her throat. Her eyes slid sidelong to the viewport, now half-filled with the *Inevitable*'s bristling bulk. The oblong lozenge of a transport shuttle lumbered past, silhouetted against the ocher planet. Probably ferrying laborers from the surface to service the sun clipper somewhere aft.

To anyone on that shuttle peering through the row of opaque portholes, the panoramic viewport of the commander's quarters on the *Relentless*—and its inhabitants—would draw the eye like a lighted stage.

"Let them look," Ben said roughly, deflecting the half-formed pushback before she could utter a syllable. "I want every sentient being in this galaxy to see you submit to me. To know you're *mine*."

Kaia's soft lips parted. Poised right on the razor's edge between titillation and protest. Her wide-eyed gaze swung to Dex in entreaty.

But damn if it didn't rev her engine. He didn't even need telepathy to know. She was electrified by the prospect of displaying herself to all three of them—and anyone else who might be watching. He'd sensed as much when he'd taken her from behind on the maintenance platform over his hangar bay. Sensed that the possibility of strangers seeing her submit, seeing her exposed and helpless and all too clearly needing everything he was doing to her, flipped every switch on her circuit board.

Clearly Ben too knew it. Knew it and was ruthless about giving the sexy exhibitionist hidden deep inside their girl everything she needed to get off.

"You heard the man, darling," Dex said with tender purpose, so guttural he barely knew his own voice. "We're waiting. And so are they. Waiting for you to make them come."

Ben gave her nipples another tweak that made her gasp and squirm.

"Right now, angel. I want to see you naked." Nero's voice thickened. "Face the viewport when you do it. Give them all a good look."

Kaia's tongue swept over her upper lip. A fine sheen of sweat glittered on her tawny skin. Eyes wide and pleading—because that's how good she was at their little game—she slipped out of his arms and pivoted to face the viewport.

Which gave all three of her future consorts a perfect view of her luscious silhouette—all tight curves and sleek muscle—as she slowly slid her zipper all the way down. Face flushed, eyes lowered, she pushed the cybersuit off her shoulders. With a whisper, the fabric slithered to pool at her hips.

Through the curtain of fallen hair, her breasts were fuller, no doubt of it, more than enough now to fill a man's hand. But still saucy and pert the way Dex adored, nipples tilted up and begging for a man's mouth.

Dex swallowed hard in a futile bid to moisten his own arid mouth. Without looking away for a heartbeat, Zorin scooped up a half-filled tumbler of amber whiskey and pressed it into his palm.

Heart jackhammering against his chest, Dex tossed back a searing swallow of liquid fire.

Ben uncoiled from the wall and prowled toward Kaia, bare feet silent on the thick Kryllian carpet Zorin must've just installed. A tangible sign of their Syndax's impulse to make his pirate's den slightly less disreputable for the four of them to inhabit.

An indulgent impulse—a protective instinct to take care of all of them—that just about turned Dex's notoriously impermeable heart to mush.

Ben padded around Kaia's exposed and vulnerable form, a sinuous shadow graceful in night-black breeches and that unlaced shirt of fragile silk Dex was aching to tear off. Supple and sinister as a stalking cat. Deliberate fingers lifted a tendril of Kaia's hair to bare one succulent breast to his burning stare.

With a flash of defiance, Kaia shook back her wine-red mane to cascade down her back. Legs spread, back arched, breasts lifted. Exposing herself completely before anyone told her to do it.

Showing them all just how eager she was to be displayed. In a silent agony of embarrassment for wanting it the way she did. But eager for the exposure.

So eager she trembled with need.

"That's right, angel," Ben purred, lidded eyes glittering amethyst with arousal. "Just think of all those crude, sweaty laborers on that service shuttle getting hard at the sight of you. Talking in graphic detail all about your body and what they'd like to do to you and how they'd make you beg for it. Speculating out loud about how you like to be fucked."

That scorching visual, lavishly embellished in all their heads with Ben's psychic paintbrush, shot straight to Dex's cock. His arm tightened around Zorin's waist. The empty glass fell from his open hand to thunk into the carpet.

Which freed his fingers to slide over Zorin's metal-studded belt and start working on his buckle.

"Neptune's knickers." Their pirate's voice was husky with lust. "Listen, gorgeous—"

"She likes it," Ben flashed, tight with sexual focus, sharp and lethal as a cracking whip. "Do you think I'd ever do anything to her she doesn't like? Anything she doesn't need? You can trust me to know. Or maybe not. Since I'm still in the doghouse with you, Zorin, aren't I?" His face hardened. "Tell him, angel."

Kaia's lilac eyes slid sideways to find her worried Syndax lover. Her mouth softened in a tender smile. "It's just a game, big guy. We can stop anytime you want. Just say the word." Silky lashes fell over her dreamy gaze. "Ben isn't the only one who gets to give the orders in this game. Is he, Dex?"

"Far from it," Dex agreed, deep and growly.

Zorin's buckle slipped open under his determined efforts. He shifted his focus to the button that closed his pirate's leather pants.

Soothed by Kaia's assurances and his own sustained attentions, the last of Zorin's resistance melted away under Dex's touch.

Which let all the arousal the big guy had been fighting to contain come roaring back.

The pirate's silver eyes slid from Ben's prowling form to the mouthwatering perfection that was Kaia, her tight gymnast's body on shameless display from the waist up, back arched, hair spilling down her back, breasts thrust forward and swollen with need.

Just begging for a man's touch.

And that unzipped cybersuit of hers clinging to her hips by a thread.

Zorin's eyes narrowed with wolfish hunger. "Long as you're a willing player, sweetheart, I'll admit I'm kinda curious to see what our boy has in store for you."

Ben's mouth curled in satisfaction. He slipped up behind Kaia and whispered in her ear.

"Show those grease monkeys on the shuttle how much you'd like all of them to touch you. Give them something to picture when they're lying in their grubby little bunks in their cargo holds tonight with their hands wrapped around their cocks, getting off good and hard while they think about you."

A hoarse sound scraped from Zorin's throat. Zorin who'd probably never seen Ben Nero play the dominant—and command the role so perfectly. Dex had to admit he too was bloody fascinated by the revelation.

And by how beautifully Kaia responded to being pushed harder and further than Dex had ever thought she'd be willing to go.

Especially when Kaia, eyes low and face burning, breaths short and quick with arousal, cupped her own breasts and offered them to the viewport.

Never mind the fact that shuttle was far enough away to make its passengers squint to see her. Unless they had cyber-enhanced vision—which would show them everything. It was the fantasy that was getting her off.

The fantasy that would make her climax.

"More." Ben breathed the order in her ear. "Show them more. Show them how much you need it."

A whimper of protest spilled from her breathless lips. But she licked her fingers and started playing with her nipples, rolling and tweaking until they jutted hard and wet and shiny between her fingers.

Her breasts had always been sensitive to being touched like that—as Dex was entirely in the position to know—but now she seemed even more sensitive. Her hips twitched at every pinch like Dex's cock was already riding her.

I am sensitive. So much it almost hurts, her voice whispered in his head. *And not only because I'm fertile, Dex. I've ovulated. Ben can tell.*

A confession that only made him more desperate to get inside her.

An impulse Zorin too was clearly fighting. His shaft was shoved so hard against the zipper Dex could barely ease it open.

But Dex was exceptionally well motivated. And Zorin wasn't exactly resisting.

By now the shuttle had almost glided out of view. With the show Kaia was giving them, he was privately amazed its pilot wasn't circling around for another pass.

Ben's voice lashed, ruthless with purpose. "Show them more."

A moan of breathless protest slipped out of her. Blushing beautifully, Kaia bent to shimmy out of her cybersuit. Leaving her wearing nothing but a scrap of sapphire silk panties and her silver platform boots. A maneuver that bent her double and exposed the taut golden globes of her ass, her crack barely covered by that narrow band of silk.

Dex barely stopped himself from closing in on her, pushing that tiny scrap of silk aside, and burying his aching cock balls-deep inside her.

But this scene emphatically belonged to Ben. Dex's turn to run the show—to command both of them—was coming.

A prospect so riveting it made his impatient cock jerk with eagerness.

At last, all his diligent effort with Zorin's zipper paid off. The stiff leather parted and Zorin's shaft sprang into view, silky skin stretched tight over sinew, ruddy head swollen and drooling with need. The sight of all that rigid length wrenching a groan from Dex's throat.

Big enough that jacking him off was going to be a two-hand job.

Dex could hardly wait to get started.

"Panties too, angel," Ben ordered. "And make it fast. I want you to give all those men a good long look at your needy pussy before that shuttle's out of range."

His hands coaxed Kaia upright and cupped her pouting breasts from behind. Lifting them to display her for whoever might be watching.

Dex was torn between the primal Mogadon instinct to possess her, protect her, pulverize to a pulp any outsider who even dared look at her—and the purely predatory instinct to start issuing his own explicit orders.

To both of them.

He settled for wrapping one hand around Zorin's cock. Savoring the hiss of pleasure that slid from his pirate's lips. Swiping a thumb through the glistening moisture at his tip and smoothing it down his shaft to get him good and wet.

Zorin's arm tightened around him. A harsh sound shuddered through him as he thrust into Dex's palm.

"You know the grunts on that shuttle are jacking off right now at the sight of you," Ben muttered darkly in Kaia's ear. "Unzipping their greasy pants and sliding out their dicks and stroking themselves while they watch you display yourself for them. I want you to think hard about that. Want you to visualize them doing it. While you do whatever it takes to get every last one of them off."

Dex honestly didn't think she'd do it. She was the Kryll maharani for gods' sake, not some pole-dancer for rent in a spaceport bar.

But he'd underestimated how aroused she already was. And how intimately Ben knew his lifemate and her limits.

Face on fire, she spread her booted feet wide and slid her panties down her hips. Leaving the silk stretched taut and suspended halfway down between her thighs. Giving all three of her consorts an eye-popping view of the saucy tilt of her outthrust ass.

And giving every grunt on that shuttle a good long look at her boldly exposed pussy. Flushed and swollen with eagerness, her hungry clit glistening with dew like a breakfast peach.

A rasp of pleasure roughened Zorin's breath. Dex dragged his eyes away from Kaia to appreciate the sight of Zorin's cock, shiny and slick with precum, wrapped in Dex's fist.

"Tell me if I'm doing this right for you," he said roughly, stroking all that impressive length from base to tip.

"Do asteroids hurt when they hit you?" Zorin gasped out a laugh. "Comets, kid."

One big hand wrapped around Dex's head and pulled him in for a hungry kiss. Over in a breath, but the man left him reeling.

From deep inside Dex, a foreign impulse surfaced. The impulse to drop to his knees and wrap his lips around another man's shaft.

At that moment, he wanted to give Zorin a blowjob so intense the man saw flaming comets. Even though he—Dex—still hadn't done that. Ever. To *anyone*. Yeah, he'd thought about it plenty with Ben. But he hadn't blasted past that final taboo emblazoned on his *verboten* list by his goddamn upbringing and his goddamn father.

While Ben, who was hypersensitive to Dex's Mogadon hang-ups and paranoid about triggering another stinging rejection, certainly hadn't been pushing.

No, whatever unexplored pleasures Ben undoubtedly still craved from Dex, he seemed entirely content deferring to Zorin to ease Dex patiently but ruthlessly past his last remaining limits.

Dex figured wrapping his mouth around another guy's cock until the guy in question cried out and shot buckets down his throat definitely qualified.

Never mind the fact that the guy he wanted hadn't even asked him yet. Dex found himself giving serious consideration to obliging.

"Sweet mother on the mountain," Zorin whispered. Molten with hunger, eyes like liquid mercury locked on Kaia as though he intended to lunge at her, push her to the carpet, hook her legs around his waist, and start thrusting inside her right there on his living room floor.

Fisting Zorin's shaft in long slow strokes to make him last, Dex swung back around barely in time to see Kaia spread her soft bare folds to expose all the slick wetness inside for whatever lucky sod was watching on that shuttle. She dipped in a finger, then swirled her own cream around her swollen clit with a hungry moan. Clearly helpless in the grip of her own mounting need, she swiveled her hips and worked her clit against her finger, her moans growing louder and more urgent.

"Juno's titties, that tears it. We're taking this to the bedroom. All four of us." Zorin's decisive hand closed over Dex's to stop him. Way before he wanted to be stopped. Wrenching Dex's riveted attention away from the electrifying scene about a breath before he would have lost it and gone after her himself like a dog in heat. "I can see you're not shy, sweetheart. But when it comes right down to it, I'm a private kinda guy."

With a whimper of protest, Kaia's startled face swung toward them, eyes blazing with passion. He didn't think she wanted to stop— not now, not poised on the razor's edge of climax. Holding Dex's gaze, she lifted a glistening finger to her lips and licked it clean.

"Yeah, that did it," Ben agreed gruffly. "You've got guys spreading their legs and thrusting hard and fast into their own hands on that shuttle, angel. Guys groaning and cursing and watching you right now while they spill. How does it feel, knowing how hard you're getting them all off?"

Kaia shivered all over in sensual response. Breath still coming too swiftly, lavender eyes lambent with need. "Not nearly as good as it's going to feel getting all of *you* off."

"Not here," Zorin said gruffly. "Bedroom. I mean it."

With a last lazy stroke just to keep him interested, Dex reluctantly unwrapped his fist from Zorin's swollen shaft. He directed his next observation at Ben.

"You're being terribly demanding on our girl. A tactic that hardly seems fair. Not when *you're* the one who's been misbehaving in here. Hasn't he, Zorin?"

Zorin grunted in heartfelt agreement.

Looking back and forth between them, Ben was all wide-eyed innocence. "She could come for us like this in about two ticks if I let her. You know that, right? Don't you want to see our girl getting off?"

A breathless little moan of agreement spilled out of Kaia. Mars, if she made another noise like that, Dex was going to ride her like a mindless rutting beast.

And he wasn't at all certain how much longer Zorin's gentlemanly restraint was going to keep the man off Ben.

"I fully intend to see *both* of you getting off," Dex growled. "In the extremely imminent future. But first we need to see *you* naked. Will you do that for Zorin and me, gorgeous?"

Ben's startled eyes slid from him to Zorin. Measuring the barely chained need lunging at both their leashes. His long lashes fell over his eyes, a hint of color rising in his face. Like a shy virgin contemplating his first taste of cock.

A fantasy that just about made Dex lose his mind.

"If that's what you want?" Ben breathed. With a little hitch in his voice like he was almost too shy to ask.

"Damn." A low groan rumbled through Zorin's chest. "You're good at this, aren't you?"

"You've no idea how good he is," Dex muttered. "You're in for a proper treat. But you're right. I'm not particularly an exhibitionist myself. Let's take this to an actual bedroom." His eyes locked on Ben. "Leave the clothes."

Ben's blush deepened—and Dex hadn't even known his boyhood best friend *could* blush. He felt like his head was exploding in slow motion as Ben wound his hands in his flowing white shirt and peeled the silky fabric over his head with a virgin's hesitant slowness. Revealing the flat hard abs Dex was just getting used to dragging his tongue over and the tight pink nipples Ben always lost his mind when he teased.

"You heard the man, angel." Ben pinned Kaia's wrists behind her back—which had the admirable effect of thrusting her breasts forward in a manner Dex fully endorsed—and nuzzled her sweating neck. "Our guys want us in the bedroom. And don't you dare climax without me."

Still flushed with exhilaration, her tawny body tight with sexual frustration, she turned her head to pout at both of them. But she gave an obedient little wiggle that dislodged the panties stretched between her thighs and sent them sliding to the floor.

Ben hummed with satisfaction, pressed his lips to her temple, and released her.

Nimbly she stepped out of her panties and started for the bedroom, naked as a newborn except for her silver platform boots and the red-gold hair cascading down her back.

The saucy swing of her delectable ass pulled them all after her like a tractor beam.

Half turned away from Dex and Zorin, Ben slanted them a sidelong look over one sinewy shoulder that smoked with sensual promise. Slowly he sauntered after her, sleek hips swaying, lazily unknotting the laces of his breeches.

Zorin beelined to Ben's abandoned shirt, scooped it up like a souvenir, twisted it into a shining rope, and stalked after him. The pirate's big leather-clad body projected single-minded purpose with every stride.

Leaving Dex to claim the cobalt scrap of Kaia's discarded panties, breathe in a groin-tightening whiff of her musky sex from the drenched gusset, and tuck the intimate keepsake in his pocket.

A pair of choices that told him all he needed to know about where both of them were coming from tonight.

Zorin wouldn't breathe easy until he'd claimed his share of everything Ben had more than promised to surrender.

And Dex wouldn't rest until he'd sired Kaia's son.

In Zorin's bedroom, he found them all waiting. Kaia and Ben standing at the foot of the pirate's massive bed, eyes locked on each other from two cubits apart. The narrow span of air between them igniting with an inferno of yearning.

Fueled by years of denial.

Looming over Ben from behind, Zorin looked purely pornographic. His leather pants gaped open, framing the colossal cock that jutted before him, slick and rigid from foreplay. Both fists were locked around his studded metal belt like he didn't trust himself to wait.

Still throttling Ben's shirt in a manner that boded no good at all for its impudent owner.

"Don't try my patience, gorgeous. I'm warning you," Zorin rasped. "You heard the man. Strip."

With a submissive little sigh that slid through the expectant stillness, Ben folded in a single lithe motion to peel out of his breeches. And just the sight of him bent over naked, muscle rippling under silken skin and ass in the air, nearly made Zorin slip his chain.

The Syndax took a single step toward him and jerked to a halt, breath rough in the supercharged silence.

Fluidly Ben straightened and shook back his gleaming hair. Showing off the long supple length of his own cock, tight and twitching with eagerness, a shining tendril of precum already dripping from his tip.

A raw surge of lust knifed through Dex and shoved his shaft against his zipper.

A moan spilled out of Kaia, who swayed with the obvious need to touch him. But she waited, like the good little girl she *wasn't*, for someone to say she could.

"Well?" Ben breathed, with a shy sidelong look that included Dex in his little game. "How do you want us?"

With a stifled groan, Zorin stripped off his shirt and sank down on the edge of the bed, booted legs spread wide. Giving him a celebrity seat for the world premiere.

Ben's head turned warily to track him. Jagged ink edging massive shoulders from the tattoo spread across the pirate's back. Cock still jutting through open leathers. Eyes burning neutron with intent under spikes of sandy hair.

Ben's fragile shirt still throttled in his fist.

A visible shiver raced through Ben's sleek frame. Although Dex couldn't see his face from that particular angle as he drank in his first real sight of practically naked pirate, he'd bet real money his boy's mouth was hanging open.

"Go ahead, kid," Zorin grated, that neon gaze sliding over Dex. "You're still wearing way too many clothes for this shindig. I wanna watch these two undress you. See all three of you together."

A primitive frisson of raw hunger coiled and snapped through Dex like a whiplash. He strode straight to Ben and Kaia.

His. Both of them. Finally, finally his. His to claim and his to command.

And he was never, ever letting any of them go.

Their heads swung to find him, twin pairs of eyes wide with anticipation. Suddenly, savagely, he wanted both of them at once—hard and fast and *now*. But this long-awaited moment, this singular first night with all of them, was way too important to rush.

Harshly he pushed out the words.

"I want to see the two of you kiss. The way you just were. Do it."

"No protest here," Ben whispered, pulling Kaia into his arms, head bending to find her mouth.

She rose on tiptoe to meet him halfway, arms twining around his neck, luscious curves pressed to supple strength. Ben's hands curled around her ripe ass, pale fingers spreading to cup golden flesh.

Both of them so breathtakingly beautiful—so transparently, rapturously in love as they sighed and panted and clung—that Dex felt his heart turn over.

Happy. They make each other happy. This is what that feels like.

I never thought I'd know.

"Nice." Zorin planted his hands on his knees to watch. "Now Dex."

A jolt of anticipation raced over his skin and kicked his heartbeat from a trot to a gallop.

They turned as one to envelop him—both his perfect Valyrian beauties, tender and devout as ministering angels. Slim fingers working his jacket open and easing off his shirt. Deft hands spreading over his chest and sliding down his ribs. The slick heat of Ben's mouth finding his, silken lips parting under his urgent press, inviting his tongue to plunge deep in a hungry kiss. The electric sting of Kaia's teeth grazing his nipples to make him groan, the burn of her nails scraping his spine.

Every nerve and synapse in his body sparked and sizzled with tingling need.

"Good gods," he managed, gasping out a laugh. "The two of you together… you're bloody unreal."

Just wait till we get going, space cadet.

That was Kaia's coy whisper in his head.

You can't believe how good we're going to make you feel.

And that was Ben's dark promise.

Ben's hands worked open his belt and slid down his zipper. The soft heat of Kaia's lips nuzzled his naked abdomen. Her jasmine-scented hair trailed down his body and tickled his thighs. His blaster went somewhere he was too busy kissing Ben to see.

Then calloused hands were easing Dex back on the bed, between the bulging muscle of the Syndax's leather-clad thighs—a shock of intimate contact that wrenched a rough cry from his already turbocharged body.

He hadn't even known his eyes were closed. Until he opened them to find himself leaning back into Zorin's naked chest, his lover's burly tattooed arms wrapped around his waist. While Kaia and Ben smoothly stripped Dex out of his pants.

And the sight of them both straddling his legs, bending over to work him out of his blasted boots—their two perfect derrières wiggling side by side for one searingly unforgettable instant—was nearly incendiary enough to derail his elaborately choreographed plans entirely in favor of a quick hard fuck.

"Sweet mother on the mountain," Zorin groaned in his ear, big hands sliding up Dex's ribs in a slow caress. The scorching length of the pirate's naked cock nudged his back and dragged from his lungs another desperate sound.

Suddenly the feel of all that menacing bulk looming over him from behind made his entire body go weak. Weak with the memory of Zorin riding him like a woman. Weak with the knowledge of just how hard the pirate's infinitely patient but ruthlessly thorough possession had gotten him off.

Despite being tender to the point of discomfort even a full day later, he knew he wanted that feeling again.

"Stars, kid," the Syndax sighed in his ear. "You and me—I'm aching to do that with you again. But you know we gotta wait. You have no idea, do ya, how many ways I want you?"

A shudder of raw need skidded through him.

"Besides," Kaia breathed, sinking to her knees between his thighs, "I need you to come inside *me* tonight. All three of you."

Zorin growled deep in response. Without warning, hackles rose down the back of Dex's neck. For a single charged moment, the titan coiled behind him was a mortal threat. Another Mogadon who wanted Dex's woman.

A surge of primal impulse shot through Dex. That primitive drive to claim her.

Mine. She's MINE. And her son is mine.

Who better to rule the galaxy than the Imperator's son?

"Easy, kid," Zorin breathed against his nape, soft words sprinkled with tender kisses. "Easy. No one's gonna take her away from you."

Dex pushed out a long breath to drain away that instinctive spurt of knee-jerk, pheromone-fueled hostility.

If our child turns out to be Zorin's… your ally, your mentor, your lover, your consort… you'll love that too, won't you, Imperator? It's the four of you against the universe. You're in love with all of them.

Kaia's shining eyes lifted to find his face. "Are you ready for us, space cadet?"

"Happy to oblige, darling." Dex voiced a chuckle to dispel that last flicker of animal instinct. *Because, in point of fact, it seems I actually am happy.* "Gods know I've never been happier."

"Right back at you," Ben whispered behind Kaia, nuzzling her shoulder, violet eyes smoking. "Finish the job with our man, angel."

Dex gripped Zorin's leather-sheathed thighs to anchor himself. Kaia peeled off his combat briefs.

Before him, the two of them sank to their knees. Both his Valyrian lovers, sultry and exquisite as fallen angels, sitting gracefully on their heels between his spread thighs. Both eyeing his eager erection under demurely lowered lashes—Kaia's ripe lips parted in expectation, Ben's chiseled face stark with need.

An endless moment suspended in time. Poised on the brink of unbearable pleasure.

Dex's balls drew tight in a spasm of anticipation so sharp it made him gasp. He pushed roughly to his feet. Determined to keep control. If they were all going to ride Kaia tonight—if she could even handle all three of them—he and Zorin both needed a break from the electric current of contact humming between them.

"Kaia," Zorin groaned. "Sweetheart. We all need you so much right now. Maybe you and Dex—"

"No." Ben's face turned toward them, blind with need. "*This* and Dex."

He wound a hand in Kaia's hair, a handspan away from Dex's straining cock. Ben's mouth met hers in a starving openmouthed kiss, their faces grazing his throbbing shaft.

The first sizzling slide of a tongue across his slit nearly made Dex climax on the spot.

Then, gods and titans of Olympus help him, they were both doing it. Sharing his cock between them, lips meeting in kisses around his shaft. Taking him into their mouths, long slow licks down his length alternating with short eager laps that circled his tingling head. The velvet seal of Ben's lips wrapped around his shaft and sucked hard enough to wring out a groan of mingled ecstasy and desperate restraint. The nuclear lick of Kaia's wicked tongue slid down his shaft and stroked his clenched balls.

A white wave of pleasure obliterated him. He barely held on by his fingernails to his own towering climax.

Desperately he clenched their hair as they both worked him over, mouths meeting around his shaft in slow hot kisses sticky with his own precum.

"Need you to—slow down a little," he rasped. "Or I'm not going to last."

"Ditto," Zorin said with a chuckle, leaning back on the bed. "And I'm just the poor schmuck watching. How about just the two of you for a bit?"

Ben's hungry gaze slid over Kaia. "I can run with that."

Uncoiling smoothly to his feet, Ben pulled Kaia into a devouring kiss. Bending her slender body backward with the force of his unleashed passion. Easing one of her booted feet onto the bed to spread her wide and expose her slick folds. Planting one hand between her thighs so he could work two fingers deep inside her with an audible wetness that brought the color racing to her cheeks.

Gasping as he whisked all control from her hands, she tried to close her thighs—regain command—but he held her spread wide.

"You're so wet for me, aren't you, angel? So ready for all of us?"

She moaned in response, head falling forward so her burgundy hair curtained her face.

"Show me what you need," he said, low and urgent.

Helpless with want, her hips bucked into his hand, full breasts bouncing gently with every thrust. Dex stood transfixed, hard and aching. And he didn't need telepathy to know she was driving Ben insane.

Especially when her hand slipped between their bodies to close around Ben's cock. Panting, sweating, feral with need—a prelude to that desperate, frantic Ben that Dex loved most to pleasure—he thrust into her grip.

Dex prowled behind Kaia for a better view. Because if Ben Nero lost his clever, calculating, maddeningly manipulative mind and came in her hand like an overeager virgin, Dex wanted to see his face when he lost it.

"Like what you see?" Ben said fiercely. Both hands reached behind Kaia to spread her ripe bottom, revealing her rose-pink pucker. A citadel Dex knew all three of them had yet to storm.

Kaia gasped and squirmed in Ben's arms. Forced to acquiesce to her own intimate exposure. When his fingers probed her sensitive rear hole, she whimpered with embarrassed need.

"Oh gods," Dex groaned, reaching by reflex for his own aching shaft.

"Easy, kid," Zorin whispered again. "Kaia needs you to come inside her tonight. The longer you wait, the harder you come, the better our chance she'll conceive. And that's what we all want."

"Me first," Ben muttered, with a hard look that warned them all not to cross him. "I've already waited nine farking years. Tell me you want me inside you, angel."

She moaned in response and squirmed into him, trying to avoid his probing fingers in her ass and impale herself on his shaft at the same time. Her hands struggled to fit him inside her.

Gods, they were both so damn desperate. Once he mounted her— once Ben thrust into her heat in the blind rutting frenzy that seized him at the peak of his need and shredded all his sexual polish like paper— Dex swore he wouldn't be held responsible for the consequences.

Dimly he was aware of Zorin unfolding to his feet to loom beside him. His breath heavy with hunger.

Muscle flexed under Ben's smooth skin as he lifted Kaia against him, hands wrapped around her ass. Her head fell back and her taut thighs closed around his hips.

"Please, Ben, please—oh gods—need you inside me so much— I'm *begging* you—" Kaia's urgent pleas ended on a sharp cry of pleasure as his hungry cock drove deep into her depths.

For a sizzling span, they both froze—both his beautiful, soul-searingly perfect lovers—breaths loud in the tingling silence.

The psychic echo of their pounding need clamped Dex's balls tight against his body and dripped a steady drizzle of precum down his shaft.

Sol's blazing chariot, if I make it through the next twenty ticks without losing my mind, I deserve a bloody medal.

"You and me both, kid," Zorin whispered beside him.

If the man even touched his fiercely aroused body, Dex knew he was lost.

Gasping for air, Ben eased their bodies a handspan apart and thrust into Kaia again, hard enough to make them both cry out. Wild with hunger, she wrapped herself around him and writhed against him. He staggered to the bed. Pinning her beneath him, he drove into her, hard and fast, fierce with the force of his need.

Dex found himself standing over them, transfixed by the searing visual of Ben's pumping buttocks bucking into her, her sharp nails digging into his muscled shoulders hard enough to draw blood, her sexy legs still sheathed in those damned silver boots clamped tight around his waist, her eager hips rising to meet his every thrust. Her shrill cries mingled with her lover's hoarse moans to urge him on.

If he—Dex—so much as wrapped a hand about his own aching cock, he knew he'd go off like a torpedoed starship in the Battle of Epsilon.

Hands balled into fists, he stalked around the bed and climbed in. Kneeling behind Kaia's wildly tossing head, he grasped her wrists and pinned her arms to the mattress overhead. Blind with arousal, her burning eyes lifted to find him. Face flushed and desperate with mindless passion, mouth open and breathless with driving need.

"You're clawing Ben's back to ribbons, darling," he muttered tenderly. "And you can't help it, can you? I'm going to hold you down for him."

Ben lifted his head to fix on Dex as he thrust into Kaia, flesh slapping flesh in the fast, frantic rhythm that always claimed him before he climaxed.

Dex couldn't help himself. He leaned over Kaia to claim Ben's open mouth in a hungry kiss. Ben's tongue tangled with his. Ben's desperate moan vibrated against Dex's lips.

When Kaia's hot tongue licked down his shaft, Dex barely held back from exploding.

"Jumpin' Jupiter. The three of you. I was just gonna watch the first time. Now I can't resist." Zorin's gruff statement was punctuated by the squirt of lube from his bedside stash.

A sound so rife with sexual promise Dex nearly lost it all over again.

Even though he knew whatever their pirate had planned in the penetration department wouldn't be with him tonight.

As Ben thrust into her willing warmth, Kaia's slick tongue stroked up and down the ridged underside of Dex's cock. Every flicker sent a lick of pleasure curling through him. Pinning her wrists with one hand, he fed her his cock and felt the earnest suction of her eager mouth closing around his shaft. Drawing him in deep until his tip nudged the back of her throat.

When her gag reflex hit, he knew he should ease back. Although his runaway maharani was a damn quick study, this was all still new to her.

But he was a bastard.

And he needed her like blazes.

"Relax your throat and swallow me, darling."

With gentle insistence, he pushed deeper. Her wide eyes found his as she worked diligently to accommodate more of him than she'd ever taken. He was patient but relentless. At last she swallowed his length with a whimper of surrender, hot silken muscle rippling around his cock. Velvet heat encased him. His eyes closed as deep waves of pleasure sucked at him.

"That's it," he praised her, guttural with hunger. "Oh darling. That's bloody brilliant. Keep doing that."

Unable to speak—because he'd gagged her with his cock—she moaned deep in her throat and swallowed him down again and again.

Ruthlessly filled by both of them—Ben's cock filling her pussy, Dex's shaft filling her mouth, both of them thrusting with swiftly mounting urgency—she clung to his hands in helpless entreaty. While he and Ben between them held her pinned to the mattress.

Forced to service both of them.

But loving every minute. Her hips rising to welcome every downstroke, her low moans rhythmic around his shaft.

Rutting into her, he felt his own desperate control slip away. Head tipping back with ecstasy, he thrust into her mouth with abandon. Precisely the way he intended to thrust into her body.

Ben was crying out with every stroke, heedless as always of how much noise he was making as his climax rushed toward him.

Then the mattress sank under Zorin's weight.

A ripple of response shuddered through Ben's lean body. His gasp of surprise snapped Dex's eyes open.

Over Ben's dark head, Zorin crouched behind Ben and Kaia's joined bodies. Working two fingers shiny with moisture into Ben's perfectly exposed ass.

"Gods and demons," Ben moaned, eyes meeting Dex's in mingled shock and arousal. "Zorin… oh comets… I don't think *now* is—"

"Not your job to *think*, gorgeous." Zorin's monumental bulk loomed over him, face hard with tender menace. "I'm about to give you what you've been begging me for all night. How about you just keep our girl happy and let me worry about the rest."

Without waiting for acquiescence, Zorin roughly grasped Ben's wrists, wrestled them behind his back, and tied him with the twisted silk rope of Ben's abandoned shirt.

Savage with need, Ben's head jerked up. Through clenched teeth he hissed, "Damn it, Zorin! I said. *Not. Now.*"

"I don't recall asking your opinion." The pirate's hard hands yanked the rope cruelly tight. "Did I."

Caught in the vise of his own imminent climax, Ben struggled and sputtered. Furious as a drenched cat, he fought to push himself up. A rough palm between his shoulders shoved him flat against Kaia.

She gasped around Dex's cock but never stopped working him, her earnest mouth so ready for his increasingly rough and rapid thrusts. And only the scene playing out before him tore his gaze away from the paralyzing sight of his own rigid shaft, shiny and slick with saliva, wrapped in the diligent suction of her lush lips.

Barely two cubits away, the Valyrian Precursor could have hurled Zorin through the wall into next week with a thought. As Dex knew perfectly well. Instead, he watched his boyhood best friend shudder and struggle to submit. Submit to the big man's brutal use.

Ben's hips flexed, driving him deeper into Kaia. Her needy cry vibrated around Dex's swollen cock.

A spasm of demand seared through him. Groaning, he eased out of the wet heat of Kaia's compliant mouth barely a heartbeat before he would have emptied his load down her throat.

Ben's ragged breaths rasped loud in the deep space silence as he pistoned into her. Punctuated by Kaia's breathless cries.

"What is it with—the two of you?" Ben gasped, lifting his head to include Dex in his question. "Always wanting to—tie me up?"

"The reason we both bloody do it is because *you* make it so bloody irresistible," Dex said gruffly, fisting his shaft in long slow strokes. "And because nothing in this world makes you come harder, does it, than a well-executed enactment of one of your violent sexual fantasies."

"Guilty—as charged," Ben panted. "It's just—he's a lot gentler—ow!—with you than he is with me."

"I'm giving Dex what he needs." Finally satisfied with his knot, Zorin rummaged in the bedside drawer where he kept his toys. "He's new to all this. You need something else. You need it rough. Like rape. Don'tcha, gorgeous?"

"When I'm with a guy—yeah," Ben growled. "Think you can work with that, Syndax?"

Zorin's tone went smooth with menace. "One way to find out."

Tasting the potent psychic cocktail of sexual aggression and raw need that swirled between them, Dex cursed and Kaia moaned. Ben's hard face softened as he leaned in to kiss her. And they were all so closely linked Dex picked up their inner dialogue as though they'd spoken aloud.

Surprised you with that, didn't I, angel?

No offense, stud pony. Her teeth sank gently into his lower lip. *But watching you with Dex? I kind of guessed.*

Open book, am I? Ben chuckled softly and deepened the kiss.

"Here's the crux of the matter." Dex's voice hardened, and Ben's head snapped up. "We intend to ensure you obtain that unsavory attention you crave so desperately from *us*. Your soon-to-be consorts. As opposed to any other, random, ill-advised individual it crosses your mind to invite to your well-trafficked bed."

"Oh, come on—only did that because I was flipped at *you*—" Ben's breathless objection broke off with a cry.

Zorin had slipped the slim black leather band of a ball gag over Ben's face.

"You said plenty," Zorin murmured tenderly. "Open up for me."

Ben's startled eyes flew wide with comprehension. His gaze clung to Dex's face in a plea for mercy. Disconcerted and unsettled in a way Dex had never seen his urbane and sophisticated lover.

While Kaia—who had an intimate view of whatever space wreck was going on in her lifemate's head—wrapped herself around him and crooned encouragement. Coaxing Ben to take whatever he needed to take. To satisfy the dominant lover in their bed.

Dangerously close to spilling himself, Dex squeezed his own shaft to slow himself down. "You heard the man. We're waiting."

"Oh gods," Ben whispered, voice shaking. His eyes squeezed closed.

Slowly, reluctantly, his mouth opened.

With tender ruthlessness, Zorin pressed the soft black ball into place, filling his mouth completely. Large enough that Ben had to struggle—groaning in discomfort—to accommodate it. But he finally managed to take it all in. Zorin buckled the black leather strap closed behind his head.

Bound and gagged, facedown and naked, Ben lay trembling and helpless on the bed. His cock still buried deep in Kaia, who watched the scene unfold with lips parted and eyes wide. When she stroked his hair and murmured encouragement, Ben only shivered.

Zorin leaned forward to whisper in his ear. "I'm gonna take it easy on you this time, gorgeous. Next time you try to manipulate me after I say no? I got a penis gag a handspan long with your name on it."

Ben's buttocks clenched and he drove hard into Kaia, wringing from her a low cry of need. Just in case Dex needed any evidence of how powerfully aroused Ben felt to be bound and gagged and helpless at the big man's mercy.

Hard and desperate, Ben bucked into Kaia while Zorin lubed up behind him. She clutched Ben between her booted legs, hips rising to meet every thrust with an eager cry. While Dex wrapped a fist around his throbbing cock and fought like blazes not to spurt all over them.

When Zorin returned to prepping Ben, easing three slick fingers into his tight hole, Ben voiced a keen of pleasure that was clearly audible even through his gag. Muscle rippled in the pirate's tattooed arm as his fingers pistoned steadily deeper. Another visible shudder rolled through Nero's body. His hips resumed their driving thrust into Kaia's eager heat.

Bucking Zorin's fingers deeper into his own hole with every thrust.

"Great flaming comets! That's so hot," Kaia gasped. Getting her own view of the action when Dex released her and backed off a little. Because he was acutely worried about how her tiny body was faring down there with all three of them looming over her.

She's fine. Nero fired the thought at him like a solar cannon. *Don't you think I'd know if she wasn't fine? She's more than fine—oh gods—I'm so close—*

"Spread him good and wide for me, sweetheart."

Zorin's hoarse command had Kaia scrambling to obey, reaching to spread Ben's ass between her hands to expose his hole. Ben groaned in humiliated protest.

Rising to his knees behind Kaia's head, Dex scored a ringside seat as Zorin crouched behind Ben, cock shiny with lube, and started working all that length and girth into Ben's well-stretched channel.

And one more joy of mating a telepath like Ben Nero was that, even with his mouth full, he begged for cock so beautifully. Just another part of that whole forced-penetration fantasy that clearly turned Ben's crank.

Gods—don't—PLEASE don't—

The unforgettable sight of his sculpted face, exquisitely twisted with ecstasy and pain, silver tears spilling from his gorgeous violet eyes, seared into Dex's brain. Along with the pornographic visual of their beefcake pirate looming over him, gripping Ben's lean hips in ruthless hands as Ben's vain and desperate pleas echoed in all their heads.

Leaning forward to nuzzle Ben's sweating back as he eased his way home.

"All right, pet?" Zorin breathed against Ben's skin. His rough-hewn face heartbreakingly soft with tenderness and wonder. "I know I'm a lot to handle. Try to relax a little for me. You're so beautiful when you take me like this."

A long low moan shuddered from Ben's throat. He buried his face in Kaia's neck to smother a convulsive sob. Her hands smoothed over his sleek hair, soothing him, whispering words of praise and reassurance.

Encouraging Ben to take more of him.

Sobbing softly in surrender, he yielded to accept the girth of Zorin's shaft.

Dex lay beside him and stroked damp tendrils of his lover's hair from his tear-filled eyes. Just the sight of elegant Ben Nero so utterly undone and out of his head with need roused a ferocious, protective tenderness in his heart. The same heart all three of them had so thoroughly conquered.

Eyes shining with lavender light, Kaia's face turned toward him. Dex gave her a slow deep kiss. She tasted of her sweetness, Nero's spice, and his own salty essence.

Gods on the mountain, he loved her. Loved all of them. And he'd never ever let anyone hurt them or take any of them away from him.

Together he and Kaia stroked Ben's shaking shoulders.

"Such a good boy," Dex whispered in his ear, kissing his tearstained face. "You're trying so hard for him, aren't you? You're going to make him feel so good when he comes buckets deep inside you. You're going to get him off so hard."

"Try to relax," Kaia murmured, nuzzling Ben's neck. "There's a whole lot more of him."

Around his gag, Ben moaned in helpless protest. But the steady rhythm of his hips was quickening.

Kaia's breath hitched and her eyes clouded with craving. "Oh—oh yeah—just like that. You want to take all of him, don't you?"

And watching Ben do it, watching him struggle to relax and submit and accept more of Zorin's cock the way Dex had done last night—Kaia's eyes locked on Zorin's face, telling him without words when Ben could handle more of him—-watching Zorin ease slowly deeper as Ben groaned and rocked himself into the pirate's massive shaft—was just about the most erotic sight in Dex's universe.

"Oh gods, baby," Zorin groaned, his gaze lifting to find Dex's fascinated face. "He's so goddamn tight and hot for me."

"I know." Dex scraped out the words. Meteors, he needed to come. Needed to come so badly for all three of them.

Needed, somehow, to wait.

Zorin leaned in to Ben's ear. "You need me to ride you long and hard, don't you? You need me to come inside you till my seed's running down your legs."

Ben's cry came muffled but sharp—a sound of desperate denial. Lost deep in the brutal game he needed so badly. A game so brutal even Dex had hesitated to play.

Just another reason Zorin was good for all three of them.

Zorin eased back, then thrust savagely into him. Burying himself all the way to the hilt in Ben's tight hole. Fucking him hard into Kaia's willing warmth. She cried out and writhed beneath them, eyes locked on Zorin's blazing face. His incandescent gaze seared through her.

Fiercely dominant, in utter command of the force and tempo of every downstroke, their pirate was riding both of them.

In about two ticks—or whenever he gave them permission—he was going to make both of them climax.

Dex had been wondering how he'd feel seeing another man— even Ben—drive his cock into Kaia. Wondering how he'd feel seeing another man—even Zorin—drive his cock into Ben. Wondering how he'd feel seeing anyone—even these two soulmates he desperately adored—getting Zorin off like a bloody rocket the way Dex ached to do himself. Even wondering how he'd feel having all of them hear Zorin call him *baby*.

Well, no more wondering. Now he knew.

It was ten different kinds of a turn-on.

#

Kaia was losing her careful clutch on her slipping sanity.

One splintered fingernail at a time.

Zorin loomed over both of them and pounded into Ben, massive chest heaving with effort, tattooed shoulders rippling with strength, craggy face harsh with need. Every thrust of Zorin's hips drove Ben's rigid cock deeper into the sweet pulsing ache between her thighs. Making her cry out with every stroke.

Fierce with satisfaction, Zorin's nuclear eyes seared through her. Burning his brand of ownership on all of them.

Staking his claim on more than her body or even her heart.

Tonight he was claiming her soul.

Ben's sinuous heat hammered her tingling body harder into the mattress with every desperate buck. Face buried in her neck, breath ragged in her ear, body shaking in her arms and slippery with sweat. Still savage and deadly as an electric eel in her bed.

Even disintegrated as he was by Zorin's brutal domination and ruthless enactment of the fantasy he needed so badly, he was the closest thing she knew to a god—a real one. Despite all the physical and sexual trauma he was willingly absorbing, the warm sparkling flood of his psychic energy never faltered.

Bathing her insides in effervescent light.

Ben wasn't only determined to make her climax. He was determined to make her conceive.

And Dex was every molecule as determined. Crouched over all of them, tawny and coiled and territorial as a sand lion, burnished hair falling in blazing eyes, cock wrapped in his own pumping fist. She could still taste the dark musk of his need coating her plundered mouth. And the only reason he hadn't come in her mouth—the *only* reason he was waiting with the same iron resolve for his turn to thrust inside her—was because he too was determined to make her conceive.

She'd never felt so claimed.

So cherished.

So loved.

But she wasn't going to last much longer. Gods of the nine unknown realms, *none* of them was going to last much longer.

Intimately linked as they all were, Zorin plucked the thought right from her brainbox. One big hand shifted from his punishing grip on Nero's hips to tuck under her knee and ease her thigh up. Deepening the angle of Ben's relentless thrusts.

Raw pleasure swelled and pulsed between her thighs. Blindly she clutched the slick plane of Ben's trembling back.

"You ready to come for me?" Zorin panted, brutal with need. "You ready to feel our boy go off inside you like a neutron torpedo? You ready for us to give you what you need?"

"Yes, please yes," she gasped, mindless and wanting.

Muscle flexed in his pumping body. Sweat glittered on his tattooed skin. "Let me hear you beg for it, sweetheart."

"Please!" The word burst from her straining throat. "Oh, Zorin, please—we're all going to die if you don't—oh gods oh gods oh gods—"

"That's what I wanted to hear." He buried himself deep inside Ben and his rugged face convulsed. "Give us a son, Kaia. Come for me—come for all of us—oh stars—"

Pulses of pleasure pounded through her frantic body, every vibration a sonic shock of exquisite sensation. Her channel clamped around Ben's shaft and rippled in spasms of desperate hunger. All of it magnified to painful intensity as she felt her lifemate's primal passion, balls tight, ass burning, climax boiling through his cock in hot gouts of release that spurted deep inside her. His raw scream of ecstasy clawed through the gag.

Love you, angel—so gods-damned much—swear to gods—love all three of you.

Ben's silent promise echoed through all of them and wrung a raw shout of triumph from Zorin's thrusting body.

Beneath both of them, she writhed in unbearable pleasure. Back arched, mouth open, cries filling the pheromone-drenched air.

When the towering crest of climax finally receded, she went limp. One hand curled protectively around Ben's damp head. He lay spent and shaking across her body.

Crushed beneath Zorin's monumental weight. While the heavy drowsing warmth of utter fulfillment seeped through both of them.

"Gods of my father," she whispered, barely conscious.

Chest heaving, Zorin leaned forward to unbuckle the gag, eased the ball free from Ben's mouth, and tossed the toy aside.

Ben stirred in her arms. A shuddering sigh slipped out of him.

Standing over the bed, his hard face etched with tender possession and fiercely trammeled restraint, Dex smoothed back Ben's hair and bent to press a slow kiss to Kaia's breathless lips.

"Talk to me, gorgeous." Their pirate released the twisted rope of fabric and leaned in to nuzzle the back of Ben's sweaty neck. "I can be a real bastard, can't I, rutting into you like that? Was I too hard on you?"

"Are you kidding?" Ben mumbled. "Don't think I've ever… come so hard… in my life. And neither has she."

Ben lifted his head to find her mouth in a languid kiss, then turned to eye Zorin. "But you… you didn't…?"

"That's goddamn right," Zorin rasped, easing out of Ben's indolent body to loom over them. Which gave all of them an iconic view of the massive boner their pirate was still sporting.

From deep in Dex's chest rose a low rumble of hunger.

Reminding Kaia she still intended to satisfy her other two lovers. Now that she knew she'd ovulated, they all deserved a fair shot at siring her prophecy son.

Zorin scrubbed a hand through his spiky hair and headed for the bathroom. "Just lemme catch my breath for a sec before you start all that, sweetheart."

Soon the hiss of the shower slid through the steamy air.

She'd just come so hard she thought she could never come again. But the thought of taking *both* of them—both her hard and territorial and fiercely scenting Mogadon males—both of them *together*—sent a soft pulse of desire rippling through her slick and tender flesh.

Ben pushed out a chuckle and withdrew. When he broke the physical bond between them, she suffered a poignant pang of loss.

Because she'd spent way too long without him.

But he softened their momentary parting with a kiss.

You're on your own this time, angel. I don't think I'll be taking any more cock... oh comets... for tonight. Gods and demons, this guy's relentless, isn't he?

A drowsy smile curved her lips. *I think it's a Syndax thing.*

The shower fell silent. Zorin ambled back into the bedroom, scrubbing a towel roughly over all those cubits of wet tattooed skin, to reclaim his terrain beside the bed. Lazy with contentment, Ben rolled to his back to eye the titan looming over them. His gaze dropped to Zorin's prodigious length and his brow furrowed.

"Not that I'm not impressed by your self-restraint, big guy. But why in the seven *hells* didn't you...?"

"Why didn't I come buried deep inside you like I threatened you I would?" Zorin pushed out a grim snort. "Sorry to disappoint, gorgeous. Far's I can tell, you got every man and woman in this sector eating outta your hand and liking it. Which makes you a little too cocky for your own good, don't it?"

Shifting to a new vantage that gave him a better view of Ben's chagrined face, Dex chuckled softly. "He's got you pegged to rights, hasn't he, love?"

Standing below the bed with feet spread wide, Zorin folded his burly arms across his chest. And just the sight of that colossal erection still jutting aggressively between his corded thighs shot through Kaia's tender depths another deep pang of longing.

"When it comes to my consorts, I'm a pretty indulgent guy. I'm pretty much gonna spoil all three of you. So when I say no, you better believe I mean it. Believe there's a darn good reason." Zorin frowned down at Ben. "You got that?"

"Yeah," Ben said softly. "I've got that. Sorry I pushed you earlier. It's just… I wanted you so much. You kept holding back and it made me so crazy. Don't be mad for keeps."

His plea of contrition eased the dangerous tension right out of their pirate's big body. Yep, that was what got her about her Syndax lover every single damn time.

That unexpected contrast between his brutal strength and his gentle heart.

"Shoot, gorgeous. I'm not the type to hold a grudge. I mighta been ticked off, but I was flattered as all get-out." Hitching his sandy brows, Zorin lifted Ben's limp hand and held it to his scarred face. "You really mean what you said back there, huh? Think you could really love me? A big galoot like me?"

"Yeah." A wistful smile chased across Ben's drowsy face. "I really think I do. Think you could ever love me back?"

Zorin turned his head to kiss Ben's curled palm. "You're the telepath, ain'tcha? Still need to hear me say it?"

"Indulge me," Ben said around a yawn.

Zorin sank down to sit beside him with a sigh. "I love you so much it scares me, Ben Nero. I'm crazy in love with all three of you. Just like our girl wanted from the get-go. Didn't you, sweetheart?"

"I did." Kaia was way too happy to stop the sappy smile spreading over her face. "I know it wasn't anyone else's plan. Not at first. But I love that you all went for it. And I was right, wasn't I? I was flipping *right*."

"Yeah, you were right. About all of us." Zorin pushed out a breath and his gaze darkened to navy. "But we gotta be honest. Being together like this—the four of us—makes us stronger in some ways. And *way* more vulnerable in others." His eyes rose to find Dex. Wary acknowledgment of shared danger flashed between them. "So, yeah, this scares the living daylights outta me."

"In that, you're hardly alone." Dex prowled up beside her to study Kaia's spent and naked body with brooding tenderness. "I fancy this journey we've embarked upon has been quite the revelation for all four of us. Not to mention the fact we're about to scandalize the hell out of all our races with this profoundly unconventional mating."

"My Syndax won't be scandalized." Zorin snorted. "That's the advantage of calling your own shots. Shoot, they'll probably throw us a party. But your Mogadon are sure as hell gonna be gobsmacked."

Dex cupped Kaia's chin in a gentle hand, brow furrowed in a probing gaze. "Are you certain we're still what you're wanting, darling? All three of us?"

"Are you kidding?" Kaia reached her arms overhead in a blissful stretch that arched her aching body. "I've never been more certain of anything in my whole life."

"Well, that's a relief," he growled, eyes flashing with warning. "If you ever change your mind, I swear I'll run mad."

"Whoa there. For your information, there's exactly zero danger of me changing my mind." She grinned up at him. "I'm pretty flipping sure you're stuck with me, space cadet. All three of you."

Her gaze roamed over Dex's proudly naked physique—suntanned skin stretched over powerful shoulders, ruddy nipples erect against smooth planes of pectoral muscle, the sculpted terrain of abs and thighs framing his fierce erection.

The Mogadon Imperator.

The galaxy's greatest general.

Not to mention her Tombola master.

He'd defied eons of sacred ritual to claim her for himself. And by doing it on her terms, he'd end the Syndax war and change the fate of billions.

If only her father, His High Holiness, allowed their union.

She shook with a sudden icy shiver of foreboding. Was it standard fear of her godlike father... or psychic premonition?

"Cold, darling?"

"A little," she whispered.

A predatory hunger hardened his face. His hand fell away and he prowled to stand between her feet. "Let's see what we can do about that, shall we?"

Her surprised giggle slipped out. "Wait a minute. I'm not sure I'm ready for... oh gods..."

Her half-formed protest drifted away.

Because he'd bent to drag his tongue up the glistening valley of her well-plowed pussy. Drenched with her own yearning and the generous tribute Ben had left behind.

"Dex." Feeling the relentless whip of desire licking between her thighs, Kaia tried to close her legs. "Angels and asteroids... *wow*... I don't know if..."

"There is no *if*. We're not anywhere close to done with you." He knelt between her booted feet, battle-hardened hands spreading her wide for another long slow lick.

Across the bed, Zorin pushed out a low groan.

"Gods of Olympus, you taste like Ben. And you taste like *you*, darling." Dex's head lifted between her thighs, butter-soft hair falling in his eyes. "You're going to take Zorin and me together now, aren't you? Then you'll taste like all four of us."

"Dex," she breathed, heart hammering with sudden need. "I want to. You know how much I want to. The three of you… the way you make me feel… I just don't know if I *can*—"

"Sure you can, sweetheart," Zorin rumbled, rising to stalk around the bed for a better view. "That's always been your game plan, hasn't it? You're gonna take Dex's cock and let him ride you till you see stars. Then you're gonna put me inside you, same as always. Aren't you?"

The slow fire of desire licked through her. In helpless acquiescence, her hands fisted in the twisted sheets. Dex held her thighs spread wide and exposed while he tongued her. And Zorin watched every flicker of response flash across her face with hawklike intensity.

Unavoidably, irresistibly, the hard nub of her clit swelled and rose to beg for more under Dex's lapping tongue. He purred with satisfaction, and insidious pleasure snaked through her tender flesh. Brow furrowed with focus, mouth wide and breathless, eyes locked on Zorin's relentless stare, she whimpered in mingled need and protest.

Too much—oh gods—it's all way too much. If Dex doesn't stop, I swear I'll die. No, I'll die if he stops—

Desperately she struggled beneath him, triggering every Mogadon instinct they both possessed.

"Wait… please… *oh*…" Her cries of protest softened, struggles growing more feeble. Until, inevitably, her hips started thrusting into the rhythm of his tongue and her cries of protest sharpened to cries of encouragement.

Ben rolled on his side to watch through a banner of disheveled hair, his supple frame still limp with release.

"Don't let her fool you. She wants it," her lifemate breathed, lids half-mast as his telepathic touch slid through her. "Yeah, you're going to make her come for you. But maybe a different angle? I rode her pretty hard."

"What would you advise, Precursor?" Dex muttered fiercely, circling her clit with his tongue. She voiced an aching moan of frustration, hips rising in mute entreaty.

Ben propped his head on his fist, drowsy interest sparking in his violet gaze. "Why don't you bend her over? She gets off imagining you doing that. Working your shaft into her until she moans. While Zorin feeds her his cock." His tone darkened. "And she *really* wants it in the ass. Wants it that way from all three of us. One after the next."

"Damn it, Ben!" she gasped, face fiery with blushes. "I never *said* I wanted—"

"Shucks, sweetheart. You didn't need to. I coulda told you that the first night." Zorin caught her embarrassed face in one big hand so she couldn't look away. "Can't say I'm not intrigued. But that's not gonna get the job done tonight. Not if we want you to conceive. Even if Gorgeous has a point about the angle, huh?"

Ruthless with purpose, the pirate held her gaze. "Turn her over for us, Dex."

A warning growl rolled from Dex. A growl that warned all of them he wouldn't be put off any longer.

Just feeling that subliminal vibration of danger against her clit made her eyes close and stars streak against her lids.

Which meant she was in no shape to argue when Dex's calloused hands eased her to her hands and knees. Especially when he leaned over her to claim Zorin's mouth with an aggressive kiss she knew would be laced with Ben's climax and her own juices.

Already that hot ache was building between her thighs. When Dex knelt behind her and spread her wide, she yielded without a protest. Her back arched and her ass tilted up. Swollen and tender with fertility, her breasts hung heavy, nipples hard and tingling and longing to be tongued.

Dex's tongue slid up her slit from behind. Spreading Ben's come up her crease. Right over the super-sensitive mouth of her rear hole. She voiced a cry of shocked pleasure and craned to look back. Because if Dex was really going to tongue her *there*—sweet stars above—she *really* wanted to see—

With gentle insistence, Zorin's big hand lifted her chin and faced her forward. His length filled her vision—engorged and slick and eager for her mouth. Her own breathless moan slipped out.

Knowing what he needed and more than ready to oblige, she wrapped her tongue around his shaft to circle his tip in a slow teasing lick. Salty drops spilled against her tongue and his husky groan tore the air.

Behind her, Dex's tongue teased and probed her hole, while Zorin's eager cock nudged her lips. She thought she'd lose her mind with pleasure.

Especially when Ben, low and throaty with arousal, whispered his own instructions.

"No more foreplay. She needs you inside her. Both of you. She's ready for both of you."

Breath rasping, Zorin's hand slid behind her head to urge her closer.

Her lips parted readily to accept his cock, her tongue quickening as it circled him. But he needed more from her than teasing. His hands closed around her head to ease her mouth up and down his shaft. Which could so easily be brutal, with his size and strength, but he held himself in check. Same as always.

Even when what she really wanted was to make him lose it.

The way he had with Ben.

Behind her, Dex stopped tonguing her hole. And her disappointed whimper would have embarrassed her if she hadn't already been well beyond embarrassment. Especially when he rubbed his cock against all that slick craving between her legs. She canted her hips and opened her mouth wider to beg him to fill her—

Zorin's shaft filled her mouth and stole her speech. Her tongue glided faster along his length, breasts swinging gently as she worked him. But there was still so much more of him to take. She wanted to take all of him, the way he'd made Ben take all of him—

"Easy, sweetheart." His hands gentled her bobbing head. "Ben needs me to hurt him a little—and not give him any choice. That's what gets him off. You don't need to be hurt. Just dominated, don'tcha?"

"Yeah, that's what she needs," Ben breathed in her ear.

She trembled under her lifemate's deft, knowing touch. Familiar now as her own hand, when the only pleasure she'd known all those years was what she gave herself. His palm eased up her torso to find one full and tingling breast.

She moaned around Zorin's cock.

"I'm entirely confident we can oblige," Dex muttered. "We all know what you want, darling. *Everything* you want. And we're all going to give it to you. But what you need more than anything else tonight is *this*."

His voice deepened as his cock nudged into her well-ridden channel. And despite everything—despite being tender and overridden and sated with sensation—her back arched and her thighs widened to welcome him.

The relentless press of his shaft surged into her, echoed by his savage shout of pleasure. Seating him deep inside her in a single thrust. A heavy pulse of passion rolled through her. She tried to back away just a little, breathe just a little, control just a little of the sensory overload before it fried her circuits.

But she couldn't.

Not with Zorin riding her mouth and Dex riding her pussy. She was trapped between them. Dex's firm hands gripped her hips as he pistoned into her, hard and fast, already close to the powerful climax he'd been reining in all night. Zorin held her steady and thrust into her mouth, the taste of salt and wolf and wanting sliding over her tongue and filling her throat.

When Ben slithered beneath her—when he applied that clever mouth to tease and tongue her swollen nipples—the need she felt for all of them swelled up sharp and desperate. She fumbled between her legs to find the aching nub of her clit and worked her finger in the racing desperate rhythm seizing all of them.

"Give us a son, darling," Dex groaned. "All of us."

And she loved him even more for saying *us*, when she knew full well the Mogadon caveman buried deep in his DNA really wanted their child to be biologically *his*.

Well, if their firstborn wasn't, the next one would be. Or the next. She longed to give children—sons *and* daughters—to all of them.

All three of the men she loved.

Ben suckled her tingling nipples, each strong pull igniting an electric jolt of arousal that shot straight to her clit and made her rock harder into the thrust of Dex's cock. With every pull on her nipples, her soaking channel clamped tight around Dex's shaft. With every pull, her mouth quickened its sliding suction around the broad girth of Zorin's cock. With every pull, the sense heightened that Ben was making love to all three of them.

A shared thought that made all three of them groan.

Gods, her nipples were so sensitive now she couldn't stand it, she couldn't. Again she tried to shift away. Instead, Ben's ruthless hands cupped her breasts together so he could suckle both at once.

Holding her in place while all three of them took their pleasure. Braced on hands and knees, she shook under the sensual onslaught while Zorin filled her mouth and Dex filled her pussy and Ben laved her nipples with his tongue. The musky smell of their passion, their Mogadon pheromones, Ben's incense and her body's eager welcome rose dark and thick in the air. A long cry of yearning rolled through her.

Dear sweet satellites, I'm going to come—so flipping hard—

Her insides were sparkling, coruscating, dazzling with the light of Ben's psychic touch. So intense, so aroused, so fertile her golden skin was actually *glowing…*

"You're so—oh gods—so beautiful like this," Dex panted. "Your skin. Your hair. Those sounds you're making. The way you want me. Love you so much, darling."

She couldn't talk with her mouth full. But she'd never needed her mouth to tell him she loved him.

Can you feel how much she needs you? Ben's intimate whisper filled all their heads. *She needs you to come inside her. Needs you to sire our son.*

"You make me so happy I swear you'll break my heart." Dex's voice roughened. "All bloody three of you."

His pace quickened, grew erratic, self-control dissolving as the climax rushed toward them. He gripped her frantic hips to hold her still and buried himself deep and urgent inside her. His harsh shout of conquest tore the air. She shuddered around the spurt and pulse as he pumped his climax into her.

An avalanche of thundering pleasure tore through her and annihilated her and made her scream. The sound muffled by Zorin's rigid cock filling her throat, sensation strengthened by Ben's hot mouth still sucking her nipples, crisis heightened by her throbbing clit still driving into her hand.

At last, with a final moan, her hand fell away from her own satiated flesh. If not for Ben's strong hands beneath her, holding her up through all of it, her limbs would have buckled.

Knowing the instant the sensation tipped over the edge from

pleasure to pain, Ben stopped tormenting her overstimulated nipples. Dex's warm weight settled over her, the heavy rasp of his breath filling the night.

With a sigh, Ben slithered nimbly out from under her swaying and utterly sated body. He wrapped himself around Dex and eased him to the mattress.

Zorin gasped and pulled out of her mouth a breath before he would have filled her to overflowing with the explosive orgasm he still hadn't released. Her limp body fell forward.

Into the certain safety of his gentle hands, trembling with desperate need.

"Need to—come inside you, sweetheart," he panted, his deep baritone stripped and flayed with the strain of restraint. "Know we're a lot for you to handle. Promise I'll be careful. But tonight it needs to be—needs to be all three of us."

"I know," she whispered, struggling to rise. "That's what we all want, Zorin. How… how do you…?"

"Here." He crawled onto the bed and sat on his heels. The towering headboard, carved with scenes of graphic conquest and sexual plunder, loomed behind him like a calamity. "Come here."

Limp and lethargic with repletion, yet burning to give him what he needed, she floundered toward him. Her body sleek with sweat, her thighs slick with sex, her core pulsing with heat.

Ah, he was so beautiful and strong and dangerous, her exiled outlaw. Last man standing in this endurathon they'd all barely survived. Fighting their way blindly through parsecs of endless space over all these endless years to find each other.

To find their way home.

Zorin's strong hands curled under her arms and lifted her heavy limbs to straddle his lap. She wrapped both hands around his cock, still shiny and wet from her tongue, and felt him pulse beneath her fingers. It wouldn't take much at all to make him spill.

To push him over the edge.

He was massive, same as always. And even exhausted, she wanted him, same as always. *How* she wanted him—

"I'll be gentle. I promise." He steadied her as she settled over him. "Stars, the way you feel. The way you smell. And the way you *look*. Dex is right about all that. You really are a goddess, ain'tcha?"

"You know I'm not. Don't listen to the hype." Chuckling, she leaned in to kiss him. Letting him taste all of them on her tongue just to hear him moan. "I'm not divine. I'm just *really* fertile. But you make me feel worshipped. And definitely wanted."

"You got that right. You have no idea how much I want you," he growled against her lips. Which only made her shiver all over. "No more waiting. What with the three of you all teasing me tonight, I've had just about all the waiting I can take. I swear I'll be gentle. Put me inside you, sweetheart."

Gasping with the force of his need pounding through her, she fumbled to fit him against her soaked and eager slit. Aware through the lifebond of Dex sprawled on the bed behind her, Ben wrapped in his arms and nuzzling his neck.

Both of them utterly spent, but fully invested in the outcome.

And Dex still a bit worried. For her. For all the wear and tear they were inflicting on her body. For how she was holding up.

But trusting Zorin to take care of her. Take care of all of them.

"Blast, he's bloody huge," Dex muttered. "How can he *possibly*—?"

Zorin's shaft slid home inside her like he'd been born and bred to do nothing else. Lubricated by Dex and Ben and her own fierce pleasure. Engulfed by his predatory mating scent, Kaia closed her eyes and let her head fall back, trusting his powerful arms around her. Trusting him to keep her safe.

Trusting him to keep them all safe.

"Just like that," Ben whispered on an indrawn breath. Feeling every erg of powerful emotion she felt, resonating through the lifebond between them. "Gods and demons, angel. Is *that* how he feels inside you?"

She was too overwhelmed to answer or even move, yet she couldn't help riding the man between her thighs. Just for the visceral, bone-deep thrill of feeling all that strength and tender violence slip his chain. Tonight they'd driven their Syndax pirate to the ragged edge of human endurance.

Now he needed her. More than he'd ever needed her. And she was damn well going to give him every single thing he needed.

The same way he always did for her.

At first his hands spread to cradle her hips as she rode him. Trying to be gentle, just like he'd promised, for her sake. But it wasn't long before his arms wrapped tight around her to pull her closer. She twined her arms around his sinewed neck and leaned in for a long slow kiss, his tongue licking deep into her mouth, their moans mingling with their breath.

Soft and yielding, she wound herself around him and surrendered to how good he made her feel every single time he had her. To the powerful connection she'd felt with him from Day One. To the slick friction of his cock filling her, the soft explosions of pleasure that ricocheted through her with every thrust.

"Jumpin' Jupiter, the way you feel," he groaned into her mouth. "Oh, sweetheart. I'm not gonna last."

"Don't hold back. I want you. Want you to fill me." She arched her back, letting her damp and tangled hair slide over their joined hips and straining thighs. "Gods, Zorin. I love the way you fill me. Love you so much. I do. I love you."

A raw, desperate cry clawed from his throat and his mouth fused with hers.

Whatever else happened with the universe or the Patriarch or the war, she was his. *She was his.* She'd been his since the day they met.

All of her belonged to all of him.

He was holding her up and driving into her, slow and steady, arms wrapped strong and fierce around her, mouth searing her shoulders and breasts and throat. Gasping out how much he loved her. How much it meant to him that she loved him back. She buried her face in the thick muscled column of his neck and moaned into every thrust, her thighs spread wide to take him deeper, her sweat-slick body wrapped tight around him.

Her heart laid soft and trembling in his hands.

"You're out of this world," Ben whispered, echoed by Dex's heartfelt agreement. "The two of you. You're so beautiful. You can't imagine how much."

Except, thanks to the lifebond, she *could.* Could see the two of them through Ben's eyes. The pirate's tattooed arms engulfing her slender back, the sinuous surge of her hips straddling his bulging quads, her sorrel skin dark against his paler hue, his tawny head bent close over her tumbled mane. His craggy face convulsed with effort and ecstasy.

Ben's whisper, edged with urgency, pushed her over the brink.

Right into the yawning abyss. "Come for him, angel. He needs you. He needs you so much."

She shook under the subterranean shudder of climax. She sobbed into Zorin's neck and rode it out. Feeling the hot rhythmic jet of his cock kicking deep and strong against the wall of her womb. Hearing his long low groan of soul-deep release burrow through her.

Give us a son, sweetheart. Doesn't matter which one of us does the job. We'll all love him and we'll all die for him. Same way we'll all die for you.

Cradled by the promise of Zorin's voice in her soul, she breathed out a slow sigh.

The soft velvet void of space engulfed her.

When the darkness lifted, she was lying safe in his arms in the blue twilight. Lying with her head pillowed against Zorin's broad chest and Dex tucked up tight against her back the way he liked to sleep, one protective arm wrapped around her waist. Lying with Ben sprawled over all of them like a contented cat, fingers laced with hers, face burrowed in Zorin's neck, the pirate's fist gripping his hair, Dex's hand curled around his ass.

All of them together. Together the way they were meant to be. Together the way they always would be.

Patriarch or no Patriarch.

No matter what her father planned to stop them.

CHAPTER NINE
The Discovery

When Dex's eyes opened to the artificial blaze of morning pouring through the ceiling panels, the first bloody thing he saw was his wrist unit lying on Zorin's bedside table.

With its infernal message light flashing.

Which was more than a trifle annoying, since he'd fallen asleep with the thing strapped securely to his wrist. An arrangement undertaken with the firm intent of waking up when someone inevitably buzzed him to resolve the latest crisis.

All of which meant his Syndax lover had been intercepting his comms while he slept.

Again.

A pattern of interference that had to be driving poor Marcus straight to bedlam. Like any good lieutenant, the man hated it when his commanding officer went incommunicado.

Dex pushed out an exasperated breath.

"Get used to it, kid," the Syndax in question mumbled in his ear, one tattooed arm tightening around Dex's waist. "We got plenty to handle with four of us in this bed. I'm not about to let the rest of the Mogadon Empire in here."

"I'm the Mogadon Imperator." Dex lifted the pirate's hand to his mouth and pressed an affectionate kiss to his scarred knuckles. "Afraid you'll have to learn to share me with the masses, love."

"We Syndax aren't the sharing type. And you're about to mate one, ain'tcha?" Zorin rumbled in his ear—a growl of playful menace. "While you're in my bed, you're all mine. All three of you."

Despite his residual grogginess and borderline annoyance, despite the drafty chill of the aging battleship and his passing interest in hunting down a Valyrian fur to throw over all of them, Dex found himself considerably diverted by the rough rasp of Zorin's unshaven face nuzzling his neck.

Not to mention the combustible friction of Zorin's hardening shaft nudging his ass.

The arousal factor substantially heightened by the incandescent vision of a lushly naked Kaia, sprawled on her back in a tangle of silver sheets directly before him. Golden skin glowing with vitality, tumbled hair a vivid magenta, lilac eyes shining with contentment.

"We should probably think about getting up," she said dreamily. Her idle hand stroked Ben's sleek head as he lay curled beside her, one cheek pressed to her tummy, amethyst eyes wide and wondering.

Like he was listening to whatever was going on in there.

Zorin propped his chin on Dex's shoulder to study them. "Morning, sweetheart. Morning, gorgeous. Want me to put on a pot of *chaco*?"

"Mmmm." Kaia's mouth curved in a sleepy smile. "You're such a dreamboat. Ben never really wakes up without his *chaco*."

Lazily Dex rolled over to watch Zorin prowl, naked and barefoot, under the battered lintel into the little galley. Because the bulge and flex of the man's unforgettable ass, beneath the awesome wingspan of the raptor inked across his massive back, was simply too delectable not to savor.

Besides, he liked watching Zorin putter about. For the scourge of the galaxy, he was a surprisingly domesticated pirate. Yesterday, after blowing every circuit in his body, this particular pirate had actually made Dex a credible breakfast—

His wrist unit warbled a *ching*.

With a muttered curse, Dex rolled over to silence the thing.

Which was when he realized Kaia's attention was decidedly *not* on the promised *chaco*. Or even the naked pirate in their kitchen.

No. She was listening. Listening in her mind with Ben, who still lay with his ear pressed to her tummy.

Ben who, *chaco* or no *chaco*, seemed to be entirely awake and entirely focused on whatever that clever telepathic brain of his was doing inside his lifemate.

"I'll have Marcus send over a shuttle to transport us to the surface," Dex murmured, without moving a muscle. He was simply too bloody contented to move. Even if the Patriarch was waiting. "I've ordered a full-fleet escort with imperial honors. Because, in point of fact, I *am* the Imperator and His High Holiness had blasted better well acknowledge—"

The sharp hiss of Ben's indrawn breath sliced through his speech. An electric current of alertness hummed visibly through his best friend's coiled body. His hand, splayed across Kaia's belly, pulsed with purple light.

"Gods of Solaris," Ben whispered.

That frisson of energy leaped to Kaia. Sharply her head lifted. Her frame rippled with sudden tension.

"No, lie still for me, angel," Ben breathed, cheek still pressed to her tummy. A look of awe and wonder softened his chiseled face.

And the visceral rush of protective tenderness, laced with a heady wallop of triumph, that coursed through the bond among them made Dex himself shoot up, sheet pooling around his hips.

Gods and titans, he *felt* what Ben felt. Felt it so vividly he was all but shouting with that thundering swell of triumph—

"That's the lifebond," Ben murmured. "Guess our girl was right about having it happen for all four of us, wasn't she?" His sultry eyes found Dex, and a sweet smile curved his lips. "Hello, lifemate."

He was keenly aware it wasn't a particularly Imperatorial impulse. Nonetheless, without any warning whatsoever, Dex found himself a whisker away from crying.

Crying for sheer sterling joy.

"Hello, yourself," he rasped. "My gods, Ben."

"Holy helium." Zorin loomed suddenly behind him, one hand gripping Dex's shoulder to steady them both. "Is *that* what this is? The lifebond? It's like all three of you are living and breathing inside my skin. Like I'm living and breathing in yours."

That bridge of physical contact conveyed to Dex more clearly than a ten-terabyte opus the vast sheltering sense of protectiveness, immense and steady as a planet, that Zorin felt for all of them. Without looking away from the singular tableau before them, he reached up to cover Zorin's hand with his.

"Yeah, that's the lifebond." Ben's gaze shifted to his own light-limned hand, still spread across Kaia's abdomen. "And there's something more, isn't there, angel? Are you feeling this?"

"How could I not? It's going to be more than just the four of us sleeping in this bed for the next nine months," Kaia said softly. "Isn't it?"

Suddenly Dex's heart was slamming like Vulcan's divine hammer against his sternum. His mouth opened, but words eluded his scattered grasp.

Ben turned his head to nuzzle her belly. His face so tender and trusting Dex's eyes started stinging.

"Yeah, we're going to need more living space. Whether it's here, on Dex's floating fortress, at the starbase or wherever the hells we all end up." Ben bowed his reverent head against Kaia's tummy. "We'd better plan for three."

Zorin's hand clenched on his shoulder. A harsh sound tore from Dex's throat.

A sound suspiciously similar to a sob.

If he'd been the sobbing sort.

Since he *wasn't*, he settled for gripping his pirate's hand like the fate of the galaxy depended on it.

"Three *what?*" Zorin breathed.

"How perfectly, gloriously appropriate." Transcendent with triumph, Kaia's blissful face turned toward them. "Three babies."

Dex found himself on his knees, every synapse tingling as though he'd been struck by lightning. Ben and Kaia were kneeling too, wrapped tight in each other's arms. Kissing, crying, carrying on, at least one of them laughing like a loon.

With a wordless shout, Dex launched himself across the bed and damn near fell into their welcoming arms. His mouth found the sweet warmth of Kaia's tremulous lips.

Her face against his was wet with tears.

Ben's silken lips met his cheek. Dex's arm closed tight around his best friend to drag him close. Then Zorin's big body was folding over all of them, cradling them to the warm wall of his muscled chest.

"Do you know what this means?" Kaia demanded, low and fierce with resolve. "It means my father will have to allow our mating. He'll have to! I mean… won't he?"

"Oh, darling." Damnation, was he actually trembling? Like a leaf in a bloody windstorm? Could that possibly be that his own voice, soft and husky with awe? "*Three* of them?"

"Yeah," Ben said, muffled against Zorin's neck. "It's too soon for a clinical test. Too soon for medics. Too soon for anything. We're talking three zygotes—fertilized eggs—barely a few clicks old. But I can swear to it, as Precursor, for the Patriarch."

"Juno." Zorin sounded positively dumbfounded. His hand convulsed in Nero's hair. "How's that even possible?"

Ben raised his head with a wry smile. "Because I'm a bona fide professional, big guy. When it comes to siring offspring, I've had plenty of practice. I can always tell. And our girl is definitely pregnant."

Zorin's dazed eyes turned to Kaia. "Neptune's knickers, sweetheart. You don't waste time, do ya?"

Flushed with happiness, she lifted her face for the pirate's kiss. "Nope. It's a samurai thing."

With one arm wrapped securely around each of his Valyrian lovers and his Syndax cocooned protectively around all of them, Dex told himself firmly the question swelling to fill his skull didn't matter.

And he knew, truly, it didn't. Knew he'd love and cherish any child they were gifted.

Yet, somehow, the longing to *know* coiled his chest tight in an aching knot of need. A longing so desperate he could barely form the words.

"Are they… can you tell…?"

Blast. For the life of him, Dex found he couldn't finish.

But thanks to the lifebond, he didn't need to.

Ben's purple eyes met his in perfect understanding. Because he felt everything Dex felt. Gently his hand settled against Dex's cheek.

"I'm going to need psi-powered diagnostics from Valyria to say for sure. And, like I said, it's really too early to go poking around in there. Even telepathically. What our girl needs more than anything else right now is plenty of love and no disturbance. But…"

Faced with his lover's hesitation, but not yet skilled enough to decipher his every thought—particularly when his own head was an utter space wreck—Dex barely bit back a groan of frustration.

"But *what*? Ben, if you don't tell me…"

"But…" Ben's sculpted face went soft. "I'm pretty sure one of them—and *only* one of them—is biologically mine."

Damn it to hell, how did men survive this sort of thing? Dex himself could barely breathe.

"Take it easy, kid." Zorin's hands settled on his shoulders to knead out the knots. "We're all excited. Speaking for myself, I'm so goddamn excited and relieved and worried for our girl and those kids and all of us I feel like I'm gonna be sick."

Dex leaned into Zorin's solid strength and pressed his brow to Ben's. The exotic aroma of sandalwood filled his head, laced with the lush sweetness of Kaia's fragrance, the feral musk of Zorin's mating scent, and his own familiar spice. He breathed it in deep and felt the mingled essence of all four of them loosen the fist of nerves throttling his throat.

Especially when Ben cradled Dex's head between his hands and drew him close for a kiss. A kiss that tasted of Ben's dark sweetness and Kaia's passion. A sensory clue that told him precisely why Kaia was looking so languid and satisfied.

Take a breath, space cadet. I've got you.

"Right." Dex exhaled into his lover's kiss and let his tension ease a notch. "You said only one of them is… yours?"

"Yeah. They're triplets—but they're fraternal. And there's a future telepath in there. A really strong one." Ben's voice thickened with pride. "He's the one who's mine."

"He?" Dex's synapses sang with an effervescent thrill of elation. More potent than a slug of reactor-fermented whiskey.

We're going to have a son.

Damnation. He was losing his blooming mind.

Clearly sensing Dex's turmoil, Kaia sighed and snuggled into his arms. Her limbs wound around his waist and her lips nuzzled his neck. The soothing slide of her supple strength and silken skin stole through him and dissolved some of his clamoring tension.

"Three sons," she confirmed softly, pressing kisses along his jaw. "That's what I dreamed last night. A prophetic dream, I'm pretty sure. Like the one that told me I needed to mate all three of you."

Three sons.

THREE SONS!

A volcano of paternal pride—exultant, exuberant—erupted in Dex's heart until he thought his chest would explode. Silently he swore to every god in the Mogadon pantheon he'd love all three of their mighty, miraculous, magnificent sons. Love them all endlessly and equally.

Still, the primitive Mogadon rooted deep in his psyche—steeped in millennia of Mogadon myth—burned with the need to know he'd made his woman conceive.

And Ben—being Ben and his lifemate to boot—Ben knew it. Understood it.

"You want my guess? Our girl is part samurai, part telepath, part goddess." Ben stilled Kaia's started blurt of protest with a gentle hand over her lips. "We're all lying to ourselves if we say otherwise, aren't we?"

Firing with agitation, she bristled in Dex's arms. But she was carrying their sons—*his* sons—and he was nowhere near ready to let her go.

"For flip's sake, Ben! I am not a god—"

"Sweetheart," Zorin rumbled, cupping her rebellious chin in his palm. "Take a gander in the glass. Your eyes are like lamps and your skin's glowing so hot you're practically radioactive. You just survived a sideways jump through cyberspace on a half-programmed chip that woulda killed the rest of us ten times over, didn't ya?"

"Yeah, I barely survived being barbecued by electron backlash! But that was *Ben*."

"It wasn't only our boy that pulled you through," their pirate said patiently. "Here's the deal. And the four of us, we gotta face it head-on. You're not just a cyber samurai. Not just that rebel maharani who ran away to join the circus. You're changing, sweetheart. You're… evolving, I reckon… into something none of us have ever seen. Not even Gorgeous here."

Color racing into her face, Kaia gripped Dex's shoulders to brace herself against the entire concept. Which meant he could feel her hands shaking. Not with fear.

With rage.

"Great gods, Zorin! No—"

"Now hang on a tick." Their pirate reached for her, but she eluded his touch.

An evasion which, given the powerful bond Kaia shared with their Syndax lover, told Dex precisely how upset she was.

"I said *no*! Do you not realize I've spent my entire life fighting this harebrained premise that I'm some kind of deity? That it's my flipping destiny to be chained to a throne and worshipped? You'd better believe I'm going to keep fighting—"

"We know, darling." Dex stroked her slim back to soothe her. "No one's going to chain you to anything. Let's just listen to Ben for a bit."

Her eyes flashed with lightning. But, faced with his entreaty, she scraped in a shuddering breath and withdrew into stony silence. A silence burning with fiery defiance that emanated from every atom.

Dex could all but hear the furious flood of words bottled up behind her mutinous mouth that howled to be spoken.

"Yeah, you all need to hear this. Because that's exactly what I'm trying to say." Ben nodded at Zorin's watchful face. "That's why the Quorum banned hybrid matings. The only reason the Kryll Patriarch was able to mate a Valyrian telepath twenty-five years ago despite the interdict was because he's on the farking Quorum. An interdict that means no one really knows what a hybrid like Kaia can do. And I mean—no one. Are you following me?"

Kaia stayed stubbornly silent, but she vibrated with contained wrath. Dex eased her angry body closer and nodded for them both.

"Yeah, gorgeous, we follow." Zorin sighed. "But what's all this ancient history got to do with who fathered those kids? Now don't get me wrong, I'm gonna love all three no matter what—heck, I love the little tykes already. Probably spoil 'em all rotten. But I know what Dex is getting at. Cuz biologically—legally—if one of 'em's *his*? We got the next Mogadon Imperator in there, don't we?"

Dex grunted in surprise. Amid the various emotional exigencies of this remarkable moment, he'd actually managed to forget he was the Imperator. And that his civilian title, unlike the military rank he'd earned by killing his predecessor in formal combat, was a hereditary honor. It had only devolved to him when the last leader's line was extinguished.

Now, someday, it would pass to his son.

You might have forgotten, but I didn't, Kaia whispered in his head, her luminous lavender eyes lifting to his. *The moment you told us you're taking the title, I knew what it meant for any child of ours—son or daughter.*

Yet you're mating me anyway. He staggered under the sudden, overwhelming onslaught of everything he felt for this extraordinary woman—his desperate love for her and his fierce satisfaction that he'd persuaded her to love him back, his ferocious pride in presenting her to his people as his Imperatrix and laying the whole galaxy at her cyber-booted feet, his violent need to claim her and possess her and protect her from every enemy.

All of which shot straight to his cock, jutting tight and tingling against her belly. Her breasts pressed into his chest, so full and taut they were nearly pornographic, just begging to be suckled. Bloody hell, he wanted her. Wanted her breathless and moaning and riding his cock. Wanted her clinging to him and begging him to let her come.

Once more, quickly, before they faced her father.

Once more to stake his claim.

And the way her eyes widened and her breath quickened and her hands slipped around to cup his ass told him his woman just might be fully on board with that plan. Even when she was furious at her fate, she wanted him.

Except there was no bloody time to execute that particular plan, was there?

And there went his infernal wrist unit again.

Chiming.

"Don't answer that thing, Dex," Ben implored him. "Not till I answer your question, okay? The rest of the Empire can wait. Kaia loves all three of us. Don't you, angel?"

In her rigid frame, Dex felt the cutting edges of her rage soften.

"You know I do," she sighed, resting her cheek on Dex's shoulder. "Always."

The simple warmth of that affirmation seeped through Dex and tightened his arms around her. Great gods, he didn't think he'd ever get tired of hearing those words.

From all three of them.

Ben leaned in to press a tender kiss to her troubled brow. "Which means she wants all three of us to be happy. And I've already told you one of her offspring is mine. You want to know who sired the other two?"

"I do," Dex breathed. "If you please."

Zorin's hands landed on his waist to anchor him.

To anchor them both.

Ben's eyes shifted to Dex's worried face and softened in a smile. "Strap yourself in, space cadet. You think it's some random coincidence she's carrying three? I'm pretty sure our girl just gave us one of each."

CHAPTER TEN
The Bargain

The Kryll were worshipping her.

Worshipping her like a flipping *goddess*. The goddess she definitely wasn't. No matter what anyone said.

Ever.

And it was freaking Kaia way the flip out.

Fierce with resolve, hands cold, stomach churning, heart cartwheeling with nerves, she marched down the exit ramp from the Imperator's command shuttle—a mobile weapon of mass destruction that made Dex's stolen *Ascendant* look like a training toy. Down from the armored fortress of Dex Draven's imperial might.

Into the sun-scorched inferno of the paralyzingly vast, sickeningly familiar open-roofed stadium where fanatical millions flooded to worship the physical manifestation of the Ninety-Nine Gods.

Her estranged and wrathful father.

Behind her, beside her, around her, forming a lethal wall of armed and deadly muscle, marched Dex's phalanx of pardoned felons. His spanking-new security detail, entrusted with shielding her slender body and its precious cargo—her sons, their sons, the sons no one else knew about—from the worshipful masses.

But no force in the galaxy could shield her from what those masses were *doing*.

In every direction, racked and stacked in stadium tiers that curved toward heaven and blurred with distance, the faithful stood swaying in the blind ecstasy of faith. The fierce chant of Apocrypha psalms swelled from a million throats—a throbbing ocean of sound deep enough to drown in. Blind and burning with holy rapture, an endless sea of Kryll enclosed her, faces bronzed from the unrelenting heat of the desert world's twin suns.

Every one of them watching the pedestal on the stadium floor where the Patriarch's empty throne loomed like an apocalypse, bathed in a holocaust of blinding solar light.

I'm going to be sick. I'm going to run. I'm going to hide. Hide in the farthest corner of the galaxy I can find—

No one's bloody running anywhere. Dex's inner voice, low and ferocious with conviction, vibrated through the lifebond that bound the four of them together—even physically separated by the formalities of the ritual procession.

She heard him clearly from twenty cubits ahead where Dex strode before her, formal and formidable in his stark black uniform, every booted footfall measured and weighted with intent.

I'm not the cash-starved soldier with a war to bankroll your father hired seven days ago to be his Tombola lackey. I command enough nuclear firepower in orbit around this dust ball he calls home to obliterate his planet ten times over. If that bastard so much as frowns at you, darling, I'll blast his entire civilization back to the dark ages.

A promise of protection meant to comfort.

Even though he wouldn't. Wouldn't murder millions just for the visceral thrill of nuking her dad. That was the buried truth she'd finally unearthed about Dex Draven. His own stubborn, stiff-necked integrity—the steel spine of his own unbending honor—would keep them all safe.

Still, her Mogadon lover's determination to protect her only cranked the jangle of nervous energy clamoring in her skull to a shriller pitch. Apprehension hummed between her eardrums. Because she really wished that winning the future they wanted could be that easy.

But killing a god was never easy, was it? Not even when you were practically a god yourself.

She fixed her eyes on Dex's fearless back as he marched before her, sweeping across the sun-blasted earth. All around him, hovering wings of Sirocco shuttles disgorged torrents of Mogadon legions— encased in blast-resistant armor, armed with lethal stun rifles, trammeled into ruthless order by their stern-faced centurions. This sea of soldiers formed fighting columns in their commander's wake.

Until Dex Draven strode at the head of an army. Coldly contained in the midst of the militant might he commanded so easily. An impression he conveyed, she now knew, at wrenching personal cost.

The medics had only just removed the nanostitches he'd been wearing since that rogue centurion knifed him in a Tombola duel.

Stray spears of sunlight slid through the hovering fleet. Sunbeams flashed on the platinum epaulets that bridged his shoulders and lit his burnished hair with a halo of fire.

Her father's faithful ought to be worshipping *him*.

Master of the galaxy.

Her Tombola master.

Her declared lover.

Because the incendiary revelation that the Kryll maharani had been spending her nights in the First Indomitable's bed, more or less since the day he'd captured her, was now blazoned all over the interstellar news.

A power move on Dex's part.

One she hadn't been asked to bless.

But one she reluctantly appreciated. Primarily because she hoped the gambit would divert the Patriarch's dangerous attention from the fate of his youngest daughter. The daughter whose hormonally enhanced, spacepox-ravaged body was reportedly isolated under quarantine on a shelf in the morgue at Quorum Central Starbase. Where Kaia's intrepid kid sister had faked her own death.

In truth, the real Kylie was tucked away tight—and chafing for freedom—amid a horde of well-armed pirates on the *Relentless* in orbit.

One more flipping crisis out of maybe a million looming disasters that'll blow up in our faces if this whole crazy plan goes wrong.

As they toiled across the parched expanse, dust rising to cake her throat, Zorin's calm voice sounded in her head—perfectly audible from ten cubits back. Unmuted by the crowd's roar.

Take it easy, sweetheart. Nothing's gonna go wrong.

That voice steadied her like a supporting hand. Steadied her and surprised her. In fact, she was flat-out relieved to hear him projecting. Because she hadn't really been sure how well their pragmatic Syndax lover would handle this permanent immersion in what he called the mumbo-jumbo. The telepathic bond that tied them all together.

I'm handling it fine, sweetheart. You know I'd handle a heck of a lot more to be with the three of you. Gorgeous and me—we got your back. And we got Dex's too.

Her lips parted on a sigh. Even as her eyes sought out the vid screens affixed to the stadium bowl. Screens erected for the backbenchers' benefit to provide an up-close-and-personal of their god. Except now, with the Patriarch yet to appear, the screens were filled with the four of them.

Kaia and her future consorts.

As the presumptive favorite among her final suitors—at least until Dex claimed her officially himself—Zorin merited his own screen.

Savagery encased in starmetal, blaster holstered at his hip, flanked by the disreputable flotsam of his dreadlocked pirates, her Syndax lover led the final, thoroughly intimidated tranche of her would-be consorts toward her father's divine judgment. The big guy stayed a decorous distance back, moving easily with a wolf's loping grace despite the incinerating heat.

A distance prescribed by the Apocrypha between a maharani and her consort at the claiming ceremony. Until her claiming was blessed by the god.

Which brought her right back to her father.

Still formidable, damn it all to hell—this whole punking setup— even after a decade away. That grisly throne, hewn from the bones of a hundred human sacrifices. Men who'd hurled themselves willingly into the death ovens under the high priest's burning stare. Men who died screaming in the flames, embracing the purifying heat that blackened their bones. Dying for the honor of shielding the Patriarch's holy flesh from the unrelenting suns.

A fanaticism no less terrifying now than in her childhood. No less terrifying than that horrific throne.

Terrifying even when it stood empty.

Terrifying with the silent promise of a god's imminent presence.

Even beneath the massed menace of a wing of Mogadon fighters, still and sleek. The Zephyrs hovered in ominous silence, loaded with precision munitions, held in abeyance at Dex's command. A single word uttered in his wrist unit would launch them.

Enough to win a war.

So numerous they were legion. Blotting out the brassy sky.

But not even a nuclear-armed fighting force could blunt the sight and sound and feel of the Kryll congregation at worship. A tsunami of awe and devotion sucked at her cyber-booted feet like an undertow.

Beneath the unrelenting burn of the twin suns, under the silver silk of her cybersuit, Kaia was sweating.

On the vid screen above, perspiration glittered on her tawny skin. A larger-than-life broadcast of her transformation that only unsettled her more. Hair a lush mane of vibrant magenta, eyes enormous pools of ultraviolet fire, the tiny spark of the cyberport flashing like a star at her temple. The platinum torques of Valyrian psi tech—Ben's Tombola gift—glowed and pulsed around her wrists.

I've been wearing these things like jewelry for days, and they choose now to start pulsing like neutron stars?

Angels of Anaxos. Zorin's right. I don't even look human.

No wonder they were worshipping her. The psychic kick of all that adulation made her hair float and her skin tingle with a tangible charge. She had to fight to keep her feet anchored to the earth.

Directly ahead, a staircase soared to the viewing platform. A perch to display the Patriarch's divine offspring for the mindless adulation she'd always renounced. Dex was already climbing, deadly with purpose, booted feet confident on the steep stone. Climbing with the graceful prowl of a sand lion under his fleet's menacing shadow. His legions lined up in ranks at his feet.

Below him, Kaia too started climbing, uncomfortably exposed despite the cyber saber riding her shoulder and the utility belt circling her hips. All around, a sea of heads turned to track her.

Awe.

Adoration.

Worship.

Inside her, the lifebond vibrated. The psychic chord that bound the four of them together. Together with each other—and, through her, the blindly adoring masses.

Why didn't you tell me? Ben whispered in her head.

She didn't need to turn to feel him behind Zorin, both climbing behind her. As Dex's neutral second, Ben's job was guarding her back.

"Tell you what?" she whispered under the chug of chanting voices.

You know what.

She'd reached the viewing platform. Dex stood at its far edge with his back to her, hands clasped behind him. Calmly confronting the throne of bone rearing on its pedestal twenty cubits away.

He might appear calm as a monk at prayer, but his famous battle sense was tingling. Thanks to the lifebond, she felt the same electric charge.

Kaia burned to stand at his side. As his ally and his consort and his equal. But the farking ritual forbade that. And her father had always been a stickler for protocol.

It's all right, darling. It's his game, isn't it? We'll play by his rules.

For now.

Still reluctant, she nodded toward Dex's still frame and stationed herself the prescribed distance behind her Tombola master. Zorin lined up the wannabes at the rear and claimed his place in their midst. His sandy head and mailed shoulders loomed over all of them—a titan among mortals.

His Syndax horde spread out below the stairs in a net of casual menace. Securing their leader's escape. Or so they hoped.

Just in case.

One lithe scramble she sensed rather than saw brought Ben up the stairs to her side. Dark and deadly as a demon in his barbaric finery, midnight hair pouring under a torque of Valyrian silver. A mantle of jet-black down floated in an inky cloud around his tall frame.

His violet eyes met hers and warmed in a secret smile.

Why didn't you tell me he's a telepath? Ben whispered in her head.

Kaia stared blankly at their Mogadon lover, an emperor standing above the teeming human sea. "You mean *Dex*? That shouldn't be breaking news, stud pony."

"I mean your farking *father*, angel," Ben said dryly. "When we met him before, he was just a hologram. Now that he's here in the flesh? Gods and demons. Why didn't you tell me he's a telepath?"

"Easy answer." Kaia planted her hands on her hips. "Because he isn't!"

"Kaia." Ben sighed. "I don't know how, but your Kryllian father's one of the strongest natural telepaths I've ever encountered. I can't see him, but I can feel him. He's close. Watching us. And he's channeling all this energy. He's feeding on it. Gorging on it like a leech." A shudder rippled the mantle around his shoulders. "Why in the seven hells didn't you tell me?"

"Look, Ben." She sucked in her breath. *How do I make him get this?* "This… gorging… this thing he does? It's instinctive. That's why he's a god. Or thinks he is."

"He's a telepath," Ben said with utter certainty. "It's just that he doesn't know. He thinks what he's doing, channeling this fanatical devotion in his, what, congregation?—he thinks it's divine. But it isn't. It's genetic. It's part of his DNA. Just like it's part of yours."

Kaia sliced a guarded glance toward the waiting throne. Still empty. Her father always loved a showy entrance.

Her gut knotted in a fist. "Come on, Ben! If he's a telepath, my mom would've known."

"I'm guessing she did know. I'm guessing that's why she fell for him. Because telepaths don't typically fall for the headblind. They fall for other telepaths."

Agitation pulsed in her chest like a heartbeat. The psi-powered torques circling her wrists glowed and throbbed.

"She fell for him because it was prophesied she'd fall for him. That was her *gift*, Ben, for flip's sake! She knew they'd have children… that same crazy dream that I'd give birth to this mythical son…"

And so I will. Three of them. Including the next Imperator and probably the next Precursor too. Ben seems sure of it.

My mother's prophecy is coming true.

A swell of dread, laced with defiance, throttled the words in her throat. Frustrated, she shook her head, the heavy mane of hair shifting around her shoulders.

"It's okay, angel," he said softly. "You don't have to say anything. Not to me."

Her lifemate's fingers laced through hers. Which was a definite breach of protocol. But who was going to say no to Ben Nero?

The silent force of the lifebond surged between them.

And the psychic energy of her father's faithful, all channeled in his absence toward *her*, arced from her flesh to his like an electric current.

Ben's hair lifted from his shoulders and his mantle billowed in the psychic wind. His violet eyes flashed with silver fire. The Valyrian torque he wore like a crown—a focusing object only a Precursor could handle—pulsed with psychic force.

And the vid screens caught every flicker. Every erg of transformation as Ben Nero—the maharani's forbidden lifemate—became a living god.

The crowd's deep-throated chant swelled and surged. Scattered through the ranks, a few figures fluttered to the floor, swooning in holy rapture.

Hand still linked with hers, Ben pulled in a slow breath.

"Gods of Solaris," he whispered. "Do you realize that's the whole source of his power? He thinks he's a god, but he isn't! He's just an incredibly strong rogue telepath. His faithful fuel his power with their worship. Hells, with all this amperage running through him, there isn't a telepath alive who could even—"

The pregnant air trembled under the toll of a great bronze bell.

Under their feet, the earth shuddered.

That sustained tremor rippled and built to a crescendo until men and women fought to stay on their feet. Kaia bent her knees and widened her stance and watched Dex do the same as the platform heaved beneath them.

Beyond her lover's still silhouette, the Patriarch's throne vanished in a blazing wall of light.

She knew every flashy stunt in her father's bag of tricks. Knew the earthquake was mechanically triggered by machines beneath the foundations that had been a family secret for centuries. Knew the blinding blaze of light to be twelve hundred teravolts of Kryllian sunlight caught and focused by a hundred hidden mirrors to conceal the god's pedestrian entrance through a trapdoor behind the throne.

Because that was her father.

Half god.

Half charlatan.

All tyrant.

Dex's hand twitched a micron closer to his blaster—an instinct she felt him squelch with ruthless resolve. Knowing if he drew his weapon, he'd unleash the full lethal force of the entire Mogadon army. Then they wouldn't have a Tombola.

They'd have a bloodbath.

When their vision cleared and the blaze dimmed to a bearable light, the Patriarch commanded the throne of scorched and blackened bones. Flowing robes the color of dried blood spilled over his gaunt frame. A towering miter flaming with gold and hammered with sacred symbols submerged his long face in shadow.

But his eyes burned with embers of holy fire.

He's not a god, Ben whispered in her head. *He's a telepath. A renegade breed of telepath I never even knew existed.*

The stands rippled in a human wave. A million men and women sank to their knees in devotion. In her peripheral vision, the well-schooled wannabes did the same. Ben Nero, political animal that he was, folded gracefully to one knee and tugged her unwilling body down beside him. She unsheathed her saber and braced it point-down before her.

Because she was a samurai, not a slave. And she wasn't walking out of here in Tombola chains. She intended to make that point crystal farking clear.

Dex stayed on his feet.

With his legions massed below and his fleet massed above.

Maybe they were all gods after all. Or whatever passed for gods in their punked-up galaxy.

Kaia swayed with a surge of dizziness and Ben's arm slipped around her waist. Zorin's steady presence at her back—kneeling too, because kneeling cost him nothing—willed patience and caution into all of them.

"I bid thee welcome, Mogadon Imperator and Tombola master." The Patriarch's voice, electrically enhanced, echoed and boomed over the cowering crowd. *"Welcome to this, the Seat of My earthly Realm. Hast thou fulfilled thy sacred Charge?"*

Ritual words that reduced the Imperator of the Mogadon Empire to an errand boy. Kaia's fist clenched around her hilt.

But Dex stood undiminished at watchful ease, legs spread and head unbowed. A mic embedded in a hovering drone projected his crisp words to the horizon.

"My charge was to oversee your daughter's auction and bring you her future consort. So I've done," Dex said coolly. "As I'm certain you're aware, the maharani's made her choice. I'm claiming her myself."

After this morning's propaganda blitzkrieg, Dex's carnal intentions could hardly come as a shock. Still, the wannabes muttered unhappily and the Patriarch leaned forward in his bony throne. His words dripped with acid.

"If indeed 'tis so, thou wouldst forfeit thy fee. Thou wouldst execute this latest of thy genocidal wars against the Syndax in the far Omega Sector without the fabled Wealth of My Treasury at thy

disposal. Without succor or supply by My merchant Fleet. What of thy war, Imperator?"

"That war is over," Dex said coolly. "The Syndax Voortrekker and I signed an armistice this morning. That accord will be enshrined in a formal treaty when I take him as a consort."

The stadium concussed with seismic shock. Kaia felt the incendiary impact of those dual revelations—a peace treaty and a male consort—reverberate through his armed and deadly legions.

Over the mutter and shift of an army of thunderstruck Mogadon, the Syndax horde gave voice to a shout of triumph. For pirates who lived outside the law, a male consort was nothing shocking.

Kaia was bemused to realize his entire horde thought Zorin was marrying up.

"I don't come to you empty-handed. Far from it," Dex noted calmly. Just as though his own men weren't poised at the brink of insurrection at his feet. Only the vaunted discipline instilled in the Mogadon legions—that and Dex's formidable, Indomitable reputation—held them barely in check. What Dex said and did in the next few moments would be critical.

"What couldst thou possibly offer," her father sneered, *"to justify this... sacrilegious Outrage? Thou didst VIOLATE—"*

"You received my bid by satellite." Dex's voice rang with an assurance Kaia knew he was fathoms away from feeling. "No other candidate can match me and you bloody well know it. You'll net a Mogadon alliance from the deal. A permanent alliance with the galaxy's dominant military power to protect Kryll caravans and Kryll markets from the ravening Swarm."

"And that's not all you're getting." Zorin ambled up to take his place at Kaia's side. An audio drone zipped to hover attentively above his head. His steely voice sliced through the restive ranks. "My boys and me, we're going hunting. Hunting for Swarm cannibals. Every one of the toothy bastards we bag is one less threat to your moneybags, Pops. That's me upping my bid right there. And you're gonna be pretty damn loaded with half the proceeds from the galactic patent on my transcription chip, ain'tcha?"

On her other side, Ben Nero flowed smoothly to his feet, hair and garments floating around his slim frame. His coronet burned with platinum fire.

"Speaking for myself, Your Holiness." The Precursor swept a formal bow. "I'm authorized by the Senate of Psychics to conclude a new trade accord with Kryll for Valyria. I'm prepared to offer preferred partner trading status and tariff-free access to Valyrian furs and metals for the next ten years. Starting the day I too mate the maharani."

In his throne, the Patriarch went rigid. His burning gaze veered to Kaia and transfixed her like a volley of flaming arrows. *"You're taking all three of them?"*

And only his momentary lapse from the honorific *thou* told her they'd finally succeeded in startling him.

Emboldened by this reminder that her formidable father could be surprised—god or telepath or whatever the hells he was—Kaia shot to her feet.

"Too flipping right I am! It's the four of us. It's the Mogadon Imperator and the Valyrian Precursor and the Syndax Voortrekker and me. They're all the ones I've chosen. And don't even pretend that's not the best Tombola deal any Kryll maharani in history's ever landed."

The Patriarch's eyes turned black with rage.

"Thou dost dare to ask My blessing for this BLASPHEMY—"

"We're not asking for your blessing." Dangerous heat surged into Kaia's cheeks, and electric anger zipped down her spine. Because she'd been spoiling for this showdown for a lifetime. "We're telling you how it's gonna be. I'm not poor sweet Kira, blindly obedient to your every tyrannical whim. Obedient until it killed her! You as good as fired that torpedo yourself, you farking bastard—"

"Take it easy, sweetheart," Zorin breathed, one hand settling on her shoulder. "You're throwing a lot at him. Give the old coot a tick to think all this through."

Unfortunately, that frisson of physical contact between a maharani and her would-be consort proved one outrage too many for her already fuming father.

"Insolence!" One skeletal arm swept up to rivet them, russet sleeve spilling from his wrist like blood. *"This infamous Heresy willst—not—stand. Thou. Shalt. Be. PUNISHED!"*

Kaia never knew whether his gesture triggered a hidden door in his dais or a flamethrower secreted up his sleeve. Because both were party tricks he'd pulled in the past. She only knew a deadly geyser of crimson fire was arcing and boiling toward them across the narrow abyss.

With barely a breath to save himself, Dex dove to one side.

But the bare platform—by design—offered no place to hide from divine vengeance.

As the firestorm raged toward them, Kaia acted on a high-octane flash of primal instinct. She shouted and seized Ben's hand. A potent current of raw energy from the worshipful masses surged through her flesh into the Precursor's lethal body. His hair and garments lashed in a cyclone of psychic wind.

Then torrents of blinding ultraviolet light poured from his eyes.

She'd never seen Ben Nero do anything like that. Because even he—a manual telepath who forged and shaped psi fire with his hands—hadn't known anyone could channel energy *that* way. Now fountains of psi fire shot from his eyes to meet the Patriarch's crimson firestorm. White light spread to form a curving shield three cubits before Dex's sprinting body.

Which gave their Mogadon lover the instant he needed to leap clear of the deadly flames. Zorin dragged Kaia from harm's way, hauling Ben's storm-tossed form with her. Behind them the wannabes scattered in screaming panic, some bolting for the stairs, others cowering on the floor.

Stoked by the binary fuel of flammable chemicals and her father's untrammeled rage, the inferno boiled and surged against Ben's psychic forcefield. A force fed and strengthened by the raw devotion of the hysterical millions Kaia kept channeling into her lifemate through their clasped hands. Around them, men and women swayed and dropped, overcome by exhaustion and rapture. The crowd's roar mounted to a howl.

Before their ecstatic eyes, the gods were at war.

Below, the battle-ready Mogadon legions pivoted to form a defensive square, stun rifles swinging toward the screaming mob.

"Hold!" Dex barked into his wrist unit, hand extended, blaster still miraculously holstered at his hip. "Every man jack of you, *hold.*"

And, gods of her father, he held them.

By the sheer force of his will, he held them.

The fountain of crimson fire dwindled and sparked and sputtered into darkness. Ben's hand slipped from hers. With the physical bond between them broken, his gaze darkened and the wind died. A breath later, the forcefield dissolved in a drizzle of violet sparks.

Shaking and spent, world spinning around her, Kaia fought for breath.

Control.

Clarity.

Ben just used power he didn't even know he had. He's a manual telepath—and he didn't even use his hands. What in the ninth impossible realm just happened?

With deliberate control, Dex uncoiled to his full height. His atomic eyes raked the platform, finding Kaia crouched with bracelets pulsing and saber slanted before her, Zorin looming fierce and protective at her back, Ben standing pale and deadly, coronet still flaming at his brow.

All of them, astoundingly, still alive.

And none of them certain how.

Dex's head swiveled slowly to find the Patriarch, rigid in his throne and quivering with wrath. A god's endless malice—an untrained telepath's lethal rage, fueled by his fanatical faithful—beat out at them and battered them.

"Careful, old man," Dex breathed, in a murmur that reached every corner of the silent stadium. "Don't try my patience any further. Don't threaten what I'll kill to protect."

"Thy lovers?" Her father's spite lashed out at them. *"Including My heretic WHORE of a daughter?"*

"She's carrying your heirs and grandchildren," Dex said in a voice like chromium. "All bloody three of them."

The riveted masses swayed in a ripple of recognition. Because every Kryll believer on the planet knew precisely what that revelation meant. If the maharani was with child, it meant the gods had blessed their union. Consecrated their mating.

From a spiritual perspective, the deed was done.

From a political perspective, this business was anything but.

Still coiled in his throne, the Patriarch trembled with thwarted violence. Over the edge of her blade, Kaia glared straight into her father's vengeful face and silently dared him to deny her.

Silence stretched between them. The silence of a galaxy perched breathless on the brink of war.

Her father's face convulsed.

"Come thou to Me." His voice scraped through the congealed

silence. *"Just thee, without thine army of militant minions. Then shalt we five... converse."*

At Kaia's feet, a hatch slid open. A staircase plunged into a yawn of ominous darkness. Slowly she lowered her blade, lungs tight with sudden nerves, chest suddenly too small to contain her hammering heart.

"Jumpin' Jupiter," Zorin breathed in her ear. "That circus trick sure got the old coot's attention. Guess we're in the front door now, ain't we?"

#

In the heart of his private sanctuary, buried deep as a grave under the stadium floor, the Patriarch was waiting. Standing with his back to them between two smoking torches under the dome before the altar where his ancestors sacrificed sobbing children and screaming lovers to the Ninety-Nine Gods.

Her childhood god.

Her supreme nemesis.

Waiting.

Waiting with the living embodiment of her deepest, darkest nightmare. Two of his harem slaves, faces blank with opium haze, bodies ripe and soft with pampered captivity. Wearing nothing but dangling jewels that pulled at their pierced nipples.

Curled in chains at her father's feet.

Kaia shuddered under the impact of that silent threat—the monstrous threat that had hovered over her head all her life like an anvil of doom. The threat of a Kryll maharani's destined fate.

The fate her father still threatened.

Sweating in the smothering heat, she felt that threat now like a body blow. Her step faltered and her gut turned to lead.

But Zorin was right behind her, big hand steady against her spine, urging her gently forward. The bulwark of his solid strength settled around her like a fortress.

The stalwart shield of her men, the intimate link that bound them together, the certain knowledge she wasn't alone anymore in this desperate struggle, propelled her into the cave after Dex's resolute frame. Their footfalls echoed from the rough-hewn walls—a sandstone canvas painted by primitive hands in sweeps of black and crimson, swirling with human sacrifice and other atrocities.

Half a Mogadon mile overhead, the distant roar of a million faithful throats screamed devotion.

Silent and deadly as a panther, Ben prowled through the narthex and brought up the rear of their wary parade. She sensed his psychic hatches battened tight in the presence of a hostile telepath. Still, his mental whisper slid through her senses.

He doesn't know he's a telepath, angel. And it's absolutely crucial he never learns. Because if he ever did? He wouldn't need to bamboozle the credulous masses with parlor tricks. He'd know what he could really do.

Shivering, she veiled her gaze and watched the rugged stone slip past beneath her boots. As if hiding her eyes could hide her thoughts. *You mean forge all that raw power into psi fire and wield it like a Precursor? The way you just did?*

She sensed rather than saw Ben's guarded nod. *The way* we *just did, samurai. I always sensed you were a stronger telepath than anyone ever believed. Hybrid or no hybrid, you inherited the same power—the difference being, you know it.*

Maybe I know it now. She chuffed out a dubious breath. *Even though I still barely believe it.*

You'd better believe this, Kaia. With billions of his faithful to feed on, he'd be stronger than any Precursor in history. Possibly including the current incumbent.

Guess that's one more secret for us to keep. A soul-deep shiver rattled her bones. *Along with, uh, Junior.*

Because she couldn't risk even thinking her sister's name. Not here in the beating heart of her father's power.

The stink of torches sizzling with human fat clotted rank and foul in her lungs. The familiar reek of blood and suffering made her stomach heave.

But she couldn't be sick now. They'd reached the heart of the sanctum.

Dex stood below the altar on its ledge of stone and bristled with deadly vigilance. Torchlight flamed in his burnished hair and flashed on his platinum epaulets. One boot planted on the ledge in a display of casual dominance. His hand never far from the blaster holstered at his hip. His wrist unit blinked in silent alarm.

A voiceless alert that he'd lost the comm link with his imperial army, buried under half a mile of Kryllian rock. The lifebond between them stretched tight with his caution.

Marking Kaia's soft tread coming up behind—or maybe just sensing her nearness—his hand lifted in subtle warning.

Still determined to protect her to the death, Dex was the quintessential Mogadon male. A wry smile curved her lips.

Lucky for him she was a Prime Class samurai. Not only his lover, but also his ally. Stubbornly Kaia took her place at his side. Where she belonged. Feet spread wide, saber riding her shoulder, hands braced on hips.

Ben slipped up alongside, hair and mantle drifting around his slim frame in eddies of psychic current. His gloves were tucked through his belt and sparks danced at his fingertips. His eyes pulsed with heliotrope fire.

Quiet and watchful, Zorin loomed like a mountain at her back. Big enough and strong enough and brutal enough to snap a man's neck with his bare hands. The way he'd done to win her in his Tombola duel. Kaia ached for the moment she could drop her guard and feel the bulwark of those powerful arms wrapped around her. Around all of them. The way they were this morning.

But the four of them stood far from safety now.

The Patriarch's voice, low and sibilant without electronic amplification, coiled through the cave. Venomous as a viper, even when he refused to face her.

The daughter who'd rejected him.

The daughter who'd humiliated him.

The daughter who'd defied him.

"You've come into your power. Your divine power as a god and a child of gods. That's how you survived my vengeance. Haven't you, girl? You came into your power when you conceived."

Her heart clenched in a spasm of grief. Before today, her father hadn't addressed her without the distant honorific *thou* since her childhood. Since way before she went off to the Psi Academy on Hegemon and slunk home stinging from Ben's betrayal, disgraced and devastated but utterly determined to defy her fate. A thoroughly unsatisfying daughter, as her father had flatly informed her. A child who'd grown up to be worthless.

A sexually awakened rebel her father could no longer control.

Composed as a guest at a dinner party while these dangerous currents swirled around them, Ben swept the Patriarch an elegant bow. "Rest assured I can swear to her condition, Your Holiness. In my professional judgment, she's carrying a son from each of us."

"Like a litter of kittens!" her father sneered. "Like a cat in heat."

Kaia bristled with resentment, one protective hand curling over her belly.

Ben slid her a lambent gaze that begged her to be patient. "As the Precursor, I can attest—"

"Save your breath." The Patriarch's red robes rippled in a sigh. Slowly, heavily, he turned to face her. "You look like your mother did when she was with child."

Kaia stared into the familiar contours of her father's face, worn with age and blasted with grief.

Because, she realized with a jolt, he was actually grieving the daughters he'd lost.

Kira the dutiful—his pet, his heir, his pampered favorite—who'd died doing her duty. And Kylie the baby, who'd supposedly died stricken with spacepox on Quorum. Both of them dead for obeying him. Leaving him grimly dependent on Kaia—this least satisfying and most troublesome of all his seed—to propagate his sacred bloodline.

And he might not be a consciously practicing telepath, but on this singular occasion she found she could read his mind.

If I had to lose a daughter, why couldn't it have been you?

Her heart shriveled under the lash of that cutting rejection. Her eyes blurred and burned with tears.

Damn the man. She wasn't going to apologize for surviving. She'd fought way too farking hard all these years to survive.

Faced with her stubborn silence, her father's brow contracted. Gently he lifted the heavy miter from his head and placed it on the altar. One hand drifted down to caress the perfumed hair of the slave chained at his feet. The girl's empty eyes, filmed with opium, stared at Kaia.

Her father's free hand knotted in a fist. His teeth bared in a rictus of dislike bitter as vinegar. But the words scraped from his throat with control harsh as bedrock.

"I'll permit this execrable mating."

The concession was so unexpected, the words so fundamentally at odds with the venom they were drenched with, that she couldn't grasp the gist. It took the hiss of Zorin's indrawn breath, the frisson of Dex's sudden vigilance, to penetrate the buzz of tension in her brain.

When it did, a lightning bolt of violent elation zinged through her. Leaving her entire body electrified. "You *will*—?"

Her father's hand flashed up. The words choked in her throat.

"Don't mistake me," he hissed, rancid with malice. His slaves trembled in terror at his feet. "This preposterous notion of mating your Tombola master and his neutral second and this—this interstellar menace who's twice your age—is a blasphemous travesty of a sacred ritual. But I'll permit it." His face hardened to stone. "I'll permit you to befoul this holy rite on two conditions."

Kaia tasted fear, sour as citrus on her tongue. Her elation vanished as swiftly as it had surged.

Steel yourself, samurai. You're not going to like this.

Deadly as a sand lion, Dex sprang to the ledge, which put him level with his adversary. An invasion that profaned the hallowed ground. An act of blasphemy, sundered from his army and buried under tons of Kryllian rock, that represented a breathtaking risk.

The Patriarch quivered with contained wrath.

"I dare say that's a prudent choice." Dex's clipped comment, delivered with laser precision, would have shriveled a lesser man. "To say nothing of being the only choice that will persuade me to refrain from bombing you and your entire barbarous civilization to stardust."

"Believe that if you like," her father jeered.

By the Ninety-Nine Gods, does he know? Know Dex lost his comms?

Did he lure us down here under half a mile of Kryllian rock to make sure of it?

Dex stood perfectly contained in dangerous stillness. In unfaltering command of the crisis and the galaxy, he projected an Imperator's unquestioned authority. Comms or no comms.

If her arrogant father had any native sense of self-preservation whatsoever, his skin would be crawling.

"For the moment, I've chosen not to put this fleeting détente between us to the test," Dex said quietly. "I trust you'll bear my remarkable restraint in mind when you name your conditions."

"Here's the first." Her father's malevolent gaze slewed toward

Kaia. "And it's nonnegotiable. As the prime maharani and my sole legitimate heir, the last living seed of my gods-blessed mating, you—Kaia of Kryll—will inscribe your name beside mine in the sacred Apocrypha. Take your place in the pantheon with the Ninety-Nine Gods. Embrace your birthright and your destiny."

The icy dash of shock slammed through her. Kaia gasped and staggered, hand falling from Ben's, legs going numb. Zorin's big hands gripped her waist to brace her.

"Steady, sweetheart. I got you," he rumbled in her ear. "He's just a sick old man. And he's heartsick. Humor him a tick while we hash through this—"

"Humor him?" The words burst from her throat as if propelled from a solar cannon. "By letting his minions fall down and worship me like a god? That's not my destiny! Angels and demons, it was *never* my destiny."

"Be thankful I don't require you to endure your godhood in chains," the Patriarch spat out, poisonous with spite. "As a strict interpretation of the sacred text clearly requires. Do you want your precious mating? Or shall I declare a kill edict against your blasphemous Tombola master?"

Zorin's hands tightened on her waist. A subterranean growl vibrated through his chest. The air thickened with the predatory musk of Mogadon aggression. Her father's threat against Dex was bringing out the beast that lurked in every Mogadon—Zorin's ferocious compulsion to protect.

If their pirate lost his famously even-tempered head and gave in to those brutal instincts every Mogadon possessed, they were punked. And Kaia knew her own surging agitation was flinging fuel on the fire.

At her side, Ben gripped her hand, eyes intent on her desperate face.

Be reasonable, angel, he whispered. *We're one word away from a planet-wide bloodbath up there. With a kill edict to follow by sunset. Even if Dex wins his battle today—gods, even if he kills your father, he'll never sleep safe again.*

Her tortured eyes swung from the slaves in chains at her father's feet to Dex's glacial gaze, burning icy and incandescent with resolve. Silently urging her to react with her clever samurai head rather than her wayward rebel heart. Promising he'd stand with her—that they all would—whatever her choice.

Suck it up, samurai. Kaia swallowed down the acid taste of bile, cocked a defiant hip, and faced down her childhood demon.

"Fine," she fired back, detesting every syllable. "Or rather—it's not fine at all. It's the farthest thing from fine I can possibly imagine. But, contrary to popular opinion, I can be reasonable. I'll go through the motions—for my lifemates' sakes. To prevent a flipping war. What else?"

Satisfaction invaded her father's ruthless face. He abandoned his terrified slaves and glided toward her.

In her ear, Zorin growled a warning that turned her blood to ice.

"Careful, old man," Dex breathed. "I tolerated your earlier assault against me and mine, but I won't tolerate another. You live only by my sufferance."

The Patriarch's teeth gleamed in a thin smile. "Ever tried killing a god, Imperator?"

Dex ruled the galaxy with an iron fist, but her godlike father never so much as looked at him. Instead, his eyes locked on hers—pools of dark matter, black holes in space, ravenous and remorseless as revenge.

She shivered under his stare.

Did he truly hate her that much?

"My antipathy toward you exists in direct proportion to the… affinity I once felt," her father whispered. Because of course he'd never utter the word *love*. His voice swelled in resonance like an exploding star. "Now hear my second condition. I'll have my sole remaining daughter fill my seat and cast my vote on the Quorum of Four."

Kaia's blood congealed to tar. She sucked in a horrified breath and felt her face freeze with shock.

"You'll represent Kryll on the Quorum, daughter—and fight to the last erg of that defiant, headstrong, unquenchable spirit. You'll fight to the death for Kryllian values—for balance, neutrality, commerce, peace—and *you'll fight to the death for mine*."

None of what her father was saying made any sense. Not when the walls of her chest were collapsing.

"Me? B-but you're the Quorum vote for Kryll. You hold that seat yourself."

"Correction," he snapped. "I *was* the Quorum vote. I've held that seat for the past forty-two years. By claiming the other seats, your *consorts* have effectively neutralized my vote. I can't overcome a three-way block in council. But they'll work considerably harder and more resourcefully to accommodate Kryll—to compromise—when it's you facing them across the Quorum chamber. Won't they?"

Kaia could only gape, appalled at the very notion. All the gods knew she wanted nothing to do with her father and his twisted values, his perverse notion of neutrality and Kryll's role in the galaxy. Nothing to do with being chained to his Quorum seat.

Dex angled his advance to intercept her father, steps measured, head bowed, brow furrowed in thought.

"A rather ingenious solution to your political dilemma, isn't it?" Dex murmured. "But that solution would require trusting your runaway daughter. You'll pardon me for noting that commodity between the two of you appears to be in exceedingly short supply."

Her father snorted in disdain, but his deliberate approach never faltered. "That's why she'll swear to it. Knowing if she violates her oath, I'll withdraw my blessing for your union. And issue the edict for your life."

A lethal stillness invaded Dex's vigilant frame. His tone smoothed to a sinister rumble. "Any day you decide you'd like to kill me, old man, you're more than welcome to try."

Ominously silent at her back, Zorin was about a nanosecond away from lunging for her father's throat. She prayed, for all their sakes, her father wasn't planning to try something stupid.

And she wondered if the old nightmare still had that flamethrower secreted up his sleeve.

"Look, forget about the farking edict, okay?" She leaned into Zorin's tense frame, eased his arm around her waist, and laced her fingers through his. Call her clueless, but Kaia still couldn't seem to wrap her head around her father's insane impulse. "You want *me* casting votes on the Quorum?"

The Patriarch's head snapped toward her.

"Not for the imperial tyranny of the Mogadon Empire nor the dangerous anarchy of the Syndax horde nor even the noble but dying Valyrian race. You'll cast your vote for Kryll and for virtue!" His voice echoed with divine thunder. "Even if it means standing against your own consorts. You'll do their bidding eagerly enough, no doubt, in your private lives—in the confines of your scandalous bed. But when you occupy that Quorum seat in the public eye, you're *mine*. You'll preserve the sacred balance in the galaxy. You'll perform your holy duty or die doing it. As I have done before you."

So it's no mistake. That's really what he's asking.
What he's actually demanding.

Her head rang with denial. She'd never wanted a political life any more than she wanted a religious one. She was like Zorin and his Syndax, a lawless rebel, a fugitive who gloried in living without rules, surviving by her skill and her samurai wits, flying by the seat of her cybersuit and loving it.

Except that she wasn't.

Not anymore.

She'd given that up forever when she agreed to be Dex's Imperatrix. She'd given it up for love. For the love of all three of her extraordinary men.

The men she could now claim as consorts.

If—and only if—she acquiesced to the Patriarch's demands.

She fought to smother the clamor of unruly emotions roaring through her skull. Fought to muster the logical arguments he'd heed.

Still, her voice slipped out in a whisper.

"I wouldn't be much of a Quorum rep for Kryll or anyone else. I'm not trained for it. I have zero relevant experience." Her hands spread in helpless entreaty. "Angels and asteroids, look at me! All the gods know I'm no politician and I'm definitely no bureaucrat."

Dex intercepted her father a breath before he reached her. Three cubits away, the Patriarch halted. Closer than they'd stood in a decade.

With the light throwing his haggard features into shadow, he was an old man. A tired man. A man steeling himself to stomach a political alliance with the daughter he despised.

Because despite his chicanery and his ruthlessness and his flaws, he believed to the marrow of his bones in the virtue of neutrality the Patriarchs of Kryll had always preached.

"I won't be any good at it," she repeated, faced with his silence, breathing in futility with every inhale. "You *know* I'd make a godawful mess. You know it!"

Her father spared her a dour smile. "You may be willful, but you're able enough. You'll set yourself to it, with me to tutor you. With your consorts here to counsel you in private—even when you oppose them in public. You'll be the living embodiment of neutrality in the galaxy, as I have been. Until your heirs grow to maturity and the pirate's son takes my place."

She fought to absorb the blast wave of this latest bombshell.

Dex's son will be Imperator. Ben's will be Precursor. Which leaves—what? My child with Zorin—my Syndax son—to be the next Patriarch?

Zorin's hands clenched on her waist as the revelation slingshot between them.

"You want a Syndax kid sitting on that ugly throne?" her pirate breathed, sounding as dumbfounded as she'd ever heard him. "You telling me you think my kid's gonna be worshipped like some kinda god? Neptune's knickers."

The Patriarch shot him an irate frown. "If you oppose it, pirate, she'll never agree."

"Yeah, well, it's gonna be *his* choice to make, ain't it?" Zorin muttered, a flicker of his trademark practicality resurfacing now that her idiot father had finally stopped threatening Dex. "Look. If that's what the little tyke wants when the time comes, I won't stand in his way, okay? Hope that's enough for you, Pops. Cuz that's all I got."

Her Syndax still sounded and felt bemused.

But not entirely resistant.

Nope. Resisting her father's formidable will was Kaia's lot in life. Same as always.

My Syndax son to be Patriarch? My son to embrace the chains I fled?

Resistance knotted her shoulders and clenched her fists. She stiffened against the repudiation she burned to shout.

And watched her father's tired face transmogrify to steel. "Swear to it, daughter. Swear to it by the blood of these men you claim to love—and I'll call off the kill edict. Instead I'll proclaim my blessing for your profane and godless union."

Her belly churned with futile rage. Which was just so punking pointless. If she wanted to sashay out of there with three consorts and no bloodshed, she needed to give him his pound of flesh. Besides, he might have her cornered—but she wasn't out of the game.

Not even close.

Hells, with her ass sitting in a Quorum seat, she'd never be out of the game again.

She angled her chin and planted a hand on her hip.

"Sure, you'll give me your blessing now. Now when I'd given up ever getting it. You'll give me your blessing so I'll give you the thing you want most. My submission."

His face flared with silent satisfaction. But he knew her well enough not to exult in her defeat.

At least not openly.

Her attention shifted to Dex, standing poised and wary at his shoulder, gaze grave and steady on her struggling face.

Give me a sign here, space cadet. What do you want me to do?

"This is your choice to make, darling," he told her tenderly. "It's always been yours. You know we'll defend you—all three of us, with all three of our armies. Whichever path you choose, we're yours. Now and always."

Immersed in the tide of love that flowed between them, her raging heart softened and her fists unclenched.

"I know that. I'll always know that. Believe me, it's the only thing that gives me the guts to say what I need to right now." She pulled in a bracing breath. "Which is *yes*."

Her father's eyes ignited with jubilation.

Ferocious with resolve, she scowled at him. "Comets and meteors! If you're fool enough to want a circus acrobat casting your vote on the Quorum, it's your funeral. I'll swear to give you what you want. And in exchange, you'll swear to give me *this*. All three of them with your blessing, and no chains and no nudity at the mating ritual. Plus Zorin's son gets to choose his fate when he's old enough. Do we have a deal?"

Narrowly he searched her face for deceit while the silence stretched and a hush descended. Except for the muffled roar of her father's faithful, still waiting to celebrate a mating—or execute a kill edict. Dex stood tautly alert, close enough to snap her father's spine… or try to… if he proved treacherous. Ben hovered barely breathing at her side, careful not to press. But he'd been her lifemate way too long for her not to know he wanted this. Zorin loomed behind, big hands circling her waist, thumbs kneading gently into the tense column of muscle along her spine. Willing her to wisdom and compromise.

They wanted this. All three of her men. Which made her realize how much she wanted it herself.

"I'll swear to those terms." Her father's head dipped in a measured nod. "Three consorts, no chains, no public viewing. And for your son… a *choice*. The choice none of us in the sacred bloodline have ever had."

Her breath rushed out in an explosion of relief.

Tempered by resignation.

"So tell us," the Patriarch breathed. "Here on this sacred soil, formally, with the gods to witness. Do we consummate a Tombola… or an execution?"

She rolled her eyes but managed to master her temper. Because she'd be needing to do a lot of that with the future she'd just agreed to. "You heard me the first time. You really need to hear me say it twice?"

She felt Zorin's soft exhale against her crown and finally, finally let herself dissolve into his solid strength. The way she'd been aching to do all day.

Her skin drank in the monumental impact of all that Syndax muscle, sleekly encased in gleaming starmetal. Different than feeling him naked in her arms—more dangerous, more destructive, and in a certain way more devastating.

Which really made her wonder if she could entice him to get horizontal sometime soon while he was wearing it.

One trick at a time, sweetheart. His amused rumble sounded in her head. *Sort of a captor-captive kinda kink, ain't it? But yeah, if that's gonna get you off, we'll give it a go-round. All four of us.*

"Considering our personal history," her father said dryly, so dryly she had to wonder again whether he wasn't reading all their thoughts, "I intend to ensure you won't change your mind… samurai."

Angels and asteroids. It was the first time he'd ever acknowledged her professional credentials—as in, *ever*—or any identity for a daughter of his other than Tombola bride and dutiful vassal. Which really made her wonder if this wildly insane impulse of teaching her to do what he'd done for Kryll on the Quorum might—just possibly— work.

An unlikely trickle of optimism bubbled through her blood. A flicker of optimism they all shared, she and her men, through the lifebond. Sensing her acceptance, Dex's face fired with the fierce blaze of victory.

While Ben, who'd already known what she'd say before she did, was barely fighting off the powerful urge to sweep her into his arms and claim a jubilant kiss.

Father or no father, Kaia gave in, one breath at a time, to a grin of triumph.

They'd just flipping done it… hadn't they? Averted a bloodbath, ended a war, and secured her father's blessing for their unconventional union.

Even if her overdeveloped caution habit made it hard to believe they were finally safe.

"Go ahead and believe it, angel," Ben murmured, loud enough so all of them could hear. "He's negotiating in good faith."

Which made the whole hoopla one hundred percent real. Because no one in the galaxy could lie to Ben Nero.

A small hiccup slipped out of her. A hiccup that sounded suspiciously like a sob. Gulping hard to hold it in, she tightened her hold on Ben's hand and reached for Dex's strong grip. Happiness hummed through the four of them like an electric current.

"A mating it is," she said, husky with suppressed excitement. "Let's go out there right now and do this thing. Before Dex's army drops from heat exhaustion. And before Zorin's Syndax start a riot."

CHAPTER ELEVEN
The Beginning

"Hey, Precursor! Aren't you going to kiss the bride?"

Under the sustained roar of a million rapturous Kryll and the raucous clamor of Zorin's Syndax playing some sort of drinking game with Dex's off-duty troops, the eager question barely reached Ben's ears. Predictably, the demand was coming from the mosh pit of desperate paparazzi jostling for the best camera angle below the boarding ramp to the Imperator's shuttle.

On the ramp beside him, breathless and disheveled from the general revelry that apparently crowned a Tombola ritual, Kaia turned toward him with a smile.

And Ben Nero, who'd never really shared the Mogadon kink for public intimacy—even after bolting more shots of Kryllian firewater over the past few clicks than could possibly be good for his besieged liver—found himself grinning back at his lifemate like an infatuated schoolboy.

Kaia might not have relished signing her name on the dotted line in the Apocrypha roster of Kryllian deities. But, for all their sakes, she'd done it.

And damn his soul if she wasn't one.

She certainly looked the part—skin rosy with excitement, eyes silver with triumph, burgundy hair tumbled down her back and cybersuit half unzipped down her front.

It was the easiest thing in the world to pull her into his arms and bend to claim the lush warmth of her mouth.

Especially when she sighed happily and melted into him, slim arms winding around his neck, sleek curves fitting into his hands and tucking against his chest like she'd been made to fit nowhere else. The quicksilver slide of her tongue spiked his senses. The potent kick of her taste infused his mouth. And the exotic tang of her fragrance, thoroughly laced with the predatory musk of both their Mogadon, short-circuited his synapses.

Flashes exploded against his closed lids. Their staccato blaze mingled with the dazzling display of fireworks that bloomed and burned and flared and faded in the twilight sky.

The well-liquored crowd roared with approval. Buoyed by that psychic rush—the electric current of energy that leaped between them—and still elated by the novelty of Kaia's sweetly clinging submission after the wintry decade of his despair, Ben himself felt damn near delirious.

I've never been happier than I am right now, he told all of them through the lifebond.

"Right back atcha, gorgeous," Zorin rumbled in his ear, one arm wrapping around his waist. "Let's all get on board this glorified terror taxi before somebody falls off the ramp."

Reluctantly Ben ended the kiss and gazed around the bedlam that reigned in the Patriarch's stadium. Zorin's big hand brushed a shower of confetti from his hair while he ushered him up the ramp toward the relative sanity of Dex's shuttle.

Dex urged Kaia along as well, their progress slowed by a fresh flurry of demands for more kissing for the cameras. Finally Dex gave in and dragged Kaia into his arms for one of those fiercely dominant kisses that always heated Ben's blood to a boil.

Even when he was only watching.

Though hopefully he wouldn't be only watching for long.

Clumsy with liquor and contentment, he wound his arm around Zorin's waist and leaned into him. He had zero plans to kiss either one of his Mogadon in the public eye, not with the cultural minefield of hang-ups the whole race was going to need to navigate in order to… eventually… accept their mating.

Or so he hoped.

Still, Zorin leaned in to nuzzle his cheek, the rough rasp of stubble abrading his skin.

A jolt of desire shot through him and made his legs go weak with need. A conditioned response his body was well primed to generate after how thoroughly their pirate had claimed and conquered and dominated him last night. Zorin had known exactly how far to push him. Blown past lines Ben hadn't even known he possessed. Made him sob and plead like a frightened virgin on her Tombola night.

And he'd flipping loved every tick.

Despite all the high-octane liquor coursing through his blood, his cock stiffened and pushed against his breeches. A husky moan spilled from his lips.

"Come on inside," Zorin whispered in his ear. "Can't wait to get the three of you alone for a real celebration."

Tingling with anticipation and desire, Ben let the pirate pull him toward the shuttle. Over his shoulder, he stole a last wistful look at Dex. All day long, he'd been sedulously careful to respect those formidable Mogadon boundaries. To let Dex set the pace of their iconoclastic mating in front of the news cameras and the Mogadon legions. Even though it would've been nice if—

Dex's burnished head turned to find him. Clearly sensing his longing. Their eyes met and locked.

It's okay. I get it, Ben whispered through the lifebond. *I get that you can't—*

Dex's gaslight gaze blazed with sudden resolve.

"Get over here." Dex's fist knotted in Ben's tunic and pulled him roughly close. "I need you to know I love the hell out of you. Now and always. Even in front of the whole bloody universe."

Which was how a rapturous Ben Nero finally found himself being thoroughly and satisfyingly kissed in public by the Mogadon Imperator.

Dizzy with happiness, Ben wound his arms around his lover's trim waist and gave in to the transcendent pleasure of being utterly and irrevocably claimed by Dex Draven. With the image blazoned on colossal vid screens in every quadrant so no one could possibly miss it.

Ben was so thrilled with the entire proceeding, he hovered dangerously close to tears.

Somehow Zorin got them all into the shuttle and the portal sealed. By the time Ben's head cleared, the four of them were standing in the subdued splendor of the Imperator's shipboard salon. Surrounded by gleaming wood from Mogadon forests and the palmate antlers of Mogadon stags mounted on paneled walls. Feeling the lush pelt of Mogadon bear sink beneath his boots. Smelling the bite of Mogadon whiskey mingled with the richness of Mogadon leather.

Not long ago, the Mogadon had been mortal enemies. But Dex was *his* Mogadon, and that made all the difference.

Unable to resist the indulgence, Ben toed off his boots and curled his bare toes into the rug with a moan of pleasure.

Dex muttered orders into his wrist unit and acknowledged congratulations that seemed sincere from his smiling pilot—by the looks of it, a patrician well satisfied to see another of his kind ascend. Of course, Mogadon males of every class were raised with hearts forged of solid titanium, hammered by rules and tempered in duty, rather than fiery human flesh. From Ben's psychic vantage, their pilot's rule-bound brain was teeming with questions and hesitation—but no outright resistance.

For now, that would have to suffice.

Kaia unslung her saber from her shoulder and drifted over to the panoramic viewport, where fireworks still bloomed and blazed in the purple Kryllian sky. Beyond her slim silhouette, a rose-colored moon was rising above the pandemonium. The turquoise sickle of a second moon floated like a primitive canoe through darkening seas. Kaia's head bowed against the polyglass with an audible sigh.

Yeah, it had been one hell of a day. For all of them.

But especially for her.

Zorin ambled over to the orgy couch and lowered his armored bulk into its depths with a grunt of heartfelt relief. Ben dug his palms into the aching muscles of his own back to loosen the crushing tension of that singular day.

Dex leveled an assessing glance at all of them, then directed his pilot softly to take the slow route home. "I mean it, Flavius. I don't want to see the *Inevitable* until at least midnight. Make it happen."

"Very good, Commander." Smothering a grin, the pilot saluted smartly and headed for the cockpit. The interior portal *shussed* closed on his heels.

Leaving the four of them alone.

Finally.

"Juno's tits, I'm done in," Zorin groaned, head falling back against the couch. "Shimmy on over here, gorgeous, and lemme give you a back rub. I'm too plumb tuckered to get up."

Ben padded across the floor and crawled happily into his pirate's lap. Which wasn't a particularly dignified placement for a Precursor, but he was way past caring. He curled an arm around Zorin's neck and lay his cheek against the starmetal that encased his muscled shoulder with a sigh.

"Forget about the back rub for a bit. Just hold me."

Because we all could have died today.

"But we didn't," Zorin said, engulfing him in his powerful arms. "Thanks to you and Kaia and that stunt the two of you finagled on the viewing platform. Honest to gods, Ben. If you weren't my own consort, you'd scare the space outta me."

"But I *am* yours." Ben inhaled slowly to savor his lover's wolfish scent and let contentment seep through him. "Not too heavy for you, am I?"

"Nope." Zorin's aquamarine eyes slid over Dex, who stood over the massive desk eyeing the tablet full of problems that awaited his attention.

"You too, kid," the pirate said gruffly. "That thing can wait till morning. It's our cotton-pickin' wedding night, ain't it? Mosey on over here and take a load off."

As a general rule, Dex responded badly to anyone's orders. But he turned away from the tablet with a wry smile and prowled across the salon to lower himself beside them. Ben felt the carefully contained vigilance ease its grip on his best friend's body.

Zorin wrapped a heavy arm around Dex's shoulders. Dex reached without looking and laced his hand through Ben's.

"You do realize we'll be doing this all over again on Mogadon," Dex murmured. "The civil ceremony, I mean, to establish our union under the Mogadon Codex. I've ordered the festivities for next week—together with my coronation. Kaia, darling, I'd love to have you here in my arms instead of all the way over there."

Smiling, Kaia turned her back on the ecstatic planet as the stadium fell away beneath them and sashayed over to the couch. "And the Imperator always gets his way, doesn't he?"

Her lilac eyes wandered over Zorin and Ben's entwined bodies and slid up Dex's sternly uniformed physique. Her lips parted on a visible shiver.

"This one has certainly formed the habit," Dex rumbled low in his throat, lids dropping over the neon lightning of his gaze. "Why don't you show me what a very good girl you can be."

Slow and sultry, Kaia straddled his hips and sank into his lap, eyes never leaving his, arms winding around his neck. Just watching the searing heat that flared between the two of them was enough to roughen Ben's breath and send all the blood racing to his cock.

"You're wearing quite a lot," she murmured, voice low and throaty. "And not a prefect in sight to undress you, Imperator."

"I'm entirely confident you'll endeavor to contrive a solution, Imperatrix. You're a terribly resourceful girl." His hands wrapped possessively around her hips and settled her eager body against his.

Kaia's deft fingers worked open the gleaming buttons of Dex's jacket and the shirt beneath to expose the hard sun-bronzed expanse of his naked chest.

Ben felt their pirate's armored body harden and raised his head to find Zorin's mouth in a kiss that smoked with his own rising passion. Their tongues met in a swirl of liquid heat. The pirate's hand fisted in Ben's hair to hold him.

"Mars, the way you kiss," Zorin breathed against his mouth. "Afraid I'm gonna disappoint you tonight. The old guy's all done in."

Which Ben might have believed if not for the colossal bulge jutting against the starmetal mesh under his searching hand.

"You could never disappoint me. You're not old. And you don't have to move a muscle." Ben's fingers tightened around that enticing bulge and worked a moan through Zorin's big body. "What were you and our girl thinking about earlier? You getting her off in your armor? How exactly would that work?"

By now Kaia had teased Dex's shirt and jacket all the way open and was licking her way down his chest. Slowly her head turned to study them, breath quick with mounting heat.

"Oh, stars." Zorin laughed, but it held a hungry edge. "The suit's designed to take it, I guess. There's kinda, uh, a hatch down there."

Ben had already found it. Because he was motivated as all seven devils. Holding Zorin's liquid metal gaze, he slithered to his knees between the guy's spread thighs. His mouth already watering for the taste of all that monumental cock thrusting down his throat.

"Don't move a muscle, big guy," he repeated, fingers busy with the mechanism. "I've been dreaming about doing this to you for days. You have no earthly idea how hard I'm going to make you—"

"Ohmygods, *gross*! Way too much PDA, people. Don't you know there's a kid in the room?"

The sudden intrusion of that brazen voice, falling from what sounded improbably like somewhere overhead, sent Ben scrambling to his feet and spinning with a gasp, dragging a hasty hand across his mouth.

Just in time to see a ceiling panel slide open and a slim female form in Syndax leathers slither deftly to the floor. Kaia's kid sister landed like a cat, planted a confident hand on one cocky hip, and flashed him an impudent grin.

"Kylie?" Kaia shot to her feet, face flaming with embarrassment. "You're supposed to be lying low on the *Relentless*. What in the cosmic night do you think you're doing up there?"

"Scoping out the sitch." The girl's fascinated gaze settled on the mouthwatering expanse of Dex's naked chest. "You didn't think I was just gonna twiddle my thumbs in orbit while you faced down Dad without me, did you? You might've needed my help."

"Neptune's knickers, honey." Zorin scrubbed a chagrined hand over the back of his neck and gave in to a chuckle. "You just about scared the bewhosis outta all four of us. Tick Tock was supposed to be watching you. I'm afraid to ask how you got past him."

"Easy-peasy." Kylie tossed her head, the copper fringe of her freshly cropped hair swinging against her stubborn jaw. "I locked myself in the *thermae* for a bath and shimmied out the ductwork. Just in time to hitch a ride."

"The starfruit doesn't fall far from the proverbial tree, does it, darling?" Dex murmured wryly, buttoning his jacket with a pointed look.

Kaia waved an impatient hand to deflect his gentle jab. "Never mind all that. Kylie—what in the cosmos are you *wearing*?"

Ben had rather been wondering that himself. Somehow Kaia's little sister had gotten her capable hands on a pair of Syndax leather pants, a ragged combat shirt that showed a bit more of her skinny navel than he was comfortable seeing, and a wicked pair of shitkicker boots. She'd cropped her flaming hair close to her cocky head in a spiky mop, but left one long fringe to brush her jaw.

In short, Kaia's kid sister looked nothing like a Kryll maharani. And nothing like a kid either.

"Standard Syndax rig." Kylie shrugged. "I figured it'd help me, you know, blend in. And look! Hotshot's girlfriend pierced my navel for me."

"Jumpin' Jupiter," Zorin said weakly, when no one else proved capable of responding. "Honey, you really shoulda asked Kaia first."

"As if." Kylie rolled her eyes and hopped up to sit on the desk, booted legs swinging. "Like I said, I wanna blend in. Hey, I hear you're sending the Syndax to find Dex's missing brother and spring him out of some Swarm lockup."

"That's correct." Determination invaded the hard lines of Dex's face and edged his voice in tungsten. "We're organizing a massive search-and-rescue operation. My intelligence service has already unearthed a possible lead. If that shapeshifter wasn't lying outright about my brother's fate, I bloody well intend to find him—and free him."

"Righto." Kylie planted a confident hand on her hip. "When you do, I wanna go with."

"That's entirely out of the question." Dex rose to his feet and looked sternly Imperatorial. "You're coming to Mogadon with us. I've already given orders to enroll you at the youth academy. You'll study with my own *grammaticus*—"

"Uh, thanks but no thanks. No offense and all, Uncle Dex, but you're not the boss of me."

Seeing his best friend floored by being addressed as "Uncle Dex"—or maybe just the revolutionary concept that there might be anyone left breathing in the galaxy he wasn't the boss of—Ben stepped deftly into the breach.

Before the kid took it into her head to start calling him "Uncle Ben."

"Kylie, if you've been holed up in the ceiling all day, you must be famished. Why don't you head down to the galley and score yourself some dinner? In fact, we could all use something more substantial than a bottle of Kryllian liquor in our bellies."

The kid cocked her head and studied him with Kaia's clever eyes. "Don't think I don't know you're trying to get rid of me. But yeah, I'm hungry enough to eat a whole sand-runner, hooves and all. I'll see what I can scare up for all of us."

She hopped down and sauntered for the door. "Don't the four of you get into any, you know, trouble while I'm gone either. Cuz I'll be *right back* in like ten ticks."

The portal slid closed behind her leather-clad rump. Ben found himself fighting an unholy urge to laugh.

"Gods help us," Dex said blankly, sinking back to the couch. "How on earth are we going to raise that child? Much less manage to do so without the Patriarch's knowledge."

"We gotta talk through how this whole thing's gonna work for all of us, don't we?" Zorin stretched his big body in a yawn. "Mosey on back here for that back rub, gorgeous, while we all palaver."

Reluctantly shelving his amorous impulses in light of Junior's imminent return, Ben squeezed in between Dex and Zorin. Dex eased Kaia down on his knee. Ben lifted her hand to nuzzle her palm and groaned as Zorin's powerful fingers kneaded the tension from his back.

"Let's start with names and titles," he said drowsily, nipping Kaia's skin just to feel her shiver. "What are they calling us back on Mogadon?"

"Right." Dex slid a possessive hand through her tumbled hair and watched through lazy eyes as she purred with pleasure. "Kaia will be my Imperatrix—my sole female consort. The two of you can choose your own titles. Or no titles at all if you prefer to minimize the ballyhoo." He slanted a grin at Zorin. "In that case, you'll simply be known as my consorts, and retain your own authorities and assets as currently recognized under galactic law."

Ben lifted one shoulder in a languid shrug, relaxation seeping through him as Zorin worked the kinks out of his back. "I never mind another title. I'll come up with something. *My lord* has a certain flair."

"Not for me," Zorin chuckled. "If someone tries *my lording* me back on Mogadon, I'm gonna do real damage."

"I'm not exactly crazy about being *my ladied* either, but I'll deal with it." Eyes bright with curiosity, Kaia tilted her head to study Dex. "What happens with our legal names under Mogadon law?"

Dex shot Zorin a wary look, clearly bracing for a struggle. "At the very least, I'd like all of you to take the Draven name. You know what that entails. It not only signifies that I'm financially responsible for the three of you—though I'm perfectly well aware none of you needs my money. It means I'm responsible for your protection. Any man, woman—or shapeshifter—who interferes with you will answer to me."

"Kaia Draven," she said dreamily, snuggling deep in Dex's arms. "I think I can live with that."

Dex's face contracted and he bowed his burnished head. "Oh, darling. You've no notion how blissfully happy you've just made me."

She lifted her face to share an affectionate kiss. "Sure I do. Telepath, remember?"

Zorin shifted his armored body with a skeptical grunt. "I dunno, kid. You gonna be responsible when me and my boys break another pesky galactic law?"

"You won't be breaking any more galactic laws, Syndax." Dex gave him a playful push, but his jaw hardened with intent. "We *are* the law now—all four of us. I'm afraid your colorful days raising hell in the outer colonies as scourge of the galaxy are behind you. From now on, you're under my protection. There's no sentient being in the galaxy who doesn't know my name. Even before I ascended."

"Look." Zorin chuckled. "You're taking two gods and a pirate for consorts. There's not a one of us needs to hide behind your name for *protection*. But I get that you want every guy in the galaxy with a cock and a heartbeat to know we're yours."

"You're bloody right I do," Dex growled, fiercely protective. The dark spice of Mogadon pheromones made Ben dizzy. "We'll be hunting Swarm spacebots and cannibals for our honeymoon, love. And we won't always be doing it together. I want every resource in the galaxy at your disposal."

"The man does have a point," Ben murmured. "And I get that it's a Mogadon thing. I can't say I'll mind being Ben Draven. If that's what it takes to placate you."

Dex's eyes flashed incandescent with triumph. He leaned in to claim a blazing kiss that left Ben's head spinning. Kaia hummed with happiness and slipped her hand through Ben's.

"Zorin Draven," their pirate muttered. "Holy hell. Your dad's gonna be spinning in his grave."

"After today, I'll wager he's already doing backflips. I've made my peace with it." Dex slanted Zorin a conciliatory look. "Why not take my surname? It's not like you're using yours, is it?"

"Yeah. That reminds me." Kaia slithered out of Dex's lap to tuck her head against Zorin's shoulder, and their pirate pulled her close.

Which pretty much reduced the four of them to a tangled mess of limbs and hair and armor that threatened to overflow the couch. Precisely the way they'd slept last night.

And Ben farking loved it.

Enough that he did what he'd been dying to do for days and crawled into Dex's lap himself.

The only thing better than the look of surprised pleasure that flashed across Dex's face was knowing he'd be sleeping in Dex's arms tonight.

And every night if he had his way.

That sounds bloody perfect to me, Dex whispered in his head and nuzzled his neck. *I firmly intend never to be without you again.*

Ben laughed under his breath. "Just try getting rid of me now, space cadet."

"What's your surname anyway, Zorin?" Kaia murmured, watching them both through languid eyes. "You never use it, do you? I never even thought to ask."

"Yeah, well, there's a reason I don't use it." Zorin pushed out a breath. "It's, uh, Theodophilus."

Kaia choked back a snort of surprised laughter, while Ben ducked his head to hide a grin.

Zorin heaved a long-suffering sigh. "Yeah. Look, it's okay with me if you wanna take Dex's. Hell, I'll take it too if that's what you really want, kid."

"Well, I'm damn well not taking yours," Dex muttered. "So I'd appreciate your obliging me, Theodophilus."

"Whatever you say." Zorin reached to tousle Dex's tawny hair. "But I'm gonna ask you to wear a Syndax tribal tattoo for me. That's how *I'm* claiming all three of you."

"You mean like the one on your back?" Kaia's head popped up from his shoulder, her expression suspended somewhere between appalled and intrigued.

Zorin's craggy face softened with tenderness. "No, sweetheart. I mean like the one around my arm. Will you do that for me?"

Eyes bright, head tilted, she considered. "All right. If you want me to. What do you think, Ben?"

Cautiously Ben examined the prospect, rather alarmed by the thought of any tattoo at all.

Zorin cocked a brow at his dubious expression and gave him a lopsided grin. "Don't you fret, gorgeous. I'll ink you myself if you let me. And I guarantee you'll dig the result."

"You'll do it yourself?" Ben's skin tingled with a lightning frisson of anticipation and arousal. "Will we be naked while you do it?"

"Turns your crank, don't it? The whole concept of lying helpless under my hands and under my needle while I do whatever I want with you?" Zorin's tone deepened to a guttural growl that scraped across his senses and made him shiver with heat. "Yeah, you'll be naked. And when I'm finished, if you're a good boy? I'll give you that shower sex you've been jonesing for."

"That goes for me as well, I suppose," Dex said dryly. "I'm hardly in any position to protest. One tribal tattoo seems a minuscule price to pay for the myriad frustrations mating the Mogadon Imperator will inevitably demand of you."

"And I'll microchip all three of you," Kaia announced. "You'll have the best avatars and the baddest exploits of any samurai in the cyberverse. There you'll be farking gods. That'll be how *I* claim you."

"Sure, if that's what you want," Zorin said easily. "You already turned us all into gods in real life, haven't you? Given us ringside seats in the Kryllian pantheon right alongside you and Pops."

Kaia stirred with a ripple of unease. "Yeah, but I'm not a god. I'm just a circus acrobat. A kid with a cybersword."

"Not to mention the Mogadon Imperatrix *and* the Quorum's newest rep for the Kryll," Zorin pointed out. "And before anyone gets any bright ideas, I'm not planting my sorry ass in that vacant Syndax seat. A pirate's gig is out patrolling the back forty in the Omega Sector. And let's not forget springing Dex's brother outta the slammer like I promised Dex I would—which is pretty much a job I can't delegate. While I'm off doing that, Kaia has my proxy on the Quorum."

"Whoa there, hold on a sec!" Kaia shot straight up in alarm. "I don't even know how I'll manage to speak for Kryll, much less the Syndax, without royally screwing the whole thing up. Nor can I believe your boys and girls would trust a punk like me to do that."

Zorin eased her agitated body back into his arms. "They're your boys and girls too now, sweetheart. You're queen of the Syndax horde, and you're perfect for the gig. They damn near worship you already."

"I don't want to be worshipped. I'm not a god!" When Ben reached to claim his lifemate's restless hand, she subsided with a fretful sigh. "I don't know why I have to keep saying that."

Beyond her exquisite profile, the turquoise orb of the Kryllian moon slid slowly into view, glowing against a tapestry of stars. Farther out, its primrose and lavender sisters floated in the darkness of interstellar night. Somewhere beyond the moons and planets that revolved erratically around the twin suns loomed the militant might of the Alpha Sector, bristling with Dex's armored legions. Astern lay the barely inhabited expanse of the Beta Sector, where the dying Valyrian race waited for Ben and his gifted progeny to restore their faded glory. Farther still huddled the hinterland of the Omega Sector and the outer colonies, terrorized and preyed upon by Swarm cannibals and their shapeshifting god. Lurking like leviathans at the edge of the known universe.

All of it waiting for the four of them—the four of them together—to claim, protect, and conquer.

Dex pulled in a measured breath. "Has it ever occurred to you, darling, that gods aren't born? They're *made*. Ben's been a god for years and he damn well knows it. You're only beginning to come into your power. Zorin and I, we're just along for the ride."

"Says the ruler of the galaxy," Zorin noted dryly. "From over here where the old guy sits, you're all a tick larger than life. None of you's exactly your average space monkey, are ya? Me—not so much. I'm just a poor schmuck who got lucky."

"I'm thinking we're all pretty lucky. All four of us." Kaia leaned to kiss Zorin and looped an arm around Dex's neck, but her tender smile was all for Ben. "Strap yourselves in, lifemates. You can call it divine prophecy if you want. But I have the definite feeling we're in for quite a ride."

THE END

READY FOR MORE ASTRAL HEAT ADVENTURES?

Discover where it all began for Dex and Nero in

Anticipated Angel:
An Astral Heat MM Sci Fi Romance Novella Prequel.

Available now!
One-click to order at https://books2read.com/AnticipatedAngel

READY FOR A CONNECTED PARANORMAL REVERSE HAREM ADVENTURE

with Mogadon, Valyrian, Kryll,
and even shifter heroes set on modern-day Earth?

Then you're ready for

Gemini Angel:
A Dark Witch Academy Standalone

I summon the lightning.
I claim my power.
The warlocks of Icarus Academy claim me.

I start my night as a cat burglar in Singapore and I end up queen of the witching world. Too bad this rags-to-riches fairytale's a gig I never applied for and won't accept. And not only because there's a queen killer on the hunt. My witchcraft is wild and lethal. Last time I summoned lightning, eighty-seven people ended up dead. I've renounced my power. I'm a fish in a tree at Icarus Academy.

But these four sexy warlocks who rule the school just won't take no for an answer.

They want me to summon the lightning. They want me to claim my power. They want me to claim my consorts.

And they want to claim me.

Because the witching world is dying, and I'm their last chance. My warlocks will end this Academy to rule at my side. But unless I learn to claim my power before the killer claims my head, there's a global extinction event looming.

With my name written all over it.

Gemini Queen is a new standalone with teacher-student forbidden love, steamy group interactions, possessive males, sexy shifters, enemies to lovers, first-time M/M, first-time gay-to-bi, and a powerful heroine who doesn't have to choose.

One-click to order at
www.books2read.com/GeminiQueen

WANT TO KNOW WHAT HAPPENS NEXT WITH KAIA, DEX, ZORIN, AND NERO?

Plus hook up with a whole new MMMF harem, some seriously yummy heroes, and the surprise heroine I never expected to write?

Coming soon!
Electric Angel:
A Solar Flare Poly Reverse Harem
Sci Fi Romance.

For a sneak peek at exclusive content and early release info, sign up for my newsletter at www.LauraNavarreSciFi.com

OTHER ASTRAL HEAT ROMANCE ADVENTURES:

*Anticipated Angel: An Astral Heat MM Sci Fi
Romance Novella Prequel
Interstellar Angel: An Astral Heat Romance #1
Renegade Angel: An Astral Heat Romance #2
The Astral Heat Romance Box Set*

OTHER STEAMY ROMANCE READS BY LAURA NAVARRE:

Fantasy Historical Romance: The *Magick* Trilogy
Magick by Moonrise
https://books2read.com/MagickByMoonrise/
Midsummer Magick
https://books2read.com/MidsummerMagick
Mistress by Magick
https://books2read.com/MistressByMagick/

Steamy Historical Romance Standalones
By Royal Command
https://books2read.com/ByRoyalCommand

ACKNOWLEDGMENTS

They say writing and publishing a book takes a village. When you're a debut reverse harem sci fi romance author with three back-to-back releases, it takes a starbase. I could never have written the *Astral Heat Romance* series without the encouragement and insight of my cosmic mate and hubby Steven—my first writing mentor, alpha reader, business partner, and CEO at Ascendant Press. And I can't rave enough about my editor, Deb Nemeth, who first acquired me for a traditional press way back when I was starting out, and works with me again now. She makes my prose sparkle and my stories sing. Also high on my eternal-gratitude list are my writing guru Angela James, my awesome cover artist Kim Killion, my diligent copy editor Elizabeth Flynn, my miracle-working formatter and uploader and hand-holder Judi Fennell, my friend and indie inspiration Dana Delamar, my marketer Heather Roberts at Elle Woods PR, and every single one of my wonderful ARC reviewers and readers! I appreciate you all to the moon and back.

ABOUT THE AUTHOR

A long time ago in a galaxy far away, Laura Navarre was an award-winning dark historical romance author for Harlequin, while her diabolical twin Nikki Navarre wrote sexy spy romance. In a daring bid to escape a global pandemic, armed only with an MFA in Writing Popular Fiction, Laura voyaged through a wormhole to an alternate universe where she crafts turbocharged, epic, hyper-erotic reverse harem sci fi romance starring three super-sexy heroes, one seriously kickass heroine, and plenty of sleek, sizzling outer space action.

Laura's intergalactic adventures are trackable by humans and aliens alike on social media here:

Facebook: www.facebook.com/LauraNavarreInterstellarRomance
Twitter: www.twitter.com/LauraNavarre
Goodreads: www.goodreads.com/LauraNavarre
TikTok: https://www.tiktok.com/@LauraNavarreAuthor
BookBub: https://www.bookbub.com/authors/Laura-Navarre
Website: www.LauraNavarreSciFi.com

9 781955 236041